FORGOTTEN SECRET: A PSYCHOLOGICAL SUSPENSE THRILLER
Copyright © 2024 by S.F. Baumgartner

All rights reserved. No part of this publication may be reproduced or transmitted in any form or by any means, mechanical or electronic, including photocopying or recording, or by any information storage and retrieval system, or transmitted by email without permission in writing from the author.

NO AI TRAINING: Without in any way limiting S.F. Baumgartner [and Represent Publishing] exclusive rights under copyright, any use of this publication to "train" generative artificial intelligence (AI) technologies to generate text is expressly prohibited. The author reserves all rights to license uses of this work for generative AI training and development of machine learning language models.

Neither the author nor the publisher assumes any responsibility for errors, omissions, or contrary interpretations of the subject matter herein. Any perceived slight of any individual or organization is purely unintentional. Brand and product names are trademarks or registered trademarks of their respective owners.

ISBN 979-8-9879494-9-8
Library of Congress Control Number: 2023923292

Edited Brilliant Cut Editing, EJL Editing, and Represent Publishing

Formatted and Published by Represent Publishing

Cover Design by 100bookcovers.com

FORGOTTEN SECRET

FORGOTTEN SECRET

A Psychological Suspense Thriller

S.F. BAUMGARTNER

AUTHOR'S NOTE

To all readers, especially residents and those familiar with the state of Florida, I wish to clarify that the town of Marian and the Mirror Estate are purely fictional creations for this series.

All characters and events depicted in this novel are born from my imagination. Any resemblance to actual people, living or dead, or to real-life events is entirely coincidental.

RECAPS

BURIED SECRETS - WHERE IT ALL BEGINS, BOOK 1

Twenty-five-year-old Dylan Roche barely has time to mourn his mom before an attorney appears with an invitation to his long-lost maternal grandmother's opulent estate. Eager to learn about the family he believed dead, and armed with a mysterious key his mom gave him before her death, he's ready to uncover what he believes are buried family secrets.

After a lifetime of scraping by with his mom, he's shocked she grew up wealthy. But, while the estate is lavish, something's off, and he can't shake the haunting feeling that he's being watched. As he delves deeper, he unearths his family's dark history tied to organized crime. His focus, however, remains unshaken, latched onto what the mysterious key unlocks.

At last, he locates the buried box the key opens. Then, along with those buried secrets, he discovers that the ever-present, sinister aura he's been sensing is his mother's twin sister, believed to have died shortly after birth. Very much alive, this ghost is now a criminal mastermind out to kill him. Although he dodges her murder attempt, he's left questioning everything he thought he knew about family, trust, and his past.

LIVING SECRETS, BOOK 2

Twenty-two-year-old hotel worker Lily Tso has grown up in Hong Kong believing she's an orphan. Then her mother, Olivia, who's alive and working for the US government—possibly as a spy—entrusts Lily with a mission. Lily is to deliver an antidote for an experimental biological weapon to her father, US Senator Simon Roth.

FBI Special Agent Kyle Peters is assigned to get Lily safely to the US and to her father. Posing as her boyfriend, he works with Dylan Roche, a young tycoon asked to assist them. But the trio soon finds themselves pursued by mysterious assailants in a harrowing life-or-death chase.

Undercover Agent Olivia Tso, code-named Phoenix, has infiltrated the organization run by the Ghost (Dylan's aunt) and thinks she can stay in the background during this operation. But when Kyle's shot, Dylan injured, and Lily kidnapped, Olivia must join forces with Simon, her former lover and Lily's father, and an FBI task force led by Ron Peters, Kyle's father.

Symptoms of the bioweapon soon start to appear among the population. After multiple setbacks, the team locates Lily. They deliver the antidote and other critical information to Simon. While a few casualties occur due to the virus, global catastrophe is ultimately contained.

Now, Lily's reunited with her long-lost parents, but a new world of familial connections and covert operations awaits this fast-becoming tight-knit group.

Relationship Chart

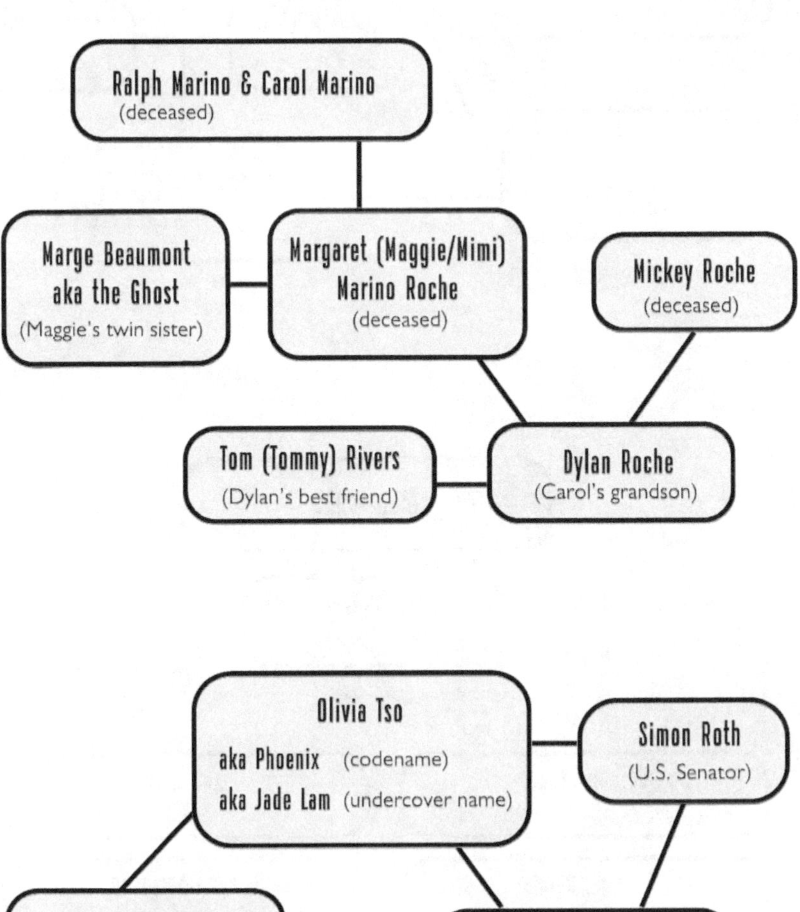

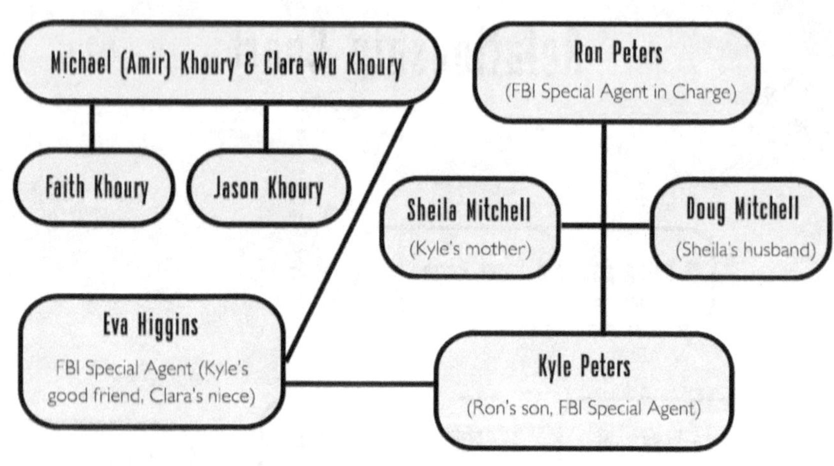

Michael (Amir) Khoury & Clara Wu Khoury
Faith Khoury
Jason Khoury
Ron Peters
(FBI Special Agent in Charge)
Sheila Mitchell
(Kyle's mother)
Doug Mitchell
(Sheila's husband)
Eva Higgins
FBI Special Agent (Kyle's good friend, Clara's niece)
Kyle Peters
(Ron's son, FBI Special Agent)

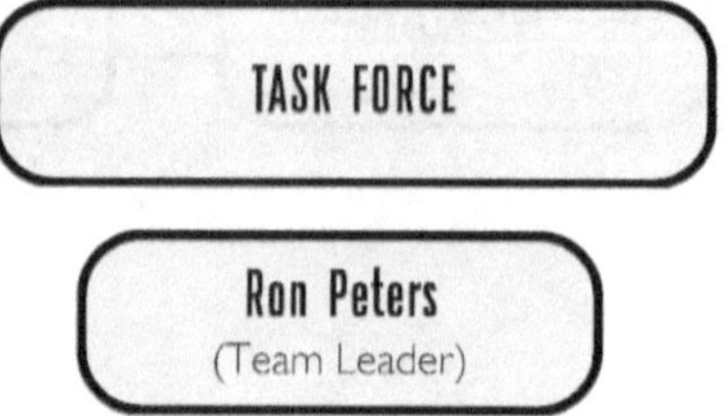

TASK FORCE
Ron Peters
(Team Leader)

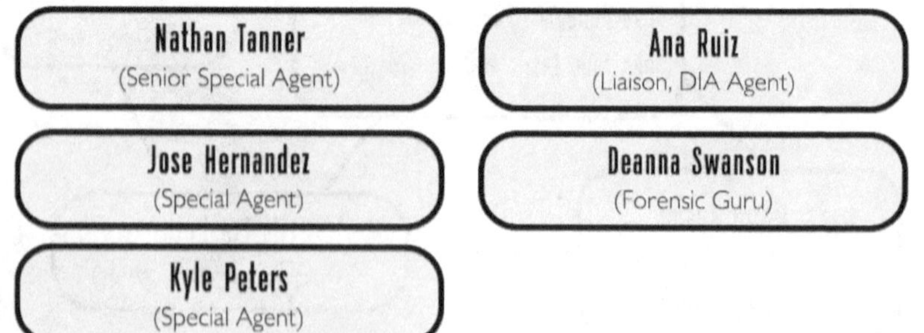

Nathan Tanner
(Senior Special Agent)
Ana Ruiz
(Liaison, DIA Agent)
Jose Hernandez
(Special Agent)
Deanna Swanson
(Forensic Guru)
Kyle Peters
(Special Agent)

PRAISE FOR BURIED SECRETS - WHERE IT ALL BEGINS: BOOK 1

I felt that the author wove a story that had twists and turns with unexpected moments sprinkled here and there.

— DELPHIA, GOODREADS

They say that dynamite comes in small packages. This one was definitely loaded with plenty of information that will blow your mind.

— TAMMY, GOODREADS

What a great story! This had enough thrill and mystery to draw me in even though it was a short novella.

— MEGAN, GOODREADS

PRAISE FOR LIVING SECRETS: BOOK 2

A great crime novel! Loved that it picked up right where the prequel left off. Loved all the chasing of Lily and who was after her. Loved the cliffhanger and can't wait to read the next one!!

— KRYSTA, GOODREADS

The book is one you will not want to put down, and if you read it at night, you will jump at every noise and check the locks on your doors and windows. Highly recommend.

— BARBARA, GOODREADS

Edge of your seat reading that keeps you guessing until the end. Plenty of drama with twists and turns that keeps you going until the end. Great characters to follow along on this adventure. Good read.

— RHONDA, GOODREADS

PRAISE FOR FORGOTTEN SECRET: BOOK 3

I am exhausted!!! This is an absolute whirlwind and it kept me guessing from the very beginning. I loved Living Secrets and I can safely say, this is even better! I'm not even going to say it's a "one more chapter" book, it's an "I read it in a day book." An amazing plot, great characters, and so many twists and turns your head will spin. I'm loving this series, if you like your fast paced psychological suspense books, give this a go!

— VICKIE, GOODREADS

WOW, TALK ABOUT NEEDING A SCORE CARD TO KEEP TRACK!! I enjoyed Clara's story, and I thought I knew who the culprit was, but I was wrong given all of the players involved! I SURE HOPE THERE'S ANOTHER BOOK IN THE WORKS!!!

— BECKY, GOODREADS

AWESOME BOOK !!! This is a great psychological suspense thriller that I would recommend to anyone. This is a fairly new author to me and I love everything I have read so far.

—MICHELLE, GOODREADS

"Human trafficking is a scourge, a crime against the whole of humanity. It is time to join forces and work together to free its victims and to eradicate this crime that affects all of us, from individual families to the worldwide community."

– Pope Francis

PROLOGUE

A relentless throb pounded in the hollow of her skull, a rhythmic drumbeat that drew her from the comfort of unconsciousness. She forced her eyes open, wincing against the antiseptic brightness. Stark-white walls towered around her, impersonal and cold, the ceiling sprinkled with tiny fluorescent lights that flickered like distant stars. She was lying on a bed, machines nearby, a thin hospital sheet barely covering her. How'd she end up here? Her breathing quickened, and her heartbeat picked up speed. Her clammy skin threatened to soak the sheet. She couldn't remember.

She blinked two figures into focus—men dressed in white coats.

"Welcome back to the land of the living." The younger, Middle Eastern-looking one leaned closer, thrusting his angular cheekbones and well-defined jaw into view and exuding a sense of strength.

Her brows furrowed. Did she die?

"You're awake." The older white man perused the hospital chart. "You've been in a coma. Because of the angle, the caliber, and perhaps distance, the bullet didn't cause any major damage.

But your brain still needed time to heal. I'm Dr. Lester Cook. This is Dr. Michael Khoury." He gestured toward the young man. "Your vitals look good. Let me have a peek. The police haven't been able to identify you. What's your name?"

Her lips moved, but no sound came out. Did he say bullet? And what was her name?

Dr. Cook did a check on her head, the bandages wrapping it making her feel like she was wearing a turban. He then asked her who the president was, what year it was, how many fingers she saw, and similar questions. She had no trouble answering them. "Now, how are you feeling?"

She tried to reply, but her throat was parched, her voice a mere croak. Dr. Khoury fetched a glass of water from the bedside table, held it to her lips, and helped her to take slow sips.

"I–I don't remember anything," she admitted, her voice barely above a whisper. Why was she struggling to say a simple sentence?

The two doctors exchanged glances. Then Dr. Cook scanned the medical chart, his brows furrowed. "You've been through a traumatic ordeal. You don't remember being shot?"

The words hit her like a gut punch, her heart pounding a frenzied tattoo against her rib cage. "Shot?" she echoed, a trembling taking over her body. "But... why can't I remember anything?"

Neither answered right away. Then Dr. Cook touched her hand. "The human brain is a fascinatingly complex organ. When it undergoes severe trauma, such as a gunshot wound, it sometimes shields itself by temporarily blocking out memories. You're fortunate to be alive."

I'm not feeling lucky! "Will I... get my memories back?"

He gave her hand a comforting squeeze. "In most cases, yes. Memory loss after head trauma is usually temporary. Your brain needs time to heal, and as it does, your memories should begin to return."

"But… who am I?"

When Dr. Cook turned to his young colleague, Dr. Khoury cleared his throat. "We haven't been able to identify you yet. You had no identification when I found you. But don't worry. We're here to help you."

He found her? Her eyes welled up. She clutched the bedsheets, searching for answers that seemed to slip through her grasp.

"Where… did you… find me?"

Dr. Khoury hesitated. "My brother and I and some friends were out on a boat on the Intracoastal Waterway. When our friends dropped us off at the dock, we found you nearby."

Had she been on the Intracoastal Waterway? The blankness in her mind failed her. "Are we… in the Outer Banks?"

"No, we're in Durham. We had to airlift you here because of the seriousness of your injuries."

"How long… have I been out?"

"Ten days."

Ten days!

The room's door swung open, breaking the heavy silence that settled upon them. Her heart quickened. Could this bring a breakthrough or a glimpse into her unknown history?

No. Just a nurse carrying a tray of medications. He exchanged a glance with the doctors, perhaps apologizing for interrupting.

Her chest tightened, but her recovery couldn't be rushed. She took a deep breath and then pushed out words with the air. "Thank you, doctors, for everything you're doing to help me."

"Don't mention it." Dr. Cook wrote some notes on the chart. "That's our job. Remember, healing takes time, and in due course, we hope to piece together the puzzle of your identity. When you feel better, we'll have, uh, a specialist to come and talk to you."

She nodded. What kind of specialist would she need to see?

Surely, a difficult journey lay ahead, but she *would* reclaim her past, no matter how arduous the path might be.

As the nurse finished his task and left, her gaze lingered on the closed door. The weight of her forgotten memories pressed upon her, urging her to seek answers beyond her hospital room.

Dr. Cook said, "Do you have any other questions?"

So many! Starting with her name, but it wasn't the doctors' fault. Her focus was on the sterile white ceiling when she heard:

Clara, Clara!

Was that—? She thought she'd seen her grandfather, but that couldn't be. He died years ago. The hazy figure was retreating, and she tried to stop him. *Come back. Don't go!*

Clara, you need to stay there. It's not your time yet.

Concerned voices murmured around her. She opened her eyes—she hadn't realized she'd closed them. Doctors and nurses now surrounded her. "What happened?" she asked.

"You gave us a scare," Dr. Cook said.

"I thought you'd drifted off to sleep until the alarm started to go off," Dr. Khoury added.

"Clara," she repeated, turning to look at the doctors. "I think… I think that's my name."

A spark lit Dr. Khoury's dark eyes. "That's a start, Clara." The encouragement in his gentle voice warmed her. "Every journey begins with a single step. This is yours. Rest now."

Dr. Cook smiled. "Your memory should start to come back."

As the doctors left, Clara stared at the ceiling, her mind a whirlwind that refused to calm. But amidst the storm, a single thought stood out. She had a name. Clara. And with that name came a glimmer of hope, a tiny flame in the all-encompassing darkness. She wasn't just a gunshot victim or an amnesiac. She was Clara. And she was alive. That had to count for something.

Exhaustion tugged at her consciousness, pulling her toward sleep's comforting embrace. But before she succumbed, she sighed. Dr. Khoury had found her and likely saved her life.

Dr. Michael Khoury, formerly known as Amir, stepped into the doctor's lounge, away from the bustling hospital corridor. He fumbled with his phone, needing to update his brother on the condition of the girl they rescued.

That fateful weekend replayed like a vivid filmstrip. His brother had given his statements to the local police while Michael had been preoccupied with saving the girl's life. After she'd been airlifted to University Hospital in Durham, Michael had gotten the chance to provide his account to the authorities.

Now, in the relative calmness of the hospital corridor, he dialed his brother's number.

When the call connected, Majid's voice broke through the static. "Amir, how's the girl doing?"

Michael had given up trying to make his family call him by his Christian name. He leaned against the wall, finding solace in his brother's presence, even if only over the phone. "She woke up. Still here at the hospital."

"Oh, good. Allah is looking out for her. Come on, what are the odds a neurosurgical fellow just happens to find her?"

"I was there at the right time. But yes, I do feel God's hand in this."

"It's been a few weeks now. Found her parents yet?"

"Nah. I'm more concerned about the cops. They got her fingerprints, but they didn't find anything."

Unspoken worries and shared understanding filled the pause before Majid spoke. "I saw a news report. The coast guard busted a boat full of illegal immigrants from Asia close to where we found her. Do you think she's one of them?"

Michael's brows furrowed as he recalled the news images—the desperation and hope on the faces of those who had risked everything for a chance at a better life. He exhaled, but he couldn't lift the weight from his chest. "I don't know. She's

Asian, but she speaks English quite well, with the slightest accent. British, I think."

"Well, we speak English quite well too. And we weren't born here."

"Point taken. So, maybe she is educated, but… I don't know. Anyway, people don't embark on such dangerous journeys unless they're fleeing something unbearable, whether it's war or political oppression. Maybe that's what she was doing." He rubbed the tightness between his brows. "By the way, her name is Clara, and she doesn't remember anything. So, I can't ask her. The cops think it's a robbery gone wrong."

"Really?"

"What I heard."

"Maybe they won't look too closely, then. And you said she didn't remember anything?"

"Yup."

"Oh, wow. Imagine that. To end up here, injured and with no memory of who she is or where she came from."

Michael nodded, though Majid couldn't see him. "You and I understand what it's like to seek a better life, to escape the horrors of war. While these immigrants may not have come from a war zone, their journey is born out of desperation and longing for a chance at a brighter future."

CHAPTER 1

CLARA

The Florida sun was a mellow presence in the sky, its rays a gentle warmth against Clara Khoury's skin. A soft breeze wafted through the minivan's open windows as she navigated the familiar Orlando streets. She glanced at the passenger seat. "I'm sure you'll make at least JV, if not varsity."

Another grunt from Jason, her freshman son. Sometimes, she wondered if Michael needed to check Jason's vocal cords.

"Dad or I will pick you up."

"Okay."

Boys! At least he said one word.

She pulled into Orlando Christian Academy's parking lot and stopped by the gym entrance. "Good luck."

Jason hopped out.

The school team had a no-cut policy, so it was only a matter of which team—varsity or JV. If nothing went wrong, Jason would make varsity. He'd been playing on elite basketball teams for years.

Her next stop was the store. She strolled through the aisles, her daughter the predominant force in her thoughts. The move had come at a challenging time for Faith in her high school senior year. They'd thought about waiting till after the new year. But the hospital wanted Michael here pronto, and they'd secured spots for their children in an elite academy.

Despite the typical teenage angst and resistance, Faith's recent breakup with her boyfriend eased the transition. The young man had, according to her dramatic narratives, made her life "miserable." The breakup had lessened her initial resistance to the move.

Now settled in Florida, she was adjusting well. She'd even made a friend, Josie. However, Josie appeared to be a trouble magnet, a wild streak visible in her languid swagger and defiant attitude.

At least amidst the upheaval, Faith maintained her grades. But navigating this crucial year of high school, the friendships she forged and the life decisions she made would need their constant vigilance and guidance.

"Ma'am, will that be cash or card?"

"Oh, I'm sorry." Clara slid out her wallet, checked out, and texted Michael for an update. As expected, he had a late meeting. So she'd go back to get Jason.

With twenty minutes to kill, she wasn't going to sit in the car. So, she went inside and joined the other parents on the bleachers, veterans whose older children had already gone through this ritual. They nodded to her, and she joined in polite conversations.

"Where are you from, if I may ask?" Sue Richards asked.

"Hong Kong, originally." Only a handful of people knew about her memory loss, and Clara kept it that way by telling people she was from Hong Kong—it sounded right. It might even be true. "But I've been in America for decades. Looks like your son is going to make a great center this year." And so she steered the conversation elsewhere.

While Jason high-fived his fellow students, Clara texted Faith, checking on her essay's progress in an attempt to maintain balance between Faith's college applications, Jason's basketball dreams, and Michael's demanding job. After waking up in a hospital with no memory, Clara began her journey to where she stood now—a writer for an online Christian magazine, the mother of two wonderful teenagers, and the wife of a successful neurosurgeon. With her therapist's help, she'd accepted that she might never recover her memories.

But sometimes, questions lingered. As the priest once counseled her, she reminded herself daily to surrender to the Lord. *Have faith!*

The cool air of Orlando Hospital greeted Michael Khoury as he stepped through the sliding glass doors. With each step, his dress shoes clicked an echo down the hospital's sterile corridors. When he started not even a month ago, a flurry of activity, sights, smells, and sounds undeniably characteristic of a busy hospital welcomed him.

Today was no different. Nurses hurried by, their shoes squeaking against the linoleum, while doctors huddled together, discussing cases in hushed tones. The antiseptic smell tainted the air, mingling with the undercurrent of coffee from a nearby vending machine.

"Dr. Khoury." Dr. Jenkins, the hospital's robust administrator, approached with an outstretched hand.

Michael returned the man's handshake, his smile easy and welcoming. "Good morning."

"Michael, these are our neurosurgery fellows." Dr. Jenkins led him toward a young man and a woman who looked eager, perhaps too eager.

"Dr. Khoury, it's an honor to meet you." A quiver slipped into Dr. Hill's voice, perhaps from nerves.

Beside her, Dr. Kim, another fellow with an equally anxious expression, nodded his agreement.

Michael extended his hand, shaking theirs in turn. "It's good to meet you both. I hope we'll have a chance to work together closely."

Michael recognized that hope in their eyes, remembered it. He'd stood there once, eager for guidance and approval. He'd offer the mentorship he yearned for during his early years.

Born as Amir in a small Palestinian village, he'd taken on his Christian name during college. Others accepted him more readily with a Christian name, a sad but enlightening reality. But it was as Michael that he had saved Clara's life, built a family, and found a home in America.

However, the path to pursuing a relationship with Clara hadn't been easy. He still remembered his conversation with Dr. Cook so many years ago. He'd been straightforward and requested to be removed from her care team in the event he might want to pursue a relationship, something he couldn't ethically do as her doctor. Dr. Cook had commended him for taking the ethical route and approved the change while warning him to proceed cautiously.

Refocusing,

Michael excused himself with a promise to catch up with the fellows soon. On his way to his office, his chest swelled. The road here hadn't been easy, but he was here now.

Hours later, he slumped into his plush chair, his palms flattening on the polished mahogany desk, such a stark contrast to the crisp white walls. He pivoted his seat toward the tall window offering a panoramic view of Orlando's skyline, the fading sunlight casting an ethereal glow over the city. Yes, this was where he was meant to be.

His cell phone buzzed with a text from Clara. She'd attached a picture of a beaming Jason in his new basketball uniform.

Michael then opened the draft email from Faith, her college essay attached. As he read her words, he let out a low whistle. What a girl! Her writing was poised and articulate. She was so much like her mother.

Dear Clara. He ran a hand over his face. He should have done something long ago. As a physician, he healed patients. But for so long, he'd been so helpless when it came to helping his wife recover her lost memories or her past. Then their move back south had unsettled her more than he'd expected, pushing him to do something he should've been brave enough to do long ago. Why did part of him still fear he might lose her if she found herself?

He typed his feedback, ensuring his constructive words remained encouraging. He was still at it when a knock interrupted him.

"Dr. Khoury, it's time for your last meeting for the day," his assistant announced.

As he closed his office door, he wondered when the PI would report back.

CHAPTER 2

OLIVIA

"She will only talk to Ms. Tso."

So many thoughts zipped through Olivia Tso's mind as Leslie Phillips, the assistant US attorney, said those words. But first, she needed to know the specifics. Phillips did say the envelope might explain things. Olivia opened it, skimming a letter from the president requesting her assistance. No other explanation.

She tucked the letter away. "Did she specifically ask for Olivia Tso?"

"I believe so," Phillips said.

It didn't make sense. Olivia Tso was "legally" dead for over twenty years. Did the Ghost know she'd been alive all this time? If so, why was she still standing? The Ghost would have had people hunt her down and eliminate her.

"Anything else you can tell me?"

"I'm just a messenger. You know as much as I do." Phillips's lips flattened. "However, we need you to come with us."

"What?" Simon Roth, her new fiancé, and Agent Ron Peters, head of the task force, spoke over each other.

"It's Thanksgiving!"

Simon held up a hand. "You need to understand. We've just gotten engaged. Can't this wait?"

"I'm sorry." Phillips pursed her red-painted lips, a finger straying to fumble with the matching cranberry brooch pinned to her lapel. "I came from my dinner too. But this is one of those rare occasions. I can chopper you back here tonight after your meeting. And depends on what her demands are, if any, we can discuss those later."

Simon was frowning. "Can we have a moment, please?"

"Of course."

Ever the hostess, Ms. Carol Marino, the Marino family matriarch, touched her grandson's arm. "Dylan, please invite our guests to have a seat."

As Ron took Simon and Olivia off to the side, the young ones wanted to join, but Ron shooed his son, Kyle, and Simon and Olivia's daughter, Lily, away with Dylan and Tommy.

"I thought you were 'dead'"—Simon's fingers formed air quotes—"to the world."

"Just what I was thinking." Olivia pressed cold fingers to the thrumming at her temples. The Company—the nickname operatives used when speaking of the CIA—had faked her death two decades ago to protect her and her yet-to-be-born baby. Even Simon hadn't known until they reunited mere months ago.

"The more important question is this—Does she know you're Phoenix?" asked Ron. Phoenix—the code name the intelligence community had given her years ago.

Her fingers moved to knead the furrowed space between her brows. "I doubt it. If she had known, she'd have killed me long ago. Something is strange. Let's say she's known I'm alive all along and for whatever reason she let me live, then the only way she'd know I'm here in the States and especially in Florida is if there's a leak somewhere."

Simon gripped her shoulders, turning her to face him. "I don't think you should go."

"I agree with Simon." Ron's rich baritone echoed in the cavernous room. "We don't know what the Ghost knows. It's too risky."

She'd been promised her days dealing with the Ghost were over. She was going to put her family first. But now this?

The Ghost only wanted to speak with her. She could do that, couldn't she? She eased back from Simon's hold. "I don't have a choice. Uncle Sam is still my employer. Besides, the big boss sent me a personal letter requesting my assistance." She took a deep breath to push out the assurance she needed to portray. "I'll go and meet with her. See what she wants. I may find out how and what she knows."

Olivia had spent over two decades infiltrating the Ghost's organization, understanding its labyrinth. The Ghost, born as Marge Beaumont, was a criminal mastermind now in federal custody who'd threatened to unleash a deadly bioweapon. Olivia had been instrumental in averting that disaster.

"You shouldn't trust her." Dylan Roche, the Ghost's biological nephew, raked his fingers through his hair as if trying to pull away the roots connecting him to the Ghost. "I bet she's up to no good."

Evidently, the young ones were listening in. The young man had become good friends with Lily in the last weeks. Olivia raised her hand, a silent plea for calm. "I understand your worries and appreciate your concerns—really, I do. But I must see what she wants. That's all."

The room fell silent again. Simon reached out to squeeze her hand, his grip warm and reassuring. Ron nodded, his stern expression softening, while Dylan stewed. As for Olivia, curiosity ignited within her. This she was eager to solve.

Then came Lily's voice, so much like her own. "But, Mom." Lily, having grown up not knowing her parents, had recently started calling her Mom and Simon Dad. "You're supposed to be dead. How would she know you're alive? And how would she know you're here in the States?"

Ron cleared his throat. "Good questions. We were just thinking about that. Don't you worry. I'll be looking into it, will plug the leak."

Olivia pulled Lily into a tight embrace, the warmth of her daughter a balm against the uncertainty. Their family had recently reunited, even Simon hadn't known about his daughter. "Oh, sweetheart, I don't have the answers. And maybe seeing her will get her to tell me something. I'll be back in a jiffy. Don't worry, baby girl."

She gave her daughter one last squeeze, then met Phillips's expectant gaze. "Let's do this."

As the heavy metal door clanged shut behind her, Olivia stepped into the secure room, her heart thudding against her ribs. She stood mere feet away from the Ghost. She'd gained the woman's trust and confidence while working undercover under the name Jade Lam. Jade was "killed" weeks ago, and she hadn't worn her "Jade" lifelike mask and wig. Today, she was coming as herself, Olivia Tso, and ditching the Hong Kong accent.

The woman lounged in a chair, her posture relaxed as if she were settled in her own living room. Her eyes, cold and calculating, took in Olivia's appearance. "Surprised?" She smirked. "I've always suspected something was going on with your sudden demise so many years ago. Just couldn't figure out where they'd stashed you."

Olivia's death. Not Jade's. *That* was the sudden demise the Ghost was speaking of. Olivia had to keep it straight and not let anything slip. Still, a chill ran down her spine, the sterile smell of the federal facility doing little to mask the underlying scent of danger, an almost electrical odor lingering around the Ghost. Olivia shivered at snippets from her last conversation with this woman as Jade. Beaumont had a relationship with the deceased retired Senator Rifkin. Rifkin must've let her know about Olivia and Simon so long ago in Hong Kong. Could that be how they found out about Lily?

"How did you know?" Olivia sat, keeping her Jade persona locked away. Surely, the Ghost didn't know she was Jade?

A nonchalant shrug was the response. "That you're here in America? Or that you're alive? Haven't they told you I have people everywhere? A little bird informed me you'd reemerged. And of all places, here in Florida."

So someone had talked. Only a handful of people knew about her past. Who could have said something? Anyway, Ron promised to take care of the problem. For now, Olivia focused on the problem sitting before her. "You asked to see me. I'm here. What do you want?"

A slow, predatory smile curved Beaumont's lips. "I want to live on the Marino grounds."

That had to be a joke. "Don't waste my time. What do you want?"

"I just told you."

Olivia sucked in a sharp breath. The woman meant it. "I doubt that will happen. There's no prison on the estate grounds."

"But they can always build something, can't they?"

"You're asking a lot. Say, if this were to happen, what would you do in return?"

"I'd help you or the task force take down other criminal masterminds."

Of all the audacity! The Ghost's organization spanned a sprawling global criminal network, from New York's grimy underbelly to Tokyo's high-rise offices. In a complex hierarchy, much like the yakuza in Japan, different families controlled distinct businesses and geographical locations. Plenty more villains were ready to step up, to carry on the activities she orchestrated.

Of course, she also had her share of rivals, organizations now thriving without her interference. If she were to help the task force take down these threats, well, such a tantalizing offer could tip the scales in their favor.

If they could trust her.

Olivia crossed her arms, narrowing her eyes. "And why would you do that?"

CHAPTER 3

RON

The bustling coffee shop created a pleasant background for their meeting. Agent Ron Peters sat at a corner table, sipping on his black coffee while waiting for his team. When Jose Hernandez, Nathan Tanner, and Ana Ruiz entered, he motioned each to join him.

Once they settled in, he leaned forward, resting his arms on the laminate tabletop. "Sorry for interrupting your holiday. And thank you for coming."

They all shrugged off the apology, all but Ana, Ron's longtime friend, the DIA agent now serving his task force as a liaison, who smirked. "Actually, thank you for saving me from dealing with extended family drama."

"I have a question for you three." He scowled into the dregs of his coffee. How did he drink it so fast these days? Shoving the mug aside, he locked his gaze onto each of them in turn. Blenders churned ice in the background, his stomach churning with the grating sound. "I need you to be honest. Have any of you talked about Olivia? To anyone?"

"Whoa, man." Tanner held up a hand in a stop motion. "Of course not."

Hernandez shook his head, echoing Tanner's response.

"Why are you asking?" Ana sipped her coffee, a crease forming between her brows. "What's going on, Ron?"

He studied them a moment longer before reclining in his chair. He had known these agents for years, trusted them, and expected these responses. Surely, they were telling the truth.

"I'm sorry." He rubbed the back of his neck, some of his tension sliding free with the air emptying his lungs. "I had to make sure. I trust you, but the stakes are high."

"What's going on?" Tanner folded his arms across his chest, head cocked to one side. "Why did you ask us about Olivia?"

Ron took a deep breath. This wasn't something a team leader ever wanted to say, but… "There's been a leak. Somehow, the Ghost has learned Olivia is alive and here in the States."

They exchanged glances. Tanner's eyes went wide. Hernandez's mouth was hanging open. Ana simply stared at him.

"Our job," Ron continued, "is to find the leak. The fewer people who know about this, the better. I'm counting on you all."

His team nodded, silent under the gravity of the situation. A load lifted from his shoulders, and he breathed deep. He trusted them. Together, they'd do everything to protect one of their own.

"I'm gonna start a deep dive on everyone," Tanner said.

Ron dipped his head. "Including me. You do everyone on the team and the office who knows about her. And Hernandez, you work on the senator, Lily, Dylan, all the young folks."

"Yeah, boss."

"What would you like me to do?" Ana swigged her drink, setting it down with the thud she used when she was ready to take off on a task.

"You and I work the other end. Who has the Ghost been in contact with since she's been in custody?"

She nodded. "If we know who gave her the info, we can work backward to find out who the source is."

"Remember, we do this on the DL."

Tanner scrubbed a hand down his face, leaving his bushy eyebrows askew. "Any idea what the psychopath wants?"

If Ron had to guess, he would bet the Ghost wanted some deal to get her off. However, he couldn't think of a leverage she could use. He shook his head. "Don't know. Olivia texted. The Ghost wanted something, but she didn't say what. I'm meeting with Olivia and Simon later today. And I hope you'll all find out on Monday."

In the soft light of Simon Roth's study, Ron breathed in slowly, inhaling the air of tension. He, Simon, and Olivia huddled around an antique oak desk, its worn surface scarred from years of use. The deep-seated leather chairs, which once might have been comforting, now seemed stiff and cold.

Simon had always been a fastidious man, and while his home was no exception, this room in particular exhibited his penchant for the orderly. Bookshelves lined the walls bracketing the credenza. Beyond the executive desk and chair, two other chairs perched at perfect angles facing the desk. Simon and Olivia now sat on the black couch in the corner while Ron attempted to get comfortable on his stiff chair, squinting in the glare from the floor-to-ceiling window falling across his face. Time to focus. He leaned back in his chair and stretched out his legs. "I'm guessing she doesn't know you're Phoenix—or Jade."

Olivia wouldn't be so calm if her cover had been blown.

A faraway look glazed her eyes. "I'm not getting that vibe from all the years I interacted with her… although most of those interactions were virtual." She blinked, her dark eyes coming into focus. "It's just how I feel. Obviously, I couldn't ask her."

Obviously. Ron smiled. No wonder Simon had fallen hard for her.

"Tell him what she wants." Simon's leg jittered.

For Simon to display his anxiety, it must be bad.

"Look." Olivia rubbed her eyes. "The Ghost is offering information that can help us capture other individuals on our most wanted list. In return, she wants… to live on the Marino grounds."

Ron jolted into a more upright position. Of all the demands he'd imagined, this wasn't one of them. He lifted his eyebrows. "Mirror Estate grounds?"

"That's right."

He gave a sardonic snort. "I doubt the AG will go for it." He clasped his hands tightly, white knuckles revealing his tension. "If we agree to her conditions, we'd be giving her a free pass."

Simon leaned back, stretching an arm across the back of the couch. The sunlight slipping past the glass highlighted the lines weathering his face, deepening the thoughtfulness of his expression. "It is tempting though. If she's willing to cooperate, it could be a big win for us."

"But what's in it for her?" Ron furrowed his brows, the pinched creases warning of an impending headache.

"That," Simon echoed, "is the million-dollar question."

Olivia sighed, that faraway look intruding in her eyes again. "I asked her. I did. But all she gave me were vague answers and cryptic smiles. 'Can't I just do something good for a change?' Yeah right. No way is she doing this out of the goodness of her heart."

Each word resounded in the following silence. The ticking of an old grandfather clock, a sentinel in the corner, was the only intrusion to their thoughts. The Ghost had never been known for altruism. Whatever she was planning, they needed to be cautious. Very cautious indeed.

"She has an angle," Olivia murmured. "I just need to figure it out."

CHAPTER 4

DYLAN

Dylan Roche sat at his desk, surrounded by spreadsheets, notes, and copies of meticulously arranged evidence. His mother's dying message directed him to unearth these documents she and his father buried. Before Dylan turned them over to Agent Ron Peters, he'd made copies of his family's dark history. Tom Rivers, his best friend, was staying over at the estate and now came to offer his assistance. Maybe, together, they'd unravel the mystery within these documents.

Tommy locked his hands behind his neck and whistled. "This is quite the collection."

"That's why I got you here to help." The only person he trusted completely. "You understand the spreadsheet better than I do."

"I'll do my best."

"Thanks, bro." Dylan slapped his friend's shoulder. "I know you will. We need to understand the Ghost and her empire."

Tommy nodded, flipping through the spreadsheets and notes. He dropped one to the hardwood floor and scooped it up. "Let's start by examining these together. Some connection or pattern might lead us to more answers."

After hours of analyzing the numbers and deciphering the coded information, Tommy slapped the table. "Look at this, would ya?" He pointed to a particular column. "These numbers seem to be transactions. If we cross-reference them with the dates mentioned in these notes, we might identify the flow of money and how it connects to the Ghost's activities."

Dylan let out a low whistle. "This is a significant break-through. What if we can trace the people involved?"

As Olivia once said, the Ghost's usual tactic was to bribe. When that wouldn't work, she resorted to blackmail. After that, he wouldn't put it past her to eliminate any obstacle. His paternal grandfather was one such victim—even though it was never proven. Her methods worked. She controlled people in high and low positions.

"You think these are bribes?" Dylan tapped the circled numbers.

"Could be." Tommy shrugged. "Your granddad didn't spec-ify, but it looks like it. Either that or blackmail. These are code names. Maybe Olivia knows who they are."

"Maybe, but I doubt she'd tell me. Classified. Need to know." Those were the standard responses from Agent Peters or other federal agents.

"By the way, have you heard anything about what your aunt wanted?"

"Again, I don't know if they'll tell us. Whatever it is, she can't be trusted—it'll benefit her somehow."

After a while, Tommy put a spreadsheet aside. "What if she found a way to go after the rumored treasure on the estate grounds?"

"I wouldn't be surprised if they exist. The Ghost always has an endgame in mind, and if there's even a slight chance she's after that, I'm gonna do everything I can to prevent it. But first, I need to talk to someone else—Fr. Phil."

Tommy's brow furrowed. "Why Fr. Phil?"

"I get the feeling he hasn't told me everything he knows about my parents." Dylan jerked up his chin. "I'm sick of secrets. It's time to confront him. Wanna come with me?"

"Nah, I need to call my sister." Tommy tossed the beer can into the recycle bin. "Let me know if you learn anything, okay?"

Dylan followed his friend outside and closed his room's door. Twenty minutes later, he entered the tranquil chapel, its hushed atmosphere calming his inner turmoil. The flickering candles cast dancing shadows on the polished pews, creating a reverent ambiance. The middle-aged priest knelt engrossed in prayer by the altar, his figure shrouded in the soft glow of sunlight streaming through stained glass windows.

After approaching, Dylan waited before clearing his throat.

Fr. Phil glanced over his shoulder, and a smile curved his narrow mouth and softened his hard jaw. "Hey, Dylan." He reached to shake hands. "What brings you here today?"

He returned the smile. "I was hoping we could talk." He turned the priest's hand, clamping his free hand atop their clasped ones. "Um, about my parents, their past, and the secrets they carried."

A depth of understanding darkened Fr. Phil's blue eyes. "Of course." He nodded toward a side door, a shock of curly gray hair tumbling over his forehead. "Let's head to the office."

As they passed the sacristy toward his office, Dylan's heart raced. Could he finally uncover the truth hidden within the priest's vault of knowledge?

"Fr. Phil," Dylan began when he took a seat at the chair facing the desk. The setting sun crept in through the window behind the desk. His fingers dug into the wooden armrests. "Do you know anything about a rumored treasure on the estate grounds? Something the Ghost might be after?"

The priest sank into the chair behind the desk and folded his hands across his lean stomach, his gaze fixed on a distant point. "Ah, the rumored treasure. That tale has been passed down through generations. Your father first told me that story, claiming when the Marinos came to this country, they had their loot with them. Apparently, the Mafia was chasing them. One of them buried their treasure somewhere around here, but only two Marinos—your great-grandfather and his sister—survived the Mafia war. His sister married Charles Townsend Sr.—"

"Wait." Dylan held up a hand. "I'm related to the lawyer? Grandma never said anything about that." The lawyer, Charles Townsend Jr. had gone to Washington State several months ago to bring him to meet his grandmother.

Fr. Phil shook his head. "Remember, it's legend. I can't vouch for its validity. Anyway, the one who buried the treasure died without revealing where he hid the money. And the survivors didn't care too much about finding it."

Elbows braced on his knees, Dylan leaned forward. "Father, if there's a possibility the treasure is real and the Ghost has her sights set on it, I need to know. I can't let her profit from it."

The priest's gaze softened. "Your determination and bravery remind me so much of your grandfather on your dad's side. He possessed a similar fire, a relentless pursuit of justice and truth. That's why he was such a great cop."

Dylan sucked in a sharp breath. "I didn't know you knew my grandfather."

Fr. Phil smiled. "I did."

"Did you know him well?"

"Well enough."

Heat flooded Dylan's being. He'd come seeking answers. He'd found more questions. Why couldn't Fr. Phil tell him about his relationship with his folks and his grandfather? And how would he find out if the treasure was more than rumors?

Fr. Phil tapped his index fingers together, his black clerical garb crinkling under his hands. "I heard your parents had buried some evidence and notes, journals and such. Did you not find them helpful?"

Dylan forked his fingers through his hair, pulling at the roots in a vain attempt to stimulate blood flow to his brain. Journals? He hadn't seen any journals. "They had journals? They weren't in the box."

"I can't say. They might have taken the journals with them when they ran away. Or, if not, they could have hidden them somewhere else."

"What else can you tell me about my parents and my grandfather? You've no idea what it was like to grow up believing my mother's family had all passed." Soon after her death, he met his maternal grandmother and learned about the family's checkered past. "I have no memory of his father since he died when I was a toddler. If you hadn't told me about my parents meeting here at the estate, I wouldn't know that either."

"What would you like to know?"

Everything! Why couldn't Fr. Phil grasp that? Dylan shrugged. "Anything."

While the priest spoke, Dylan sank back in his chair. If his parents hadn't left with the journals, they would have hidden them too. He'd go back to the site and dig deeper. He'd stopped digging when he hit metal, so he could have missed something. Maybe they'd buried more than the box.

CHAPTER 5

OLIVIA

Inside the austere Sensitive Compartmented Information Facility (SCIF), the hum of electronic equipment created a consistent background noise, its whir an embodiment of the tension thrumming through the sterile space. Braced for the discussion, Olivia sat with Ron and Simon at the central table, a secure virtual conference line connecting them to Leslie Phillips, the AUSA, and Ron's team outside the room. Olivia's CIA credential was still valid. Technically, she was still an intelligence operative. But to get Simon admitted, they'd had to designate him as a special consultant to the task force, even though he'd recently been a ranking member of the Senate Intelligence Committee.

After they updated Phillips on the Ghost's demand, Phillips scoffed. "I highly doubt I can sell that up the food chain. She'd escape easily."

"No," Olivia countered. "If we proceed, we'd need to construct a secured enclosure on the estate. Armed guards, the works. She wouldn't be free, but she wouldn't be in a traditional prison either."

"But we would still need the cooperation of Ms. Marino and the grandson," Phillips interjected via the conference line. She pulled off her glasses, her face grave on the screen. "Even then, it's a long shot. And how can we be sure the Ghost—or should I call her Marge Beaumont?—wouldn't go back on her word? About helping us capture others on the most wanted list."

Wasn't that obvious? Olivia tugged a stray hair behind her ear. "If she decided not to help, she'd win a one-way ticket to supermax."

"Come to think of it." Ron held up a hand, an old scar on his palm flashing white in the LED lighting. "Where would we construct this enclosure?"

After a brief silence, Simon cleared his throat. "The closed orphanage, or at least, parts of it, could be converted to this makeshift prison. It's on the estate grounds."

Simon would know. Few people knew about his past—that he had spent years at the orphanage. He'd told Olivia about the place, its lively atmosphere, and the nuns in their habits among the lay teachers. Toward the end of Simon's time there, Fr. Phil, a transitional deacon at the time, joined the teachers. Then after he graduated came the final blow—the cessation of government funding. While the Catholic Church ran the school, the orphanage had received state subsidies.

"Hello, are you with us?" asked Ron.

Simon rubbed his eyes as Ron's voice appeared to bring him out of his reverie, and Olivia spanned back to focus as well. "Sorry. Spaced out for a minute."

"I was saying, you guys need to get the Marinos on board before I try to run it up the food chain." Phillips slid her gold-rimmed glasses back in place.

"That makes sense. It's a private property," Simon agreed.

With that, they adjourned the meeting.

The door clicked shut behind Ron, leaving Olivia with Simon. His gaze warmed her, not in a scrutinizing way but more like someone piecing together a complex puzzle. He'd been like that, observing the changes in her since they'd reconnected. The spirit of her past, a burning desire for the adrenaline-pumping world of espionage, still simmered within her. Yet, alongside it was a newfound tranquility, a sort of stillness she had managed to cultivate.

"You're thinking about it, right?" He broke the silence. "Getting back in the game?"

Her gaze drifted toward the screen, veiling her internal struggle. When she finally spoke, her words came out soft, almost a whisper. "A part of me still craves it, Simon."

"But?" His knit brows and his tender expression somehow conveyed a nuanced understanding of her internal battle. He leaned forward, making it not an interrogation, but an intimate conversation. "But?"

The meeting of their eyes was like a secret language, an understanding only they, with their shared history, could comprehend. "But I'm back with you and Lily. That has to be my priority. Our family."

A palpable relief stole the tension from his features, his shoulders unwinding. Yes, he understood the gravity of her choices, the potential sacrifices involved. She was choosing them, choosing family, over a life she once lived and breathed.

"So you're okay with being the mediator between the Ghost and the task force?"

"Yes." Unwavering, she locked her eyes onto his, revealing a depth of conviction that needed no further explanation. "For now, that's the plan."

CHAPTER 6

CLARA & ROOK

Clara was cleaning up after dinner while Michael watched the evening news. She seldom watched the news, preferring to glance at the headlines on her phone. An intriguing segment on the science of memories had just concluded—a discussion on how our memories, even the ones buried, continue to shape our lives.

She scrubbed the marbled counters, mentally going over her to-do list for the evening and next day, but unable to shake the TV report on memories, an interesting, albeit distant, echo.

Then a name uttered by the newscaster jolted her. She pivoted and focused on the TV. Images on the screen displayed a dilapidated building and a swarm of police officers. The news anchor's voice took on a somber tone. "During the demolition of an office complex, workers made a grisly discovery—the remains of a body hidden within the walls. Police have identified the victim as one Linda Boroski...."

Clara sucked in a gasp, gripping the waterfall island counter between the kitchen and living room as the name stirred a dormant memory, a forgotten face. The news segment transitioned to an old photograph of a smiling young woman—Linda Boroski. How eerily familiar the image seemed. Clara rounded the island, edging into the living room, her jaw clenching so tight her teeth hurt.

"Michael?" Her voice hushed, she kept her gaze fixed on the screen. "Does the name Linda Boroski sound familiar?"

"Linda Boroski?" he echoed, the name rolling off his tongue as he tried to place it. "Can't say it does. Why?"

She chewed her lower lip, Linda Boroski's fading image still on the television screen. "I don't know? The name… and her face. It seems familiar, but I can't remember from where."

"Boroski is not a common name. I'd have remembered."

Her teeth ground together. "Exactly. But I know that name."

A phone number flashed on the screen, urging anyone with information about the twenty-year-old crime to come forward. Clara fumbled for her phone, typing in the number. She wasn't sure why, but something urged her to dig deeper into this mystery.

As the evening morphed into night, she couldn't shake the unsettling news and the victim's haunting image. Each time she closed her eyes, she could see the old photograph, the woman's eyes beaming with an innocence that contrasted her fate.

Restless, she pulled the decorative cream and gold pillows off their bed, turned down the rich navy spread, and plumped her pillow behind her before settling in with her laptop. She typed in a few keywords, hoping to uncover more about Linda's case. The top articles were all from various news outlets, reiterating the same information. So, tucking her feet up underneath her, she searched for something about memory triggers. Could this name help her recover her memory? She scrolled the countless search results and stopped at a different article: "The Architect of Identity: The Crucial Role of Memories in Shaping Our Lives.'"

As she delved into the piece, her fingers knotted around the plush comforter, and her mind hummed with the words of the experts interviewed. Dr. Laura Patterson's analogy of memories serving as the mind's filing system resonated, while Dr. Mark Fields's insights on shared experiences and memories strengthening bonds were thought-provoking. What an intriguing concept—memories not only as snapshots of the past but also as architects of one's identity.

The soft padding of bare feet on hardwood flooring preceded Michael's entry into the room, his brows furrowed as he eyed her. "Still thinking about the news?"

She nodded, gesturing toward her laptop. "I found this article about memories. It talks about how they shape our lives, our identities."

Michael settled on the edge of the bed. "Memories are powerful." He reached over and rubbed her back. "They can bring joy and sorrow or even guide our decisions. They're a fundamental part of who we are."

Her shoulders sloped, her spine sinking against his warm hand. "But I have no memory of half my life."

His grip circled her waist, drawing her in against him. His breath warmed her hair as he spoke. "Not entirely true."

"Yeah, yeah." She turned in his grip and cupped a palm to his face. "I know what you're gonna say. I speak Cantonese, even though I don't remember when I spoke it or how I know the language. I know the places in Hong Kong. I know what dim sum to order at a Chinese restaurant and whether it's authentic or not—"

"That's right. Your memories are just locked in your head." He covered her hand on his cheek, then brought it to his mouth, and kissed her palm. "But, honey, you've been making new memories."

"Yes." She nestled into him. "Good memories too."

But how do I unlock those hidden memories?

A chill hung in the evening air as Rook—code name for one of the Ghost's trusted lieutenants—ascended the winding path to US Attorney General Koenig's sprawling Virginia residence. Situated atop a hill, the grand mansion loomed like an intimidating fortress shrouded in the deep hues of dusk. However, the imposing façade did little to deter Rook's mission.

From his vantage point, his footsteps reverberated with a controlled, rhythmic cadence as he crossed the expansive foyer. Meanwhile, Koenig radiated nervous energy in his grand living room. His fingers entangled in restless motion, and worry lines creased his forehead.

Koenig's head tilted with immediate recognition when their eyes met through the security monitor. Koenig must be aware of why Rook was there. The Ghost had sent him, and when the Ghost sent someone like him, it meant business. The Ghost was no petty criminal. She was leagues above that, which must heighten Koenig's anxiety.

As the housemaid led Rook into the living room, Koenig dismissed her, seeming desperate to keep their conversation private. How amusing to see such a powerful man rendered so weak, especially while, for Rook, it was just another day on the job.

"I can't spring her this time, Rook." Koenig crossed the plush carpet, his voice echoing in the silence, his gaze darting around, refusing to meet Rook's penetrating stare. Shadows accentuated the stress lines around his eyes and mouth, even with his face flushed.

Rook shrugged. "She doesn't want to be free. She wants to live on the Mirror Estate grounds."

Koenig's pacing halted. His head jerked up, his eyes wide. "She wants what? Why would she want that?"

Chuckling, Rook flashed his signature chilling smirk. "You want to question the Ghost's motives, Koenig?"

His hand delved into the pocket of his tailored suit, retrieving a tiny cassette tape. He held it up, the dim light glinting off its plastic casing.

Koenig's face paled, his breath hitching. "What's that?"

Rook twirled the tape between his fingers, enjoying the moment, the power and control. This was why he worked for the Ghost. Sure, the pay was good, but nothing beat making men who thought they owned the world squirm. "Remember our little conversation, Koenig? The one you had with the Ghost? The one about your daughter?"

The blood drained from Koenig's face. The man had been desperate when his world collapsed—the brutal murder of his daughter, the miscarriage of justice. The fool had sought the Ghost's help and maybe even made himself believe that secret was safely buried with the painful past.

Rook leaned in closer with an intensity that likely sent a chill down Koenig's spine. "If you don't comply, Koenig, this will become public consumption."

"But–but this is a big case. Lots of senators are involved."

"Don't worry. You'll have the support of the White House counsel."

Rook's smirk widened, his fingers closing around the empty cassette. The real one was safe with the Ghost. The implied threat was more than enough to push Koenig to the edge. In their world of shadows and secrets, perception was often stronger than reality. And the Ghost? She always got what she wanted.

CHAPTER 7

EVA

As Eva Higgins stood on the Mirror Estate's beautifully landscaped lawn, Uncle Bill's words kept repeating themselves in her mind. Even years later, she remembered them clearly. His countenance, usually jovial, had been etched with grim lines as he said, "I'm convinced Clara didn't vanish. I fear she might have fallen prey to human trafficking."

Those words impacted her decision to join the FBI.

Now, she strolled with her new friend, Lily, who was still unaware of this theory. With her dark, straight hair cascading past her shoulders and her brown eyes reflecting her mixed heritage, Lily displayed innocent curiosity and strength.

"I never believed she ran away," Eva confessed, her voice barely more than a whisper against the leaves' soft rustling. She paused before a nearby rose, the crimson bloom basking in the sunset. Her fingers strayed to touch one delicate petal. "She promised me, Lily. Promised she'd be at my dance recital."

As a cool breeze swept over them, Lily gathered her long

tresses into her hand, then released them to fan down her back. "And she never showed?"

Eva shook her head, the pang of her childhood disappointment still alive in her heart. "I was five. But I remember." She swallowed, summoning the courage to continue. "The police didn't investigate seriously, claiming no foul play. She was a legal adult, blah, blah, blah. They believed she ran off. Of course, I know now missing persons cases aren't a priority unless it's a senior, a kid, or a VIP. But my aunt Clara—she had plans. She wouldn't have just disappeared." Eva swallowed hard, her heart pounding with the weight of her next words. "I think… I think she might have been a victim of human trafficking."

"Why would you think that?" Lily's eyes widened, but she held steady. "Oops, the photo! Mom wasn't around when I went home the other day after you told me about the photo. You know, the one with your aunt being the third girl with my mom and godmother. I forgot to tell her about Clara. You watch, once I tell her, she'll know what to do. And we'll find out the truth."

Eva didn't want to believe her aunt was trafficked, but Uncle Bill's words and Clara's journal told a different story. But was she ready to share it with Lily? Then again, Lily's mom was a CIA Officer. She might be able to help. "My mom retrieved all Clara's belongings. Among other things, there was this journal. I started reading it and kept it since. Some entries in there made me think her disappearance was more sinister than it looked. She was investigating a human trafficker."

A frown crinkled her friend's flawless forehead. "I thought you said she was a graduate student."

"She was, but she had a part-time job as a staff writer for a magazine. She met this figure during one of the events she covered."

"Oh, wow! Who? Who did she meet?"

"I don't know."

"I'll tell my mom. She'll know what to do."

"Thanks. I hope so." But would Olivia know? Aunt Clara had met the Ghost's public persona of the Ghost. Clara even saved a few articles she had penned as a junior staff writer.

A Night with the Visionary:
An Interview with Marge Beaumont, CEO of the Beaumont Foundation

Beaumont Hotel's grand ballroom, replete with futuristic art pieces symbolizing hope and progress, hosted the Beaumont Foundation's annual gala, "Building Tomorrow." Symphonies played, champagne flowed, and chandeliers illumed the city's elite—philanthropists, social leaders, and visionaries, all coming together for a common cause. But the most captivating presence was Marge Beaumont, the Foundation's young and dynamic CEO.

This journalist was granted an unexpected opportunity for an interview when Marge expressed interest in talking. We found a quiet corner and settled into plush velvet chairs. Her presence exuded grace and authority, and her eyes sparkled with a genuine passion while her warmth set the tone for our conversation.

Beaumont Foundation was her parents' dream, focused on empowering others through education and healthcare. After their tragic accident, Marge carried on their legacy, becoming the CEO contrary to her planned path and determined to turn the Foundation into a beacon of hope.

"The evening's building-tomorrow theme signifies the Foundation's commitment to the future," Marge Beaumont said. "By investing in education and healthcare today, we're nurturing a brighter tomorrow for all." Marge went on to speak passionately about their focus on STEM education for girls and collaborations with hospitals to make healthcare accessible to those in need.

When I asked about the balance between being a CEO and maintaining a personal life, Marge acknowledged the constant challenge but emphasized the importance of family support and self-care. "Though my days are often filled with meetings and hands-on involvement, I find time to recharge and reflect on my goals. Without goals, any person, any foundation can stagnate."

Those goals shine through Marge's work. Her drive comes from a deep sense of compassion that makes it obvious her goal is not just to grow the Beaumont Foundation but also to touch as many lives as possible. She has faced challenges, such as funding and skepticism, but has overcome them through transparency, alignment with the right partners, and a clear vision.

Among the success stories, Marge shared the story of a young girl named Aisha, who is now studying medicine and is determined to give back to her community. "Her story epitomizes what the Beaumont Foundation stands for," Marge said, "symbolizing hope, empowerment, and the ripple effect education can create."

The evening continued with a gala dinner, a silent auction, and speeches that moved many to tears. Marge's speech was a highlight, filled with conviction, inspiration, and a call to action. Her words resonated, leaving an indelible mark on this journalist and seemingly all present.

As the night wore on, I reflected on the experience. The grandeur of the ballroom, the glamour of the guests, the sumptuous food, and the eloquent speeches were all part of a beautiful tapestry. But the core of the evening was Marge Beaumont herself. Her dedication to a cause, her unwavering belief in humanity, her vision, and her ability to turn dreams into reality set the night apart.

Marge Beaumont is more than just a CEO: She is a symbol of hope, a beacon guiding us toward a better future. Through her leadership, the Beaumont Foundation is not just a charitable organization but also a force for change, a movement that promises a brighter tomorrow for countless lives.

Her story is a testament to the fact that age, gender, or circumstances don't define us—our actions do. It was a story of dreams realized, of barriers broken, and of a young woman's relentless pursuit in making the world a better place.

As I left the grand ballroom, now bathed in soft lights, I knew I had witnessed something special. A night with Marge Beaumont was not just an event: It was an inspiration.

The article only proved Aunt Clara had met the Ghost. However, the next few entries disturbed Eva the most and persuaded her Clara's disappearance was more sinister than the police thought.

CHAPTER 8

OLIVIA & ROOK

In the Mirror Estate's great room, afternoon sunlight shone through the wall of windows, gleaming off antique mahogany furniture and those faded family pictures on the walls. The room smelled like old wood, overplayed by a little whiff of roses coming in from outside.

Olivia stood with Simon just outside the door, talking in hushed voices. "I promise, that's all I'm doing. Just a go-between for the task force and the Ghost." She tipped her face, catching the warmth from the fireplace. When Simon didn't say anything, she kept going. "No one knows I'm Phoenix. But Ron will figure out who's leaking info and stop it. This needed to happen, like, yesterday."

Simon nodded, his hazel brown eyes dimming to a muted shade. "I agree. It's a priority. Knowing him, he's already started."

They stepped back inside, joining Ms. Carol, Dylan, and Ron in a nook of cream-leather wingback chairs clustered over a

Persian rug. With a deep breath, she explained the Ghost's proposal.

"Are you serious?" Dylan gasped out, jerking upright and gripping his chair's arms. "Let her *live* here?"

Ms. Carol let out a soft sigh. "She's still my daughter and your aunt, Dylan. If she wants to live on our grounds, she can."

"But—" His knuckles whitened, his fingers clawing into the leather. He loosened his grip at a stern glance from his grandmother. "You know she has to have an agenda. And it's not good."

"Be that as it may." The older lady's chin rose, dignity in her pose as the sunlight falling over her shoulders cast a halo's glow on her gray hair. "Where is your Christian charity? These good people won't let her roam about freely. And I may get to see her finally."

Ms. Carol had offered to help and wanted to see her daughter whom she had assumed to be dead, but the Ghost had refused. That might motivate the matriarch to allow Marge Beaumont to live on the grounds.

Dylan palmed the back of his neck, kneading it as he ducked his head and mumbled, "Whatever."

He plucked at one of the brass studs beading the front of the armrest. Poor kid. After all, he was the one the Ghost tried to kill several months ago. Facing down the barrel of a gun wasn't something one would forget.

The grandfather clock's soft ticking marked their silence until Olivia cleared her throat. "Ms. Carol, you're right. She won't be roaming about. *If*—a big if—the AG office accepts the deal, she'll be in a maximum-security ward, with an ankle monitor."

Dylan snorted. "But where would this maximum-security ward be? Last I checked, there's no prison on the estate grounds."

"Right." Simon held up a hand, acknowledging Dylan's

sarcasm. "They can convert a portion of the old orphanage. It's not being used anyway. If I'm not mistaken, it's on the estate grounds. With enough security, it could work."

Ms. Carol nodded, the weight of her decision apparent in her expression. "We could do that. It's settled, then. You'll need to ensure it's properly equipped and guarded."

"Yes, ma'am," Olivia responded alongside Simon and Ron.

"Ensure it's more than properly guarded." Dylan crossed his arms over his chest, his expression stern. "She's a criminal mastermind, remember? She'll have something up her sleeve."

"*I* know who she is, Dylan," Ms. Carol said, her tone sharp. Yet, her gaze softened on her grandson. "But *you* need to know she's also family."

Simon slapped his raised hand on his thigh. "We're all aware of the risks involved. That's why the maximum-security ward, the ankle monitor, and of course, the guards."

It all sounded feasible, but Olivia's heart weighed heavy. "The Ghost will have to stay put in the Federal Detention Center until the arrangements are complete."

"I suggest she gives us a name as a good-faith gesture before any deal is signed," Ron said.

"Good idea." Olivia nodded.

"But keep your eyes peeled," Dylan warned. "If she tosses us some small-time player, it's smoke and mirrors."

"Good point." Ron smoothed his slacks as he stood. "Better be someone on our wanted list."

Olivia dipped her head. "We'll see. First, we need the AG to approve the deal."

At the Federal Detention Center, Rook sat at the cheap table, disliking the cold and uninviting facility. The drab-gray walls contained a sterile antiseptic scent strong enough to make anyone's nose scrunch. Yet there he was, adopting the persona of the unassuming attorney Adam O'Shea to report his progress to the one they called the Ghost.

At least the concrete attorney visitation room provided sparse impersonal furniture and a single frosted window filtering the feeble sunlight. Only the occasional hollow echo of guards' footsteps broke the oppressive stillness as Rook focused on the woman across the table.

A beautiful woman, now devoid of any makeup, her brown hair cut into a short, practical bob. The kind of woman one would always take notice of. For years, she'd portrayed herself as a successful businesswoman. Only a trusted few knew her other persona, her true identity. She'd also used a body double, had perhaps even made her doppelganger undergo plastic surgery so they were almost identical. But nobody could mimic her steely eyes, stare, or seductive voice, if she needed to use that.

Those eyes now held his attention as they projected an unspoken challenge to anyone who dared meet her gaze. And few would, for this formidable woman inherited a regional criminal organization and turned it into a global empire while maintaining her philanthropist persona. Admirable, really.

He scanned the dummy papers in front of him. "I've established contact with the AG. Your demands will be met."

"Excellent work, Rook." She flattened her small hands on the steel tabletop, her tone just as flat, devoid of unnecessary sentiment. "Find out about Jade's death. It supposedly happened in Bishop's house. Something about the FBI getting involved."

He cocked his head. "Didn't it happen a few weeks ago?"

"Yes, but I'm not getting the details. Find out who shot her. She was a great computer geek. I don't know what got into her mind to confront Bishop. I told her to get him here to see me. Instead, she went to avenge King...."

Rook stayed quiet while she ranted. He never met Jade, but he'd heard about her—a Hong Kong chick, a computer genius.

All the encrypted communication had gone through her, the Ghost's loyal confidante.

Finally, the Ghost stopped and addressed him again. "So, what else did you find out from your source?"

She'd known about the source he'd cultivated. She never asked who it was, and he never offered. This was a delicate situation. He needed to protect his source. "Other than Olivia Tso is alive and in town, not much else. Her daughter is here, so is the senator, uh, former senator."

"King spent years grooming Roth. I saw early on that one wouldn't bend. But King never listened. Got attached instead. Well, no use lamenting past failures. Any other news?"

Rook shifted in his seat. "I'm still tracking our friend, Phoenix."

Her demeanor changed, her alert eyes lighting up. "What have you learned?"

"The information is"—how to say it?—"sparse. They've been cautious, leaving almost no traces. Only a few people know of his real identity."

"So, Phoenix is real?"

He crossed his legs and laced his hands on the top knee, the nearby steel table chilling him even without having touched it. "I believe so. I mean, he's an urban myth among the spooks. But the intel has to come from somewhere or someone."

She narrowed her eyes. "I trust that you're making every effort to unearth more?"

"Every resource is being utilized."

"Good. But remember, time is a luxury we don't possess. I need information—especially on Jade's killing—and I need it soon."

Rook swallowed, the urgency in her voice bringing a clog to his throat. "Understood."

Her gaze bored into him. "See that you do."

After a whirlwind of cryptic exchanges and clandestine

plans, Rook walked out of the cold building and into the warm afternoon.

He jiggled his car keys, quickening his stride to his car. This wasn't just another assignment. The Ghost had cared about Jade. Now, she'd avenge her death. First, he'd need to dig out who the agents were. If he had to guess, Peters would be involved.

When the Ghost gave an assignment, failure wasn't an option. And of course, he still had to look into Phoenix.

CHAPTER 9

LILY & OLIVIA

Caught in the whirlwind of wedding plans, Lily tucked her feet up on the barstool's rungs, pivoting the seat in short turns before their kitchen island, looking back at the last couple of months. So many things had changed since she was literally plucked from Hong Kong to Florida to deliver an antidote to her father—a man she hadn't known until then. And she met the mother she'd thought was dead. Her father was a senator then, and her mother, a superspy. *How wild!*

Simon's Thanksgiving proposal had delighted all the friends —until the AUSA's arrival put a damper on everything. Nonetheless, Lily offered to help plan the wedding. Oops, she should be focusing on that. She tugged her open laptop closer and tapped to awaken the screen, her recent browsings for reception venues coming back up. Fr. Phil had scheduled their marriage preparation. Check. They had reserved the chapel. Check. Now, they needed a reception venue.

The garage door opened, and Olivia walked in, followed by Simon cautioning her to be careful of the Ghost. And Mom told him she knew the Ghost very well as Jade, and yes, she'd be careful.

Lily hopped from the barstool, her bare feet slapping cool tile as she hurried over to have her say. "Mom, are you sure they don't want you to go undercover again? Or do spy stuff?"

Mom smiled at her. "I'm only going to be the liaison."

Dad huffed, but Lily avoided eye contact as she said, "Okay, if you say so."

"I do say so. Enough of that. Now, tell me, who's the boyfriend of the week? Dylan? Kyle?"

That got Dad's attention. He'd been rooting for Kyle, while Mom was on Team Dylan. However, Lily wasn't quite ready to pick either one.

"They're not boyfriends." Lily slid her long hair over her shoulders, then flicked away a fallen strand stuck to her long-sleeved top. "Actually, I don't know. We're all friends. I never go out with just one of them. It's always a group thing."

After crossing to her side, Olivia gripped Lily's shoulders, her mother's touch a comfort she'd yet to take for granted. "Yes, but I sense some underlying tension between the two guys whenever they're together. Hmm, wonder why that is."

Lily could sense the tension herself. It was subtle, and everyone acted friendly. But she could tell. "Well, what am I supposed to do? I like them both. Am I supposed to pick one and stop being friends with the other?"

Mom patted her shoulder. "Baby, I'm lucky I didn't have to choose." She stepped back and hooked her arm around Simon's waist. "I met your father, and that was that. As you said, you're all friends. But when you're ready, you'll know. Your heart will tell you."

As they kissed, Lily averted her gaze. She'd learned to tolerate their display of affection. They had only reunited when she got dragged into a dangerous operation. Now, they couldn't keep their hands off each other. The only time she had witnessed them arguing was soon after her ordeal a few months ago. Mom had wanted to look for a place and have Lily with her so she could keep her safe. Dad had wanted to get to know his daughter. In the end, Lily settled the argument. No way would she live like a child of divorced parents, one week with Mom and another week with Dad. They would all live in Dad's house. Everyone had their own room. Problem solved. After all, the house was big enough to accommodate many.

Having a heart-to-heart with her mother was a new thing. She'd been raised by her uncle and aunt. Then her aunt had passed when Lily was ten, so she'd missed a mother figure in her adolescence years.

At last, her parents finished lip-locking, and she could follow through on a promise. "Mom, do you remember the photo on Auntie Marie's desk?"

Olivia's brows furrowed. She clattered her purse onto the counter. "The one with her and me and Clara, the girl who immigrated to the States years ago?"

Lily swallowed the lump in her throat. "Yes, that one. Clara —she's Eva's aunt. You all looked so different then. The hair, clothing, everything. And you were like, what, thirteen?"

Olivia's hand paused, almost knocking the purse to the floor, her eyes widening slightly. "Clara is Eva's aunt? Really? Small word. And yes, we were about thirteen then. We lost touch after we started high school. Marie managed to stay in touch longer. Where's she? I'd like to reconnect." She touched Simon's arm. "We were best friends back then. And then Clara's family immigrated to the States."

Lily inhaled deeply, preparing for the next part. "Here's the thing. She's been missing for twenty years. Eva thinks she didn't just disappear. She thinks she might have been… trafficked."

A low breath hissed from Mom's lips. "What makes Eva think that? What did the police say?"

Dad, who'd gone to grab something to drink, strode back and

handed Mom a mineral water. "Trafficked? That's quite an accusation. Does she have any proof?"

Rocking back on her heels, Lily tucked her hands into her trousers pockets. "The police didn't take it seriously. They thought she ran away. Eva said missing persons cases weren't a priority, especially with no suspected foul play. But she read her aunt's journal. Clara was investigating a human trafficker. I don't know if that counts as proof."

"Really?" Mom grew still, her lips pursed. "Was she in law enforcement?"

Lily fiddled with the change in her pocket, warm coins jiggling and slipping through her fingertips like Eva said clues slipped past her grasp. "According to Eva, she worked part-time as a staff writer for a magazine. She had somehow met or seen this human trafficker at one of the events she attended." Lily clenched a quarter, holding tight. "What do you think we should do?"

Mom glared. "*We* don't do anything. *I* will see if there's anything I can do."

Later that afternoon, as Olivia entered the plain meeting room at the Federal Detention Center, the air-conditioning's cold smell hit her. Beyond the steel table, the Ghost reclined in her chair, nonchalant amid the severe surroundings.

Swallowing, Olivia took a seat, her heart steady, her gaze unflinching.

You got this. You've talked to her many times before.

But never as Olivia.

Did you forget your Thanksgiving visit?

Oh, shut it! That was different.

What's the difference? Just channel your Jade persona.

But I can't let her know I'm Jade.

Oh, relax. You got this.

She shook her head to clear the voices and chose her words with care. "Your proposal… it's under consideration." But she spoke too high, her voice echoing off the cold walls. *Calm down. Don't let her see you rattled.* "Now we need something in return. A name. Someone significant. And any useful intel you might have on them."

The Ghost met Olivia's gaze with a scrutinizing stare. A heavy moment passed before a hint of a smile curved her mouth. "All right. Ray Ho."

Olivia's heartbeat quickened.

The Ghost didn't miss a beat, her eyes glinting. "I assume you're familiar with him?"

Lily and Dylan's kidnapping surged in Olivia's mind, her pulse thudding in her ears. The confirmation was unexpected, yet it shouldn't be surprising.

"Tell me more." Good, her voice remained steady despite her internal chaos.

"He's the spider at the center of the web, controlling the triads in Hong Kong, Macau, and southern China. Human trafficking is his main line of business. The method is classic—lure them in with visions of the American dream and shackle them with unpayable debts. Of course, he also has a smuggling side business. Clients pay a bundle to get to America."

The all-too-familiar narrative mirrored the brutal strategies the Mexican cartels employed. Olivia folded her hands on the cold steel tabletop. "So the victims… they're put to work in factories, as housekeepers, in restaurants, and such? Or does his operation extend into prostitution?"

The Ghost shrugged, a casual motion that belied their conversation's severity. "That's for your task force buddies to find out."

Olivia followed up with a few more questions, only to be met with similar answers.

"In the meantime, you'll need to stay put." She told the Ghost, the room once again falling into silence. "We're checking the orphanage, seeing if we can convert a part of it into a max-security ward. Architects, contractors, the works. It's a process, and it'll take some time."

The Ghost nodded, her gaze never leaving Olivia's face. As Olivia rose to leave, the sterile scent of the facility lingered, a stark reminder of the high stakes involved.

They had a name and basic information. But many more questions. The Ghost was giving up Ray Ho, which confirmed Olivia's earlier inkling that Beaumont had nothing to do with Dylan's and Lily's kidnapping. So, had Ho tried to take over the Ghost's position?

CHAPTER 10

CLARA & DYLAN

Clara adjusted the angle of her laptop camera, ensuring she appeared professional and composed for the videoconference with her editor in her home office. The screen flickered to life, revealing Ellen's familiar face. Clara tucked her hands out of sight in her lap, gripping them tight as if she could hold herself together. Ever since she heard the news, she thought of little else. And she'd had a nightmare for the first time in years.

"Good morning, Clara," her editor greeted, her voice emanating from the speakers. "How are you today?"

"I'm doing well, thank you." Clara managed a slight smile. "I've been thinking about a potential article idea, and I wanted to run it by you."

"Of course." Ellen leaned forward. "What's on your mind?"

Deep breath, then plunge into the pitch. That's the way she always did it. Never mind that this time was personal. "Well, I've been following the recent news about the remains found by the police. It may not make the national news. It's a case from about twenty years ago."

Ellen dropped her gaze to the keyboard. "Give me the victim's name and location."

Clara did and waited while Ellen typed, her eyes scanning another screen. "Ah, here it is. The police are asking for information, hoping to solve the crime after all these years. What about it?"

Here goes. "I believe I could contribute to the efforts by writing an article. Even though I'm not an investigative journalist, I'd like to ask some questions, delve into the details, and jog people's memories. Maybe, just maybe, we can bring closure to the victim and her family."

Ellen's eyebrows rose. "You write lifestyle and faith-life pieces. What kind of angle?"

"Like I said, I'll write a story offering hope and healing."

"Are you confident you can handle it?"

Clara nodded, her jaw set. "I understand this is a big gig for me. But I was trained in investigative journalism."

Whoa. The words just came out. She hoped she hadn't lied.

She couldn't explain it, but somehow Linda held the key to her memory—or part of the key. Perhaps, by pursuing her story, Clara could uncover something about herself.

After a moment of silence, Ellen raised a hand. "All right. If you think you can do this, then I trust your judgment."

Clara's taut muscles loosened, and she released her tight grip on her hands. Embarking on this investigative journey would be challenging, but easier with her editor's unwavering support.

"Thank you, Ellen." Clara pushed as much gratitude as she could into her voice. "I won't let you down."

Now, if only the headache and nightmare would go away.

Ellen smiled. "I believe in you, Clara. Start working on the article. We'll discuss the details and provide you with any resources to assist. This could be a remarkable piece that offers not only answers but also healing and closure."

Her chest swelling, Clara breathed in deeply. She had been

given an opportunity to delve into a forgotten crime, bring justice, and perhaps uncover a missing piece of her own identity.

Dylan crouched beside Tommy where Dylan had dug up his parents' box close to the chapel, though still on the estate grounds. If he hadn't been driven already, the Ghost's proffered deal further urged him to search for the rumored treasure. The sun cast long shadows as he ran his fingers over the disturbed earth around his feet, ready to unearth the secrets dormant within.

Then he sprang to his feet. "Let's do this."

Shovels in hand, they began to dig, the scratch and scuffle of metal chewing into earth and dirt being displaced ground into the normal daytime sounds. The earth yielded, its resistance met with their persistence. The cool breeze carried the smell of damp soil, invigorating his senses.

As the hole widened and deepened, his anticipation heightened, and he gripped the shovel's handle firmly.

"Hey, what's this?" Tommy jammed his shovel aside and kicked at something. He knelt and clawed away loose chunks of earth, pried at something edged beneath, then lifted a stainless-steel container covered in a layer of dirt and time.

Heat pulsed through Dylan's veins as they cleared away the dirt. "It looks like one of those time capsule thingies."

He set his shovel aside as well and helped pry open the container's stubborn lid.

Photographs, weathered and yellowed, depicted people long gone, their stories preserved within the fragile frames.

Dylan's traced the edges, his touch delicate. Each image held a story, a glimpse into lives once intertwined with his own. Now, the faded hues and smiles seemed to transcend the years.

"What a glimpse into my family's history," he whispered. "I

don't know if my parents buried this. Mom never said anything about a time capsule in her message. She just wanted me to find the box with the evidence."

Tommy craned over his shoulder, his sharp cologne invading the space. "I wouldn't know. But this is a treasure trove."

As they examined each photograph, Dylan imagined the lives of those captured in the images, the moments they shared, and the stories they could tell. Their faces carried hints of laughter, joy, and perhaps even sorrow, inviting him to piece together their existence.

He tucked the photographs aside and unfolded old news articles, their faded print depicting significant events, glimpses into historical moments and local happenings, a window into the world that had shaped his family's narrative.

"Look at this." Tommy pointed to a map tucked among the articles. Its yellowed parchment suggested its age, its delicate creases a testament to the journeys it had once guided. "Wonder if this is where the treasure is hidden."

"I don't know. Maybe." Dylan let out a low whistle. Was this the reason the Ghost wanted to live on the estate grounds? No way would he allow her to get ahold of the treasure. She'd done enough harm. "Thank goodness we found it."

"The ink is fading. Kind of hard to see. And I can't even tell which way is which. No directional sign." Tommy thrust the map to Dylan.

Jagged edges demarked one side. Dylan ran his thumb along them. "This may not be the whole map. It's like someone tore off half of it."

Tommy felt the edges. "Sure looks like it. Or whoever drew this map tore it off the notebook or whatever this came from." He then slapped Dylan's shoulder. "Anyway, good luck, man."

CHAPTER 11

CLARA & MICHAEL

Clara took a seat across from Skip Hunter in his sleek law office, a stark contrast to the quaint charm of the Orlando suburbs where she lived. The air conditioner's cool hum disturbed the quiet stillness while glass walls allowed sunlight to filter in, casting a bright glow on the polished mahogany desk. The immaculate room was a testament to the lawyer's precision and attention to detail.

A tall man, Hunter sported a tailored charcoal suit that accentuated his lean figure. Gray speckled his sandy hair, a clear indicator of the passage of time since Linda Boroski's case, but his intelligent cobalt-blue eyes studied Clara with quiet curiosity.

"First of all," she began, "thank you much for seeing me. I am trying to write a piece on Linda Boroski's case. I got your name from the case detective. He said you might have information."

Hunter leaned back in his leather chair, crossing his arms over his chest, his gaze never wavering from hers. He sighed, a sound that carried two decades' worth of unanswered questions.

"Linda… Yes, I remember Linda." His voice took on a soft, somber tone. "I only knew her briefly. We met at a party. She was vivacious, full of life. We hit it off and decided to go out on a date."

Emotion flickered in his eyes—sadness or regret or something more? "Our last communication was a phone call on the day the police now believe she disappeared. She seemed… happy, excited about her future."

"And the last time you saw her?" Clara poised her stylus over her tablet.

Hunter's gaze dropped to his clasped hands, his fingers tracing his knuckles. "That would be our date. She looked stunning in a red dress that matched her fiery spirit."

Clara jotted down the information, an invaluable glimpse into Linda.

He focused on something far beyond the room's glass walls. "We were planning another date." The faintest hint of a smile touched his lips. "I had arranged for a boat ride, thought it would be romantic, and Linda seemed enthusiastic. We were going to double date with my buddy. Well, it was his boat—or his parents' boat."

His smile faded. "But she never showed. And now, of course, I understand why."

Clara shifted in her seat, her heart aching for the young man Hunter once was, for the woman who would never arrive. "Do you know who she was going to bring to the double date?"

He shook his head. "I believe she said she'd bring her best friend."

"Can you recall anything else? Nothing is too insignificant."

His lip curved up. "You sound like a detective. But then I suppose an investigative journalist is kind of like a detective. And no, I don't remember anything else. But if I do, I'll let you know."

"Thank you, Mr. Hunter." She tucked her tablet into her

oversized purse. "Your information is invaluable. Linda's story deserves to be told, and you've given me a place to start."

As she rose to leave, she glanced back at him. He was staring out the glass wall, lost in the past with a vibrant woman in a red dress.

Leaving the law office, Clara headed to the dilapidated building where Linda's remains were discovered. The place had an eerie quietness, the bustle of the city's life seeming to fall away. The police tape that once marked the crime scene was gone, leaving a nondescript construction site, the skeleton of a building interrupted mid-transformation.

Climbing over a wooden barricade, she examined the site more closely and edged around recent construction work, stacks of bricks, coils of wire, and heavy machinery standing idle. But what she was most interested in were the layers of history hidden beneath the ongoing renovations.

At a nearby coffee shop, she did some research on her tablet. After contacting the construction company, she found out the property had changed hands multiple times over the years. Each transaction led further back. Persistence and a lot of calls later, she unearthed the critical information.

The building was being renovated when Linda disappeared. It had been a construction site then, just as it was now. A shiver tacked down her spine. Linda's story had taken Linda to this place twice, two decades apart, both times the building frozen in a state of becoming something new.

How easy to imagine Linda's excitement on that last phone call, the young woman unaware that, instead of a boat ride, her date would be with a lonely construction site and a tragic fate. Clara took a deep breath, clenching her hands tight. She would give Linda the justice she deserved.

After a long day, Clara made her way to Orlando Hospital. As she stepped inside, she blinked against the fluorescent lights, such a stark contrast to the dwindling daylight, and sterile disinfectant replaced the city's dust and grime.

Spotting her husband in his white coat, she smiled. Despite the long hours and heavy responsibilities, Michael always retained a certain energy. He turned, and his tired eyes brightened.

"Clara! Over here!" He gestured for her to join him and the two younger doctors with him. Once she approached, he wrapped an arm around her waist, drawing her close. "Clara, meet Dr. Kim and Dr. Hill. They're our neurosurgery fellows."

She poked at his side. "I remember you were one of them when I met you."

"I wasn't so eager, was I?" He winked.

Dr. Kim, a tall man with dark hair and a friendly smile, extended his hand. "It's nice to meet you, Mrs. Khoury."

Dr. Hill followed suit, her gaze serious. "Yes, very nice to meet you."

Their introductions were a pleasant conclusion to Clara's day of investigation. After chatting, Clara and Michael left the young doctors to their rounds.

"That Dr. Hill worships you." Clara slid free of her husband's arm.

Michael waved a dismissive hand. "Nah, she's just me twenty years ago. I was always trying to impress Dr. Cook."

Michael would make a good mentor, providing what the fellows needed just as he gave her unwavering support in her pursuits, no matter where they led her. Today had been a long day, but she'd see this case through to the end, for Linda's sake.

His phone's shrill ring cut through the night, jolting Michael from his sleep. He squinted at the screen, the bright light searing his sleep-heavy eyes as the screen flashed the contact for Dr. Harris, Clara's therapist.

"Michael." The voice that greeted him was crisp, carrying the distinct undertone of professionalism, yet an unmistakable hint of concern laced the word. "Apologies for the late call. I lost track of the time difference. I'm in the Bay Area attending a conference."

He brushed off the apology with a weary wave of his hand, despite knowing the gesture wouldn't translate over the phone. He had Clara's medical power of attorney, so Dr. Harris often discussed Clara's treatment with him. "It's okay, doctor. What's the matter?"

After a brief pause, Dr. Harris resumed. "I've been going over Clara's recent episodes these last few days—these nightmares and headaches. It's curious. They seem to have started around the news report about Linda Boroski's remains. The report might be acting as a trigger, stirring something in her subconscious."

Michael ran a hand through his hair, his gaze drifting to Clara asleep beside him, her face pale in the moonlight, a sheen of sweat on her forehead. He winced at a pang of helplessness. "What should we do, doctor?"

"For now, reassure her. If these nightmares persist, we may need to consider a more intensive therapy approach."

As he ended the call, Clara was thrashing, her brows furrowed. He reached out, running his fingers through her hair, a silent promise to stand by her through the storm.

Clara jerked upright, gasping. Her wide, fearful eyes found his, and in that moment, he knew their journey was only just beginning. "It's okay," he whispered, pulling her close. "You're safe. We're going to figure this out together."

Her fingers clung to his shirt, her trembling body seeking solace in his. As he held her through the remainder of the night, he ground his molars. Just what was her subconscious trying?

Should he tell her what the PI found out?

CHAPTER 12

DYLAN & EVA

The office building, a towering monolith of concrete and glass, dominated the downtown skyline. Dylan was with executives from M&M Enterprises, assessing the mostly deserted structure as a potential acquisition. They toured the building, their whispered debates on its merits and renovation prospects echoing off the empty walls. But the map and photos kept intruding on his focus.

They were about to descend the staircase from the penthouse floor when an Asian woman headed toward the rooftop. In this near-empty building, her presence seemed out of place. Excusing himself, he moved toward her, suspecting she might be lost. "Can I help you?"

The woman glanced at him with a vacant smile but shook her head and continued her journey. Could she be contemplating something drastic?

Not wanting to overreact, he followed her discreetly. The woman seemed dazed, moving with an eerie calmness. Maybe Lily could help. As if his thought summoned her, Lily called.

"Hey, just the person I need," he answered the phone and explained the situation.

"You want me to call the cops?"

"I don't know. Why don't you try talking to her? Maybe she'll listen," he said, "in Chinese, I mean."

"How do you know she's Chinese? Maybe she's Korean or Japanese?"

"We won't know until you try. She doesn't look like she understands me."

A beat later, she said, "Okay, put me on speaker."

He did.

Lily started speaking in fluent Cantonese—that would be his guess. Since he didn't understand a word of it, he looked at the woman's face. There was a hint of something, like the woman recognized Lily's voice, which was impossible. The woman halted as if responding to a command. Her body then went limp, collapsing.

He raced to catch her fall. "Lily, call 911!"

While he held the woman, ensuring she was safe from the building's edge, he asked Lily what she'd said to her. She was talking to the 911 operator on another line, probably the hotel landline.

"Hang on," she asked the 911 operator, then to him, "Just trying to calm her. She literally stopped when I told her to. So weird."

"That's an understatement. She collapsed like a rag doll. Thanks. Later." He hung up.

As he waited for the ambulance, the reality hit him. Something was terribly wrong with the woman, and he'd stumbled upon it in the unlikeliest of places.

When paramedics arrived, they rushed past him, their movements precise as they attended to her.

"She's heavily sedated," one paramedic murmured.

A police officer approached Dylan, pen and notepad in hand. When did he arrive? Dylan had no idea. Maybe the 911 operator alerted the police. He gave his statement, recollecting every detail, while another officer delved into the woman's purse, procuring her ID and a card for emergency contact.

The officer raised an eyebrow. "Her emergency contact is a Dr. Michael Khoury."

One of the paramedics turned. "Dr. Khoury, the new chief of surgery? This must be his wife."

Nestled in Mirror Estate's secluded guesthouse, Eva clutched her encrypted phone, Uncle Bill's voice barely more than a murmur in her ear. His words, though hushed, hummed with a heightened urgency that sent adrenaline through her.

"They might start an investigation soon—against a known human trafficker." Layers of technology distorted his tone.

"Understood. I'll keep you posted." Her wavy dark hair hung around her face, tickling her cheeks as if to ease her pensive mood as she stared at her encrypted device.

Eva opened Clara's journal in her other hand to reread the one entry:

Dear Journal,

An odd day today. As I left my writing class, a man approached and flashed a badge identifying himself as Officer Bill. I inspected it carefully—you know, in light of everything that has happened—and it appeared to be genuine.

The look in his eyes was sincere, if somewhat hard, like

he'd seen more than his fair share of life's darker corners. His words, however, left an impression. He warned me to be careful of Ms. Beaumont.

Even stranger, he mentioned that a guest at the event, seemingly an innocent businessman, was suspected of being involved in human trafficking. A terrifying prospect.

I didn't know how to react or what he expected me to do. But I thanked him, promised to be cautious, and parted ways. As I walked away, fear and curiosity churned within me.

I now feel like I'm peeling back layers of a town I once thought was simple, unassuming. Dark secrets hide beneath the surface. It's daunting, but I can't ignore what I know. I'm teetering on the edge of a mystery far greater than anything I'd ever imagined.

Later,
Clara

Eva closed the journal. Had that suspected human trafficker been the one Uncle Bill said the task force would investigate? If so, it would be time to insert herself into the investigation. This might be her only way to find out about Clara.

She headed outside, beneath an ancient oak on the grounds, his words still echoing in her mind.

"I need to know everyone you've come into contact with at the estate." Eva agreed, her mind mapping the faces she'd met so far. "And I have a feeling they'll be calling on you."

"To do what?" she'd asked.

"You'll see." He'd disconnected.

Now, she was about to meet Kyle, a childhood friend turned FBI special agent. She had buzzed him in moments ago. Security at the estate was stringent. He approached the gazebo as she'd requested.

"Hey, Eva. What's up? You sounded serious."

After a friendly embrace, she attempted to keep her tone light. "Wanted to ask you something, and I didn't think it should be over the phone."

"Shoot."

"Have you heard anything about a possible human trafficking case?"

A flicker crossed his face as he hesitated. "There's been some talk. Why do you ask?"

She shrugged, her nonchalance practiced. "Just… I'd like to be a part of something meaningful. If you guys are working on a human trafficking case, do you think your dad would grant my request to join the task force this once?"

Kyle raked a hand through his short brown hair. "You know how it goes. He doesn't tell me that kind of stuff."

Birds chirped melodically in the background.

She kicked at a dried leaf in the dewy grass. "Didn't he get you on the task force?"

"That's only because of the last case with Lily. They had to read me in on some classified stuff. Since I've had dealings with the Ghost, Ana nudged Dad to get me to stay on."

"Ana and your dad… are they a thing?"

"Don't know. He hasn't said, and I'm not about to ask."

Several gnats flew by, and he swatted them.

She touched his arm, imploring. "If it's a human trafficking case, you know there's a chance—"

"I know." His hand covered hers. "But we don't know if this case has anything to do with your aunt's abduction."

So, there was a case. She scooped up the leaf, the only thing out of place on the immaculate grounds. She'd have to believe Uncle Bill's "prediction" that Kyle's father, Agent Peters, would call on her soon. He'd already told her Agent Peters would get her working with the Marinos, and it came true.

CHAPTER 13

CLARA & DYLAN

Surrounded by comfortable familiarity, Clara found the situation almost surreal. The ER hadn't seen fit to admit her yesterday although they'd run a lot of tests on Michael's insistence. Now, she was sitting on her brown leather couch opposite Detective Clive Jordan, and his intensity left a cold knot in her stomach.

"Mrs. Khoury, you mentioned you have no known enemies, no one with a motive to harm you."

"That's correct." She twisted her hands together in her lap, a nervous habit, then smoothed out her pants. The sole thing she was working on was the article on Linda Boroski. So far, she'd only interviewed the lawyer and dug up some background information. That couldn't have anything to do with the incident.

He hesitated, the lines of his forehead creasing as he formulated the next question. "And your marriage? It's… stable?"

Defensive irritation sparked within her. "Yes, Detective. Very."

"Any issues at all? Affairs, past or present? Either you or your husband?"

"No! We don't have heated arguments or fidelity issues. I'm not sure where you're going with this."

He held her gaze, unblinking. "Your husband's a doctor, right?"

Something thrummed at the base of her skull. She moved her hand to grip the cushions on either side of her, grinding the leather into her palms. "Yes?"

"And as such, he'd have access to medical substances, including GHB? Ketamine? Rohypnol? And other substances?"

She shivered. He'd just named date rape drugs. The lab had found traces of a drug, gamma-something-acid, in her system. "Are you implying that my husband might be behind this? That he… drugged me?"

Jordan raised his hands in a placating gesture. "We have to consider all possibilities. It's procedure."

A fire ignited in her chest. She sprang to her feet. "Well, you're wrong, Detective. Michael could never hurt me—he *saved* me!"

In the silence after her outburst, she sat back down, smoothed her pants, and struggled to calm her breathing, to cool the heat sluicing through her veins.

"I understand your frustration." When he spoke, his tone was softer. "I'll continue looking into other leads. But I had to ask."

She sat still, the heat receding to a dull simmer. She trusted Michael. The culprit was still out there, and Jordan better focus on finding them.

"What's your last recollection from the day of the incident?"

Clara took slow breaths, her brow furrowing. She rubbed the pinched spot between her eyes. "I, um, had an appointment with a therapist in the morning. My usual therapist is based in Chicago where we lived before moving here. I was trying to find a therapist locally."

She paused, a blank void in her memory where the rest of the day should have been. "After the session…" The pinched spot throbbed now. Her temples started thrumming too. This would be one of the more brutal headaches. "Um, I'd planned to return home and finalize the arrangements for our Christmas party."

The detective poised his pen over his notebook. "Was this appointment held at the hospital your husband works at?"

She shook her head. "No, it was in a medical office adjacent to it."

"And that's the last thing you recall?" His question was gentle, almost reverent in the face of her growing distress.

Her vision blurred as she stared at some indistinct point beyond the detective. A nebulous shape skirted the periphery of her recall. "There may have been someone—I can't be certain."

The elusive figure remained just out of reach, an echo dissipating in the recesses of her mind. *Why can't I remember?*

In the bustling hubbub of M&M Enterprises, the residual sound of hushed phone conversations, the tapping of computer keys, and the murmur of ongoing meetings melded into a symphony of productivity. Dylan had barely returned to his office from a meeting when the duty manager called to let him know Dr. Khoury was here to see him.

Just what would the doctor want? Had Mrs. Khoury taken a turn for the worse?

After a light knock, a figure emerged from the glass and steel foyer. A cautious relief tinged the man's weary eyes, but his person carried the weight of sleepless nights and worry-infused days, despite the firm resolve in his stride.

"Mr. Roche." The man extended a hand, his grip strong. "Dr. Michael Khoury. You saved my wife's life."

Dylan stood. "Dr. Khoury. I'm glad I could help. And please, call me Dylan. How is she now?"

"Stable, and it's Michael." Dr. Khoury's voice caught slightly. He swallowed hard. "She was drugged. The police are looking into it."

Dylan grimaced.

Michael's next question jarred the silence. "Who was the young woman who spoke Cantonese to my wife? Clara mentioned her. She'd like to meet her."

"Lily. She works at Marino Hotel. Would you like me to take you there?"

"If it's not too much trouble?"

"Of course, it's not." Dylan reached for his keys, jangling them in his palm. Perhaps he'd go to lunch after this. Maybe Lily would join him and Tommy.

The hustle and bustle of M&M Enterprises faded into the background as they exited the building and ventured into the Marino Hotel in the adjacent office tower, connected by the elevator bank. The aroma of freshly brewed coffee and the pleasant chatter of guests infused the lobby where Lily lingered by the concierge desk, multitasking with an effortless grace.

"Lily, this is Dr. Michael Khoury."

"Oh!" Lily's luminous eyes widened, and her plush little mouth curved up as she reached for Dr. Khoury's extended hand. "It's a pleasure to meet you, Dr. Khoury. How is your wife?"

"Recovering, thanks to you both, and it's Michael." The doctor reached his free hand to cover Lily's holding on longer than necessary. "You, dear girl, were a calming influence when she needed it most."

The praise left Lily blushing as she freed her hand, and it fluttered to tuck escaped wisps of her glossy hair behind her ears. She always wore her hair up at work, a mistake to conceal her long, glossy tresses. "I didn't do anything. I just talked to her, Dr. —uh, Michael."

Michael rested both hands on the marble-topped concierge desk, his fingers drumming out nervous energy. "My wife and I would like to invite you both to dinner. It's the least we can do to show our gratitude."

Lily and Dylan shared a glance, a silent communication passing between them before she smiled at the doctor. "We'd be honored. Thank you."

After they finalized plans for the dinner, they exchanged cordial goodbyes with Michael.

Once he was out of earshot, Dylan gripped Lily's arm. "His wife was drugged. That's… that's serious."

Lily winced. "That's terrifying. If you hadn't stepped in, she might have… and it wouldn't have been suicide. It would have been murder."

Neither of them spoke for a while. Not long ago, they were abducted and held captive. Another, longer look between them conveyed a shared understanding. Not getting involved.

CHAPTER 14

OLIVIA, KYLE, & RON

The Ghost had summoned her. Why? The task force was just starting to review all the case files related to Ray Ho. Ron had someone talking to the local human trafficking unit. What did the Ghost want now?

The guards led the prisoner in, secured her, and left.

Olivia clasped her hands on the cold tabletop. She'd always thought the Ghost's eyes were the most intimidating. Today was no exception. "You asked to see me?"

"There's an auction coming up." The Ghost leaned back in the chair, her face devoid of emotion. "On the dark web, next week."

Olivia slid her phone from her blazer's pocket. "Can you be more specific? What day next week?"

"I don't even know what day it is today. It's always on the weekends."

"Where?"

"I'm not finished."

"Excuse me."

"The bidding will be online. But they will also host a local auction here."

This disclosure was significant. An auction in the underworld of human trafficking—it was repugnant, yet invaluable in their ongoing investigation.

Bracing her forearms on the table, she leaned forward and firmed up her features. "Do you know where it will take place?"

In this secretive world, information was a precious commodity, often held close to the chest.

A flicker of something—amusement?—crossed the Ghost's serene face. "I can't do all the work for you. You might want to try Ray Ho's local lieutenant, John Liu."

Olivia swallowed. The taste of the cold coffee she'd consumed earlier lingered in her mouth, now bitter and faintly metallic. "You've got to give me more than that."

The Ghost sat back, her eyes steady, but her fingers were tapping a rhythm. A few beats later, she exhaled. "Well, when you locate John, mention that I sent you."

Olivia frowned. "I don't work for you."

"In a sense, you do. If you want his cooperation, you'll do as I say."

If this was the way to get to Ray Ho, Olivia could do that. But would Ron go along with it? He was the one in charge, even if the Ghost would only talk to her. Olivia took a breath. *I'm only a messenger. Nothing more.*

She stood up, smoothing out her coat. "Thanks for the tip. We'll do our best to use it."

The Ghost nodded, her face a still mask. As Olivia moved toward the door, she could feel her gaze following her.

The door slid shut. It would be nice if the team could put someone on the inside, and better yet, have someone else go in as a bidder.

The human trafficker brought Clara to mind. If Eva were correct, the abduction had happened twenty years ago, and the odds were against finding her. But Olivia promised to look into it, and so she would. *What happened to you, Clara?*

Later that day, Olivia entered the squad room to the low buzz of voices. Sunlight slanting through the blinds striped the shiny furniture and gave the place an institutional feel. Even with its brightness warming the place, a tense chill lingered. As she headed over to Ron by Tanner's desk, everyone started looking her way, and the room went from chatty to dead quiet.

"We're all waiting to hear the latest." Ron broke the silence.

Olivia plopped a stack of papers onto the nearby desk and straightened her shoulders to carry the seriousness of their task as she updated them.

"Assuming it's next Friday or Saturday. That's not a lot of time." Ron signaled for Hernandez to start a new electronic white board. "And we don't know where it's gonna be."

Ana Ruiz, a DIA agent now serving as a liaison and a familiar face since Lily's kidnapping, sat down at her desk and began tapping the keyboard. "I'll start digging on Liu. His network, his hideouts, everything. Tanner and I can work through his known associates."

"We'll also revisit all the evidence and the witnesses and unsubs in Lily's case." Tanner, Ron's senior agent, sat back down at his desk, picked up the phone, and put in a request.

Olivia asked Hernandez to bring up everything they had on Lily's case on the big screen. Of course, they would re-interview and follow up with all the unidentified suspects in the previous case. "The human trafficking unit should have sent over all the pertinent documents."

"We need all the information we can get." Ron stared at the screen, now filled with images of statements, arrest records, etc. of Lily's case.

Simon watched all the discussions, though he didn't voice his thoughts.

"Ideas?"

"I will talk to this Liu character." Olivia clenched and unclenched her fists. "I'll ask around the Chinese restaurants and shops. Discreetly." She was still an intelligence operative, but she wasn't a field agent. Since Ron was in charge, she'd need his okay. She cocked a brow at him, waiting.

His subtle nod gave his approval. "All right, folks. We need to attack this from all angles. Hernandez, can you delve into the dark web? Scour for any leads."

"Definitely." Hernandez's hands were already working their magic on his laptop. "Olivia, I might need some assistance."

Tanner held the receiver in his hand, ready to place another call. "I'll reach out to our contacts in the human trafficking division. They might have additional intel."

As the team members delved into their roles, Olivia glanced at Simon. She had another idea, a bold one that involved Eva. While risky, it could provide them with an edge. "We should have Simon pose as a bidder."

"Me?" Simon raised his eyebrows. "I can't be undercover. I'm not trained. And I was a senator. People will recognize me."

"Exactly. Now that you've resigned, you can be, shall we say"—she formed air quotes as her lips twitched—"bored?"

"Right." Simon's eyes glittered. "A man of my age, now jobless, perhaps I am looking for a little excitement in my life."

His comment provoked stifled laughs while Ana's smile widened into an outright grin. "You'd make a convincing bidder, Simon. I mean, your engagement to Olivia isn't public knowledge yet, right? The media hounds are none the wiser."

Tanner then gestured theatrically as if parting an imaginary curtain, his voice taking on the dramatic flair of a newscaster. "Ex-Senator Resigns! Hidden Involvement in Underground Minor Auction?"

More laughter erupted, Ana chiming in amidst her chuckles. "The press would be on you like bees to honey!"

Simon feigned a look of horror, holding a hand to his heart. "Now you're tarnishing my sterling reputation."

"Don't sweat it, Senator." Kyle winked. "I'll be there, covering your back."

"All right, settle down," commanded Ron.

Olivia cleared her throat. "I also propose an agent on the inside."

The room fell silent at the severity of her suggestion. The risks were tremendous, yet the potential reward could be a game changer.

"An undercover agent could offer us a first-hand account of the proceedings." Ana tucked her curly bob away from her face. "It could be the breakthrough we need—as long as we can assure their safety."

Ron waved. "Elaborate."

She breathed in deeply. "I was, um, thinking we need a fresh face, young, attractive."

"No, no." Simon stiffened. "Not Lily."

Ron let out a low whistle. "I don't think she meant Lily. She did say agent. Who do you have in mind?"

"Eva."

"Who?" several asked.

Olivia waited for Ron to answer. When Olivia met her, Eva had introduced herself as Ms. Carol's personal assistant, which hadn't felt right. And Olivia's intuition had proven correct after she'd checked with her old contacts.

"I'll think about it." Ron pursed his lips. "She's currently in an undercover operation. We'll need to plan this. But I agree, a two-pronged approach might be our best shot."

After the meeting, Ron pulled Olivia aside. "Wanna tell me how you knew?"

She shrugged. "It takes one to know one. I was in deep cover for half my life."

"Who else knows?"

"I didn't tell anyone. Not Simon, not Lily." She gathered her long hair away from her shoulders, smoothing it into a loose ponytail and letting it go. "I don't know what your objective is, but Dylan's a good kid. And *you're* the one who told me Ms. Carol had never been involved. By the way, the Ghost wants me to talk to Liu."

"Why?"

"She said this would be the only way to get his cooperation. I'll be able to speak to him in his dialect to make him more comfortable and therefore more willing to cooperate."

"I see." He clapped his hands and rubbed them together in his let's-get-this-done gesture. "All right, let's get to work."

But he didn't answer her question about Eva. *What are you really up to, Ron?*

The meeting had just ended, but its potential implications jarred Kyle. Eva joining the task force? Even if temporary, he'd not anticipated this. He moved away from the team mobilizing, pulled out his encrypted phone, and dialed her number.

As he waited, he stood at the office window, the cityscape serving as a backdrop to his anxious thoughts. They'd been best friends as long as he could remember, so how could he handle her joining this dangerous mission?

"Kyle?" Her voice crackled through the line.

"Hey, Eva." He forced a casualness. "Olivia knows you're undercover."

"How?"

"I don't know, but she, um, mentioned you during the meeting."

Silence. Then her throat cleared. "And?"

"And Dad might be open to reassigning you for a while."

Another pause, longer this time. "Really?"

"Yeah, really." He ran a hand through his hair. "Just… be careful. This isn't some kind of game. It's dangerous."

"I know." Her voice softened in stark contrast to the steely determination girding it a moment earlier. "I'll be careful. I promise."

He let out a long low breath, staring at the cityscape. For Eva's sake, he hoped she could keep that promise.

After the briefing, Ron joined Ana far from the preparation noise. "Talk to me about the Ghost's contacts. What have you found?"

She tapped her phone, her brow creased. "I've gone through all the lawyers. All legit. Olivia posed as a lawyer once to get to her, so that name, Jade Wong, is good. However, there's this one guy… Adam O'Shea."

He rubbed the back of his neck. The name didn't mean anything to him. "Who's he?"

"That's the thing—I can't find anything about him. No social media presence, no footprint, nothing. Yet he's on the approved visitors' list."

He moved his hand up from the prickles at his nape and through his hair. "I thought everyone on that list had to be vetted."

"They do, technically." Ana shrugged and rolled her eyes. "But you know how things can be. Sometimes people slip through."

Ron nodded. "Look into it, Ana."

"Will do." She strode back to her laptop, already on it.

CHAPTER 15

EVA

S ettled in with her homework, Eva opened Clara's journal.

Dear Journal,

These galas are going to be my undoing! Tonight's spectacle again offered that wild mix of work and fun that makes these things so thrilling, but my attention remained anchored on one person—Ms. Beaumont. My interactions with her had always been cordial, even pleasant, but since Officer Bill's warning, I started looking at her with new eyes, the eyes of suspicion. Tonight felt like I was tiptoeing around a mystery, a riddle I must solve.

Amid cocktail-dress-clad women and tuxedoed men, I noticed a young Chinese man speaking with her. I decided to listen in, taking cover behind a group of giggling debutantes.

The man, Ray, was describing Shenzhen with an infectious enthusiasm. "The tech scene is extraordinary, Ms. Beaumont," he insisted, hands waving as he painted a vivid picture of a city on the precipice of greatness. "The government is supportive of foreign investments and most interested in cross-border ventures."

Ms. Beaumont's eyes gleamed with what I can only describe as a predator's instinct, clearly finding the prospect of a new, untamed market attractive as she asked him to clarify the special economic zones.

"They have been a game changer," Ray replied. "The incentives for businesses are unlike anywhere else." Then someone called out for Mr. Ho, and Ray excused himself.

Their conversation seemed normal, even promising. But Officer Bill's warning cast a shadow over the interaction. What hidden layers did this have? What was I missing? The questions continued to whirl as I retreated from my hiding spot, more intrigued than ever about Ms. Beaumont and her dealings.

I guess only time will reveal the truth.

Until tomorrow,
Clara

Dear Journal,

I've been rattled since Officer Bill gave me that cryptic warning. I can't shake feeling like something's lurking beneath the surface, something much more dangerous than I suspected.

Seeing Ray Ho and Ms. Beaumont together oddly heightened my suspicion. So I've begun snooping, online at least. If something's to be found, the internet is my best bet. Of course, this investigation is still a secret from my editor boss. I dare not raise any alarm until I have something substantial. If I can gather enough evidence, hopefully, I can sell the story to a newspaper. But do I tell Stella?

So far, digital channels haven't yielded much. Ray Ho, it seems, is quite the social butterfly. He appears in a handful of articles hobnobbing with some celebrity or socialite. This glittering façade to his life, a veneer, distracts from any potential underlying menace.
But then I shifted my focus to Hong Kong. There, Ray Ho isn't just a wealthy socialite—he is a prominent underworld figure, a gang leader according to the tabloids. I find myself fascinated and terrified in equal measure and left with more questions than answers. How can a man with a criminal past move so effortlessly within the world of the elite? What's his connection to Ms. Beaumont? And more importantly, what does this mean for me now that I've tangled myself in their world? I need more information, more concrete evidence, but I must tread carefully, make sure I don't alert anyone. Maybe it's time to look beyond the internet.

This might turn out to be the biggest story of my career. It might even put me in real danger. Either way, I can't back down now.

Clara

Eva closed the journal, her hand lingering over its spine. Was Clara investigating Ray Ho? Had that contributed to her disappearance?

She caressed the fabric cover. Uncle Bill might've been right. Clara might've been abducted. Was Uncle Bill "Officer Bill"?

Ray Ho was wanted in a few countries, including the US. The task force believed he'd ordered Lily and Dylan's abduction—and had intended to put Lily up in an underground auction. Could this be the one human trafficker the task force was now focusing on? It couldn't be a coincidence that Clara had encountered him at a business event and seen him speaking with the Ghost.

Agent Peters had called earlier and wanted to meet. Maybe it was to assign her to the task force.

She set the journal aside. A girl could hope, couldn't she?

An old chandelier lit the drawing room, throwing shaky shadows on the fancy furniture and expensive paintings. Surrounded by the scent of old wood and shiny leather, Eva sat in a tall chair, her heart going crazy like it wanted out. All that rich stuff made what was about to go down feel even more serious.

In her last conversation with Uncle Bill, his voice strained as he said the words *kingpin of human trafficking* and divulged the task force's new undertaking. The memory added weight to the opulence around her, reinforcing the stakes.

The towering double doors made a creaking sound, and in walked Agent Ron Peters. The big guy seemed way out of place in the fancy room, and the twinkle in his eye had given way to a chilling seriousness. As he greeted her, she checked behind him to ensure they were alone, then relaxed.

After all, they'd known each other since her teens. He sat across from her, the leather of the chair creaking under his weight, and when he cleared his throat, the small gesture somehow enhanced her anticipation. "How are you liking your role so far?"

"It's good." Her heartbeat raced, and her hands wouldn't stop fidgeting. "I reported everything as requested, sir."

"Yes, I got them." He crossed his legs and gripped both hands on his knee. "I may have a new assignment for you. But I'm giving you the option to stay put."

Eva nodded, her palms clammy against her jeans. "Thank you, sir. I–I want to help in any way I can." Her words echoed in the vast room. Oops, she hadn't meant to speak so loudly.

Head cocked to one side, Ron studied her for a beat. "I'm not going to lie. It's a dangerous situation. The plan Olivia proposed involves a high-risk role for an undercover agent."

"I understand." Chin high, voice steady, she met his gaze head-on.

"Good." The slightest twitch at the left of his mouth revealed his approval. "We need someone to pose as one of the trafficked girls. I want to make it clear—if you're not comfortable with this, we will not hold it against you."

"I'm ready." She meant it. "More than ready—I *want* to do this."

"Attagirl. Then be at the task force office first thing tomorrow morning. I know it's Sunday, but when we have a case, we work. Although if you need to go to any church services, you may, just come in as soon as you can. We have extensive briefings and preparations to cover and a deadline to make."

He shoved to his feet, but as he turned to leave, he glanced over his shoulder. "Here's what you'll do. Explain to Ms. Carol you have a family emergency and need to take a leave of absence. She'll have no problem with it. If there's any problem, let me know."

His figure receded into the shadowed corridors, leaving Eva alone in the dimly lit room with emotions surging through her— fear, anticipation, exhilaration.

Yes! She was in. Was this the first step toward finding the truth about her aunt?

CHAPTER 16

CLARA

Feeling more like herself, Clara carried a mug of coffee to her oak desk in the master bedroom. Once she settled in, she typed in various keywords, sifting through articles, forum threads, and archived digital records. A neighbor's bright security light filtered through the curtains, lending a gentle illumination to the bed. The soft radiance turned the navy spread into a shade of deep indigo and gave the creamy walls a warm, inviting hue. The click-clack of her typing offered a comforting rhythm, an echo of her returning strength and resolve as she attempted to trace back to the company in charge of renovating the building where Linda Boroski's body was found.

"Yes." She gave a fist pump as, after countless dead ends, she found it—a construction company still operating after all these decades. Her heartbeat quickened, and her lips curved up. She dialed the number. Their website said they were open on Saturday.

The phone rang three times before a woman answered, crisp and professional. "Goodman Construction. This is Marlene."

"Hello, Marlene. I'm Clara Khoury with the *Christian Living Magazine*. I'm researching the Linda Boroski case and wondering if you might have records or employees from the time —um, about twenty years ago. You guys were working on a project, the old Lawson building?"

Papers shuffled on the other end. "Twenty years ago? Most of the employees from back then have long since moved on. The only person who's been here that long would be Mr. Goodman himself, the owner. Is there anything specific you're looking for?"

Clara's breath caught in a sudden lurch. "Yes, actually. Would it be possible to speak with Mr. Goodman? As I said, it's about the Linda Boroski case. I believe he might be able to help."

Marlene paused again, this time longer. "I'll have to check. Can I take your contact information and have him call you back?"

Clara agreed and provided her details. Jittery as she ended the call, she sprang to her feet and paced to the bedroom window. She opened it to the warm breeze, breathing deeply of the roses beyond as she grounded herself. Was she getting closer to uncovering what happened to Linda Boroski? Or was this the end?

And why did it feel… personal?

The familiar doorbell chime sent a soft echo through Clara's home. An unusual tension twisted her stomach as she approached the front door, unsettled by the unexpected visit. Through the door cam, Detective Clive Jordan's piercing gaze peered at her, and the tension loosened its grip as she unlatched the door.

"Mrs. Khoury." He inclined his head. The formal politeness reinforced her discomfort. "May I come in?"

"Of course, Detective." She stepped aside to let him in. She didn't bother inviting him to sit. "What brings you here today?"

"Mind if we sit?"

She took a deep breath and gestured to the front room. "Sure, please."

He claimed the cream-toned accent chair, seeming impatient as he waited for her to sit in its twin across from him. "I've come across some information in my investigation pertaining to a life insurance policy on you—for a million dollars."

Clara's eyebrows furrowed, but she kept her composure. "I'm aware of that policy. Michael and I thought it was a sensible decision for our family's security."

Jordan maintained his steady gaze, his expression impassive. "Dr. Khoury has also made several substantial withdrawals from an investment account jointly owned by you both. I'm interested in knowing if you were aware of this."

The air around Clara seemed to turn cold, her breath hitching in her throat. How long ago had that been? Yes, Thanksgiving. She'd been hanging out in the crowded living room, the mouth-watering smell of roasted turkey overplaying her guests' laughter and chatter.

Then, amid the family fun, Michael and his brother edged away from the crowd, near the fancy windows, their faces serious as they leaned into each other deep in heavy conversation.

When she asked Michael about it later, he'd chuckled, his answer casual—too casual. "Oh, that was just Majid being Majid."

But hadn't there been something she'd missed at the time—a quick flicker in his eyes, like he was nervous or something? He hid it fast, and she'd ignored it with all the holiday fun. But that shadow now looked way bigger and turned the memory into something… creepy.

"I…" She cleared her throat, then raised her chin. "No, I wasn't aware of that." That quiver in her voice gave her away. She firmed it. "But Michael wouldn't need the money. We're comfortable."

The detective's unwavering stare held fast. "That may be the case, but the facts suggest a different narrative."

"I'm sure there's a good explanation. I'll ask him when he comes home tonight."

"Please don't. This is an active investigation."

She recoiled at his words. The detective seriously thought Michael would harm her? "So? What's that got to do with me asking my husband why he withdrew large amounts of money?"

Jordan's attitude cracked for a sec, and he rubbed his tired, rough face. His palm rasped against a days-old beard, and the tough glint in his eyes made her stomach flip. "If you were to confront your husband, you might alert him to our investigation. It could lead him to change his actions, cover his tracks, or even take steps against the investigation."

A shiver ran down Clara's spine. Could Michael be capable of such things? The man she built a life with, the father of her children… a suspect in a criminal investigation?

"Are you implying—Are you saying Michael is a suspect?" The headache started pinching the back of her skull. The room had been plunged into icy cold. Her breath should be visible in the chilling silence.

Jordan held up a hand. "I'm just doing my job. Right now, we are following the evidence."

"But this is—it's absurd!" But even as she protested, a small voice in her mind raised the terrifying question: What if it wasn't?

He stood. "Bear with us, ma'am. I've got to go now, but I will be in touch."

And like that, he left her there in her big, fancy house, a house that suddenly felt like a stranger's place. And beyond the pounding at the base of her skull, the words reverberated again and again. Even this house she loved seemed distorted somehow in his wake, creepy, with the fancy lights she'd selected throwing weird, spooky shadows on the walls.

No, Michael had nothing to do with this. There had to be a reason for the withdrawals.

Later that evening, Clara hunched over her laptop on the kitchen island. Michael sat across the room in a reclining chair, watching TV, Jason at basketball practice, Faith in her room. Another ordinary evening.

"Dad, where are you?" Faith yelled from upstairs.

"He's down here watching TV," Clara hollered back.

In a rush of thumps and footsteps, the teenager bounded down the stairs. "Hey, why didn't we tour Northwestern before we moved?"

Clara stifled the urge to roll her eyes. "Do you know how expensive the tuition is?"

"Oh, she'll get a scholarship." Michael put down the recliner's footrest and pushed to his feet to wink at their girl. "Right, sweetie? When you get that, we'll talk."

"But shouldn't we tour the campus?"

"Fifi, I never toured any college campuses. I went with the one that offered me a full ride."

"He's right." Clara shut her laptop, spinning the barstool to face them. "You've got to be practical." Not that the words *practical* and *teenager* meshed well.

"Seriously? That's your solution?" Faith raised her eyebrows, turning to look at Clara and Michael back and forth. "Guys, that's not how we do things these days. How do I know if I'll fit in?"

"Well, go ahead and apply." Michael passed her, patting her shoulder on his way to the fridge. "If you get in and get a scholarship, we'll go tour the campus and visit friends."

Faith uttered some unintelligible words as she ran up the stairs while Michael poured filtered water from the fridge.

Clara spun back to reopen her laptop. As she scrolled through their bank statements, she fixated on the large withdrawals. They never had money issues, so why the sudden need for liquid cash?

"Michael?"

He raised his glass. "Want one, hon?"

"No, I…" How could she put her question delicately? She blinked at the screen again, the numbers seeming to mock her. "I just…"

What about what Jordan said? Had she promised or just not responded? She shook her head, forcing a tight smile. "Never mind."

Michael gave her a puzzled look, swigged the last of his water, and rinsed the glass, but he didn't press her.

She returned to her screen. The detective's words thudded in her head, the headache she'd been fighting all day insisting on returning. *Don't let anyone know our progress.*

A cold stronger than that ice water coiled in her stomach. Was her husband a suspect?

Of course not. How outrageous even to think it.

And yet… the question tainted her otherwise peaceful evening. She glanced at Michael again, her heart heavy.

How am I going to prove him innocent? And what did he and Majid talk about?

CHAPTER 17

EVA

Eva's heart started pounding when she walked into the task force office. From the outside, it looked like nothing more than a warehouse, but man, inside it was alive! Energy practically pulsed in the air. A strong coffee scent added vitality to the whispering in the background, and a cool techie vibe provided the buzz you only get from computers humming away.

Kyle's welcoming grin eased her nervous excitement. With a hand on her back, he led her deeper into the operation's epicenter and leaned closer to tease. "Welcome to the hive."

Rapid intros followed.

Tanner—an experienced agent with a rugged look and eyes that said he'd seen a lot.

Hernandez—a tech whiz with restless fingers and circles under his eyes that said he'd spent too much time lost in his glowing screens and data.

Ana—a DIA agent and acting liaison with poised shoulders and alert posture that said she was crazy smart.

"Oh, and Deanna, our lab tech, is in her lab," Kyle tossed in. "I'll get you two together later."

Eva raised herself onto her toes to crane around. "What about Officer Tso and the senator?"

Kyle shrugged. "They drop in as needed. Perks of being consultants—ah, speaking of…"

At the elevator, Senator Roth and Officer Tso walked in together. Officer Tso—Olivia—was one of her aunt's best friends and one of the girls in the photo. Her features had matured with age, but similarities remained from her teen years. Of course! No wonder Lily looked familiar. She resembled her mom.

They both greeted her and welcomed her to the task force.

"Please, call me Olivia." Officer Tso shook Eva's hand. "I'll talk to you in a bit. Why don't you get settled and read up on the case?"

"Sure thing," Eva said.

As Tanner ushered her toward a temporary desk and handed her the login credentials, a profound sense of purpose steeled her. She was here, on the precipice of something that mattered, something that could make a difference. This was it—the start of her journey with the task force. And she couldn't have been more ready.

Then she stifled a gasp. The trafficker was Ray Ho!

Hunched over her temporary desk, Eva immersed herself in Ray Ho's files. A knot tightened in her gut. If her aunt had fallen prey to this network, Eva didn't want to speculate on her survival odds.

Could she hope the police's initial assessment was correct? Hope her aunt had run away? Hope she was somewhere out there, safe, oblivious to this nightmare?

No! She quashed that thought with an indomitable resolve. She wouldn't allow fear or wishful thinking to sway her. *I will find out what happened to you, Aunt Clara!*

Whatever it might be.

An hour later, she plopped down at the conference table across from Olivia. The intelligence officer appeared relaxed, her hands resting on the table, her gaze steady and lips curved like she knew they were about to dive into something big. Her not-so-stiff look lightened the room's serious vibe.

"Eva," Olivia said, "we're in the process of getting more intel on the whereabouts of our target, Ray Ho. Credible intel indicates there is an auction in five or six days. We need you to go undercover. The local human trafficking unit will help insert you as one of the girls being trafficked."

Eva nodded.

"It's going to be dangerous." Olivia folded her hands on the table and leaned over them. "You need to be ready. But we've got your back."

Eva swallowed, forcing her fear down. "I understand. I'm ready."

"I'm going to be your handler. The local unit has a confidential informant, a CI, who will be your inside contact. If I need to communicate with you, it'll go through him. If you need to communicate with us, you'll do the same. Ordinarily, we'd set you up with a wire and earbuds. But in case they have you change clothes or something else, we won't risk it. Speaking of, I hope you're prepared. Since it's an auction, there's a chance they'd want to pretty you up, that's why we're communicating the old-fashioned way."

"Yes, ma'am."

"All right, then." Olivia stood. "Go study your cover identity, backstory, and related information. It'll be your defense against exposure as an agent."

"Yes, ma'am." Eva rose as well.

That afternoon, Olivia pulled her aside with pointers about staying undercover. Then Eva was off.

"This is Detective Annie Kwok, from the organized crime division of the Metropolitan Bureau of Investigation." Tanner introduced a stern woman in her late thirties or early forties dressed in plain clothes. "She'll get you set up with her CI."

Kwok looked Eva up and down, nodding. "You look young enough, but you're too well dressed. To make this work, you'll need to speak with an accent, and I'll get you dressed accordingly. Let's go."

After a round of instructions, a change of clothes to a T-shirt and short jeans, and more prep work, Kwok took Eva to meet her CI, David Chun, a worker in a Chinese restaurant. With his assistance, she'd soon be assimilated into a hidden factory, presenting as another unfortunate caught in human trafficking, working off an imagined debt to the Chinese equivalent of a coyote.

With sizzles, clinks, and whispers enlivening the restaurant's atmosphere, Eva became Mei-Yee. Behind this Chinese restaurant was a hidden factory. Smart, but creepy. Her heart was thumping so loud it overrode the other sounds as she stepped inside, walking right into trouble.

The manager, a cold, calculating gaze set in his hawkish face, approached immediately, his eyes raking her from head to toe, sizing her up. "Where'd you come from?"

Beside her, Chun stepped forward. "Her debt, she's here to work it off."

The manager's scrutinizing gaze didn't waver. He seemed to weigh Chun's words before nodding. "Come."

Then he led her away from the factory, through the restaurant, and into a basement.

Eva steeled her jaw to control her fear. She was Eva Higgins of the FBI, not a victim. Inside a dimly lit room, a group of teenagers huddled together, their eyes wide with fear and hollow with exhaustion. Girls and boys, no older than sixteen or seventeen. A pit opened in her stomach, a grim reality setting in.

The manager whispered something in Cantonese to a burly guard. Then she and a few others were separated, grouped into another category, and the apprehension in her fellow captives' expressions sent chills down her spine.

The dim basement lights cast haunting shadows across their huddled forms. They were kids, really, their young faces hardened with a forced maturity.

"Eva—no, Mei-Yee," she reminded herself. Sticking to her cover was crucial.

She moved toward a girl, her face pale and her clothes loose on her thin frame. "Hi. I'm Mei-Yee."

The girl's brown eyes flicked toward Eva, and her lips pressed into a thin line but remained silent.

"It's my first day," Eva confessed, hoping her vulnerability might build a bridge.

The girl gave a stiff nod. "Ling."

Eva pressed forward, "Do you know what are we supposed to do here, Ling?"

The girl let out a bitter laugh. "Survive, Mei-Yee. Just survive."

CHAPTER 18

DYLAN

Dylan paced his apartment living room, a sleek, modern space with an expansive view of the Orlando cityscape. The glass-topped coffee table and matching dining table, as well as the granite bar separating the kitchen, played host to the papers, documents, and photos he and Tommy recovered from the estate. Once again, Tommy acted as his "Dr. Watson." Tommy now hunched over the map, its edges worn and faded, its lines and words barely decipherable.

Forking his fingers through his hair, pulling at the roots, Dylan joined him. He reached out and traced his index finger over the faded lines and smudged words, squinting to make out any meaningful information. He'd already pulled up a topographical map on his laptop, the screen's brightness turned to the max to help align the old map with the crisp digital version. His brow furrowed, the crease pinching as his focus intensified.

Across the table, Tommy now directed his attention to the stack of black-and-white photos. He picked one up, his fingers framing the fragile edges.

"Dylan, is this your grandfather?" Tommy extended the photo toward him.

Dylan frowned at a man he bore an uncanny resemblance to. "Could be. I can't say. I've never seen a picture of him when he was young. Wait a minute." He grabbed the photo. "I wonder if this is my cop grandfather. They all said I looked like my dad. I can't imagine this is my mom's father. But, if so, why would his photo be with these other ones?"

"No clue. Could be he was undercover?"

"Hmm. A mystery for another day." He handed the photo back and returned to the maps. "This is impossible. I don't even know if it's a full map, and I can't see any obvious landmarks or directional signs."

"What about the people in these photos? They must be significant somehow."

But were they? He pushed to his feet, frustration driving him to pace again, the soft living room carpet giving way beneath his bare soles. "Maybe. But unless we can identify them, they're not much help."

"What's the deal? I understand the pictures. You'd want to know about your ancestors. But the map. What gives? It's not like you need more money. Who cares where they buried the treasure?"

Seriously? Dylan pivoted and stalked to his friend. "Dude." He shook a finger in Tommy's face. "*You* know I'm not doing this for the money. I don't want my aunt to get the treasures. Why else would she want to live on the estate grounds?"

Tone it down, man. Tommy wasn't the enemy. "Um, sorry, dude."

Tommy waved. "Don't sweat it. And beats me. She's a psychopath. Anyway, what's your plan? How do we go about locating it?"

Dylan returned to his side of the table, hands braced alongside the map, the shadow of his head showing the mess he'd made of his hair. "My grandmother might know the people in the picture, but she might not know about the map. Even if she did, she wouldn't tell me. She never wanted me to get involved in the old family criminal business."

He pushed himself upright and smoothed down his hair as if a calm presentation could calm the thudding in his chest. Didn't work. "Max, the loyal butler/majordomo, might know something. I'll ask him. But Fr. Phil…"

The priest might be able to help. Dylan gripped Tommy's arm. "Did you know he was a Navy SEAL before answering the call? Do you think the Navy teaches the SEAL to decipher these maps?"

"You're asking me? How would I know?"

"Right, I'll ask Fr. Phil." He grabbed his keys and followed his Watson to the door. "You coming along or heading out?"

"I'll leave you to it. I got a big day tomorrow."

Forty minutes later, he was back at the chapel again. Only yesterday, he was here for the evening Mass with his grandmother. The big trees were like old friends, and their leaves seemed to whisper stories about the old days. He could almost see ghostly images of his family from way back, laughing and hanging around. He had to shake his head to snap out of it. Since he got here months ago, he'd had this creepy feeling someone was watching him. It never went away, especially when he was walking to the chapel by himself.

His steps slowed near the chapel, the old stone structure a testament to the years gone by. Fr. Phil was standing by the entrance as if he knew Dylan would be here.

"Dylan." The priest's eyes crinkled at the corners. "Miss me already?"

Dylan returned the smile. "What can I say? Your homily is very… deep."

"Good to hear."

He held up the rolled parchment. "I was hoping you could shed some light on this, Father."

The priest motioned Dylan inside. They settled in the rectory, ensconced with the musty scent of old books and well-worn wood. The stained-glass windows painted a kaleidoscope on the stone floor.

When Dylan unrolled the map on the wooden table, his fingers smoothed out the creased parchment. Fr. Phil stood over it, peering at the lines and markings.

"This is… unusual," he said after a long silence. "I recognize some landmarks, but the overall layout—it's not accurate. As if it's meant to confuse or mislead."

Dylan's shoulder slumped. He rubbed the back of his tense neck. "Great. Here I was hoping for a breakthrough, and you've given me more questions. Are you sure, Father?"

Fr. Phil gave him an empathetic look. "I'm sorry, Dylan, but this isn't even a full map. These notations here?" His thick index finger thudded three spots. "I believe they're codes. You'd need a code breaker to decipher. It's designed to keep its secrets well-guarded."

Dylan cocked his head. "Code, you say? Perhaps I should be more intrigued than disheartened. This thing's a true puzzle, one my ancestors left behind." And while he had yet to unlock its secrets, he'd find the key to solve it somehow. "I'd need the code breaker and the rest of the map. Is that what you're saying?"

"I'm afraid so. See here?" The priest pointed to a triangle. "This tree's close to where you located the box. But then this"—he outlined an oblong shape—"should be the pond."

"But that's not where it is. It should be closer to the estate."

"Correct. So not only is this not drawn to scale but it's also misleading. I'm sorry."

"That's okay. Thank you, Father."

CHAPTER 19

CLARA & FAITH

After her peaceful morning prayers, Clara trusted Michael hadn't done anything wrong. She needed something solid to hold onto, an anchor in a storm. And prayer lifted the weight off her shoulders. Now, she had to find the right time to ask him.

Pushing those thoughts aside, she refocused on Linda Boroski. As she reviewed her work, she gasped. Engrossed in Linda's death, Clara overlooked Linda's life. Understanding Linda as a person might help uncover the circumstances of her death.

With her newfound determination, her fingers danced over the keyboard as she hunted for traces of Linda's past. Then she picked up the phone, calling the police station for another round of questions.

"Officer Johnson, please forgive me for pestering you. This is Clara again. From *Christian Living Magazine*."

"Good morning, Clara. Yes, I remember you. How may I help you?"

"I'm still on the Linda Boroski case. I'd like to know more about her. Can you help me?"

After a pause on the other end, Johnson replied, "Sure, I'll see what I can share with you from the files."

Phone music overtook the line before Officer Johnson returned. "I have something." His voice seemed higher, hinting at excitement. "Boroski was a student at Orlando University enrolled in the business school."

Jackpot. "Thank you, Officer. I appreciate the tip."

"You bet. Best of luck with that."

She hung up, then grabbed her keys to head over to the big Orlando University campus. Maybe wandering the halls Linda used to would help.

Shortly later, she parked under a big oak tree on the campus. Lit up by the sun, the brick buildings looked fancy but friendly. Students clustered together, sat reading alone, or hurried to class. The whole scene felt kind of homey, but a weird déjà vu hit her.

She shook off the uncanny sensation, clutched her tablet and purse, and stepped out of the car. Inhaling the scent of freshly cut grass overplaying the faint aroma of coffee from a nearby café, she moved toward the administrative building.

A cool blast of air-conditioning and the quiet hum of productivity met her as she approached the reception.

A young woman offered a welcoming smile and pushed glasses up her nose. "May I help you?"

Clara checked the woman's name tag—Stacy—then took a deep breath, steadying herself. "I hope so. My name is Clara Khoury, and I'm researching a former student named Linda Boroski. She would have been here about twenty years ago, in the business school, I believe. Might there be any old records, or perhaps even someone who knew her might still be around?"

Stacy's brows knit together, the motion edging her glasses downward again. "I'm afraid those records are archived and not easily accessible. And we don't give out such information without the student's consent unless there's a court order. And as for Ms. Boroski's acquaintances, most of them have likely moved on if it's from as long ago as you say."

Clara nodded. "I understand. Thank you, anyway."

Stacy slid off her glasses and wiped them, crinkling her nose. "You know, you might try speaking with Professor Evans. He's a professor emeritus, but he's here teaching a course. He's been here forever and knows practically everyone. He might remember something."

Yes! A lead. "That sounds like a great idea. Where can I find him?"

Armed with directions to the professor's office, Clara thanked her before heading off. The déjà vu hit her again as she navigated the hallways. The feeling only intensified when she met Professor Evans, an affable older man with a warm smile and a shock of white hair.

After a brief introduction, he frowned at her. "Were you in one of my classes?"

"I'm, er, I don't think so." It was the only way to answer honestly. Why did she feel like she knew the campus so well? She didn't remember this professor, but something about him felt familiar. Did she go to college here?

"Oh, well, I've taught so many students over the years. Probably got you mixed up with somebody else. Why don't you come into my office and tell me what I can do for you."

In a cluttered back cubbyhole, he gestured for her to sit. He listened as she repeated her story, his eyes clouding over. "Linda Boroski," he murmured. "The name sounds familiar, but twenty years, you say? As I said, I taught so many students over the years."

Clara tapped her phone a couple of times to locate the photo of Linda she'd downloaded from the internet earlier. She presented it to the professor. "This is her."

He studied the photo. "She does look familiar. Or rather,

did." He returned the phone. "You know, I'm pretty good with faces, not so much with names. If memory serves, she always hung out with that student from Hong Kong who I thought was you. Isn't that the darndest thing?"

The Orlando Christian Academy cafeteria was a simple place, really—just long tables, benches, a spot to grab food, and a big noticeboard displaying school stuff. But with its buzz and laughter, it felt homey, revitalizing even with its backbeat of energy. The tall ceiling took in all the noise, turning what could've been a crazy racket into a nice background hum. And the smell of lunch? It mixed right in with the sound of chatty teens and the flip of books and papers, making the place just what Faith needed to unwind.

She bit into her chicken salad sandwich, her mind wandering to her history paper. Josie, her new friend from her homeroom, was next to her, half-heartedly poking at her salad.

"Have you gotten started on the outline for Mrs. Scott's paper?" Faith asked, trying to reel Josie into her world of assignments and deadlines.

Josie made a face, rolling her eyes. "You can't be serious! We're teenagers, and there's a massive party coming up." Lowering her voice, she added, "Rumor has it Chase will be there."

Faith's eyes widened. Chase, the school heartthrob, had made quite an impression since he transferred in from California. "Wow, Chase?"

Josie's grin spread out, revealing the cilantro stuck in her teeth. "Yup. The Chase. It's going to be a blast!"

Bella and Sophie, two of their classmates, arrived at their table and launched into excited chatter about the party, leaving

Faith torn between the mounting academic pressure and the lure of a social life.

Then the cafeteria doors opened, and Chase walked in with the easy grace of an athlete. Wow, his gaze landed on her. Her heartbeat sped up, and a slice of avocado plopped from her sandwich. Oops.

He sauntered over. A flick of his head sent his light brown bangs back from his eyes. "Faith, isn't it?"

"Y–Yes." Double wow, he knew her name.

"I remember seeing you with a guy at the soccer camp last summer in Chicago."

Seriously? He'd noticed her then? "Oh, that was Liam, my ex. You were in Chicago?"

He shrugged, his smile warm. "You have a distinct look. And beautiful. I was just there for the soccer camp."

Blushing, she fumbled for words and managed a mumbled thank you.

"No worries. Hope to see you at the party." Then he was walking off.

When he was out of earshot, Bella squealed and slapped the table, jostling their water bottles and pop cans. "I don't believe it. Did that just happen? Chase likes you!"

Faith's cheeks heated even more. She didn't know about that, but the upcoming party now seemed like a much-needed diversion from her academic worries. So how was she going to convince Mom to let her go?

CHAPTER 20

RON & OLIVIA

"Hey, Ron. Got a minute?"

Ron rolled his chair back from his desk, surrendering to the need for a break from paperwork when Ana tapped his doorframe. He sank deep in his chair and folded his hands across his middle, letting the agent know she had his focus. "Sure. What is it?"

"It's about Adam O'Shea?"

A knot tightened in his stomach. The lawyer had been a menace since this investigation began.

"There's no such person, at least not the one we've been dealing with."

His head jerked up. He moved his hands to his desk and leaned over it. "What do you mean?"

Ana crossed the room and brought up a profile on her tablet, showcasing a friendly-faced, middle-aged man. "*This* is Adam O'Shea. He's a lawyer, just like our guy, but he's on a sabbatical in Hawaii. His wife writes for a travel magazine, and they've both been there for the past few months."

"That's not possible." Ron took the tablet and scrolled the images. "He was at the federal detention center."

"I know." She slid the tablet from his hands and sat on the edge of his desk. "But I've confirmed the real O'Shea is in Hawaii. I've spoken with the school administrators, his students, even the local police. He's been teaching classes there, hosting seminars. His wife's been reporting on local culture and food for her magazine."

Ron rubbed his eyes, stalling as he processed. This fake lawyer had to be connected with the leak.

"So, our guy is an imposter. Using a stolen identity. Have we got anything on him yet? Fingerprints, photo matches, anything?"

She gripped his desk on either side of her, one leg jiggling out her excess energy. "We're working on it. I've requested footage from the detention center. We'll run facial recognition, see if we can get a hit."

Hands laced in his lap again, he scowled at the papers on his desk. "I've been hoping to plug a leak—and here, you've discovered an imposter visiting the Ghost. Why doesn't the real O'Shea have any digital footprint?"

"I don't know. It's unusual, but there are still some people living off the grid. Or trying to. Didn't you scrub Dylan's online presence?"

"Yeah, but…" It was for Dylan's safety. Could it be this real O'Shea was hiding from someone or something too? "Whatever his reasons are, we can't worry about him now. We need to identify the fake one. Keep me posted on the facial rec."

"Yes, sir."

"Notify the local law enforcement and have them start searching for any lawyers who've recently gone off the grid."

"Understood." Ana hopped to her feet, her petite form reminding him of an espresso—a small cup but watch out for the wallop of caffeine.

"Good work, Ana." Man, he loved his team, but he'd need more coffee to keep up. He shoved back from his desk and headed to the break room. Whatever the Ghost was up to, they'd have to stay ahead of her.

As Olivia pushed her way through the bustling Asian grocery store, the marketplace offered a familiar comfort. Shoppers were negotiating prices, vendors hawking wares, and children running amok. But through it all, she scanned for one face in particular—Henry Chen.

Back at the office, she had peered over Tanner's shoulder at the information passed by the human trafficking unit while he was on the phone with the police detective. As soon as she overheard the name of someone who might help, she took it upon herself to do some fieldwork.

She found Henry in the produce section, stacking fresh bok choy with the practiced ease of a longtime employee. She sidled up to the vegetable stand, giving him a casual nod, and remarked in Cantonese. "Nice selection of greens you've got here."

His brows knitted. "Thanks. Do I know you?"

"Just a friend." She offered a casual smile.

As the conversation meandered on, his posture relaxed, his answers becoming less clipped. Then she steered to her topic. "Heard about any interesting happenings around town?"

He drew in a slow breath, then released it as if afraid to let the words out. "There's a... banquet scheduled at Fu Gardens Restaurant."

Satisfaction jolted her, but she hid it behind a nod. "A banquet? Sounds fancy."

"Yes, you know, the kind where all the high rollers show up."

Ah, so the word *banquet* was code for an auction.

"When is it?"

"It's always on the weekends. Saturday."

"Thanks." She'd be in on planning the op. She stepped out of the store, dialed Ron, and pressed the phone to her ear as she walked.

"Ron, it's Olivia." She scanned the busy sidewalk, then kept her head down. "I've got a lead—a, um, 'banquet' at Fu Gardens Restaurant."

"That means we need to move fast. We'll have to scope out the place. Get Simon and Kyle prepped. Can you secure an invitation?"

"I'm not sure. But I can try."

She turned on her heels, headed back to the grocery store, and found Henry Chen in the same spot, now arranging a crate of dragon fruit.

"Hey, Henry. This banquet at Fu Gardens. Is it open to anyone, or do you need an invitation?"

Henry glanced around before leaning in closer. "Well, it's not public. But if you're famous or rich, they might let you in."

"And if I'm not?"

Henry hesitated, then edged in closer, and lowered his voice to a whisper. "Just tell them… Fat Uncle invited you."

She nodded. Fat Uncle. Simon, as a former senator, might not need that. However, it was best to be prepared.

Poor Simon. He'd never been an operative. Would he be convincing enough to act as a bidder?

If only she could go along to ensure his safety.

CHAPTER 21

CLARA

Seated at a round table waiting for their dinner companions, Clara scooted her chair closer to her husband's. "Do you think I went to Orlando University?"

Michael stretched his back, stiffening in his crisp mint polo shirt. "Er, that would be a crazy coincidence, wouldn't it? To end up here again? I mean I found you at the Outer Banks. Not here. Although I suppose you could have taken a trip up there."

"You didn't see the professor. He believed I'd been a student of his."

He shrugged. "I'm not sure what to tell you. Maybe you can ask the registrar."

"If I did go there, my social wouldn't be the one I'm using now." Majid had somehow procured a packet of identification for her long ago. They'd thought she was an undocumented immigrant, and Michael wanted to protect her from trouble with the police. Neither of them asked where Majid obtained the documents.

Michael didn't say anything, just pressed his lips together.

But the line that drew his thick brows together when he was pensive appeared, and the skin tautened over his well-defined jaw.

She touched his hand. "There are these little things I know. Like I believe I'm Christian and I have a strong feeling I'm Catholic since all the prayers are familiar to me. And I can drive. It's so weird."

He turned his hand to grip hers, swallowing it in warm comfort. "Memories aren't motor skills. Dr. Cook was hoping your memory would start coming back once you remembered your name. But then—it's like you wanted to forget. Have a clean slate."

"Did you really think I was an undocumented immigrant?" Her throat clogged. "Do–do you still think so?"

He looked around to make sure no one was paying attention. "Well, there was that big bust of illegal immigrants right where we found you. So, yeah, it seemed likely. But, after knowing you, I doubt it. If you were, you'd have come here long ago."

Before she could say anything, their guests approached. Dr. Jenkins, the hospital administrator and chief medical officer, and his wife, Rhonda, orchestrated the evening intending to get better acquainted. They'd also invited Dr. Miller, chief of the emergency department, and his wife.

Dr. Miller's eyes widened, and his mouth slid open as he sighted Clara. He staggered, his hand fumbling for the back of a nearby chair.

His wife, Elaine, rushed to his side. "Ben, are you all right?" She steadied him with her arm. "You're not having another episode, are you?"

He regained his composure and shook his head, though his gaze remained fixed on Clara. "No, I'm f–fine, Elaine."

But with the way his voice wavered, he didn't sound fine.

"You sure?" Michael got to his feet, ready to take action.

Dr. Jenkins also leaned around Clara to better focus on the disturbed doctor.

"I'm okay, really. Let's sit." Dr. Miller sat with his wife and again assured everyone he was fine.

Once the awkwardness was dispelled, dinner proceeded, their conversation ranging from hospital politics to personal anecdotes.

"Yes, Faith is a senior. She's hoping to go back to Chicago for college. But we'll see." Clara sat sideways in her chair, facing Elaine, whose daughter was a freshman at the University of Miami.

"Well, at least she's at a good school." Elaine raised her water glass, ice tinkling before she took a sip. "Ben's son, Chase, is a senior at Orlando Christian Academy. He's just moved to live with us recently from California. He was staying with his mom."

"Small world! Faith may know him, then."

Soon, Clara found herself explaining her intermittent memory lapses. "I suffered a head trauma years ago." She'd used that half-truth before to evade deeper questions.

"Head trauma can indeed have lasting impacts," Dr. Miller murmured, his gaze steady on Clara.

"If you don't mind my asking, what happened?" Rhonda Jenkins asked.

"Oh." Clara waved beside her head. "It was an accident."

"I heard about the golf fundraising thing. Tell me about it." Michael, her hero as always, saved her by changing the subject.

As Michael left to retrieve the car and Elaine excused herself to use the restroom, Clara stood alone with Dr. Miller. The Jenkinses had left. Dr. Miller's previous behavior had left her somewhat wary, but she maintained a friendly demeanor.

"Clara." He reached as if to grasp her hand, then stopped himself, and crossed his arms over his chest. "I was intrigued by your comment about your head trauma earlier tonight. May I ask how severe it was?"

Taken aback, she fumbled with her purse straps. "It was serious enough. I lost a lot of my memories. It's why I often seem lost or out of sorts."

His intent focus never left her face, as if he was trying to find something hidden in her features. "I find your case… interesting. Head trauma is a fascinating area of research. So much is still unknown about the brain's resilience and its ability to recover."

Clara shifted. His interest felt too personal, too focused. But it must just be professional curiosity.

"It hasn't been an easy journey," she admitted.

"I can only imagine. I'm spearheading a research project about the long-term effects of head injuries and how the brain recovers. It's groundbreaking. We're looking for participants who've suffered from similar experiences. Would you consider participating?"

He was working on this very thing? She blinked, then nodded. "I-I'll think about it. It sounds interesting. Let me discuss it with Michael."

"Of course." His arms dropped from their tight hold across his chest, and his taut features relaxed. "Take all the time you need."

Michael's car pulled up to the curb, and she slid into her seat. As the car hummed to life and they left the parking lot, she touched his arm braced on the console between them. "What do you think about him? Dr. Miller, I mean."

He shrugged, still focused on the road. "Ben seems friendly enough. Another doctor." There was a pause, a flicker of curiosity as he glanced her way. "Why do you ask?"

"Nothing. Except he was talking about a research project he's leading. About head trauma and brain recovery. He asked if I'd be interested in participating."

He arched his brows. "He did? Interesting. I haven't heard about this project before. I'll look into it."

"Also"—she lowered her voice—"did you notice his reaction when he saw me? It was, um, odd."

He stopped for a red light, eyeing her again. "Odd how?"

"I don't know, really. He looked shocked, almost scared. You know, like when they say someone had seen a ghost."

The light changed. A few blocks passed by in silence before Michael broke into a light chuckle. "Ben? Scared? You're over-thinking this. He recently had a mini heart attack. It might just be his health."

Maybe. She nodded, but she wasn't convinced. She'd drop the subject for now, but she couldn't shake the nagging feeling. Surely, there was something more to Dr. Miller's odd reaction.

CHAPTER 22

CLARA

Clara settled in her home office, a sunlit corner in the master bedroom, soaking in the quiet, the room's silence accentuated by the ceiling fan doing its thing and the old grandfather clock ticking away next door. Papers covered her wooden desk, all messy but somehow making sense, each one scribbled with her notes on Linda Boroski's case. Getting ready for her chat with Dr. Harris, she kept thinking about Michael's suggestion. Maybe she should call the registrar at Orlando University, where Linda attended college and Clara might have gone. It wasn't a bad idea.

Would they demand her social security number? And what would she tell them? She rubbed between her eyes but couldn't push the questions to the back of her mind. "I might as well be trying to untangle an endless knot."

Steeling herself, she dialed.

"Orlando University." A woman with a crisp, professional voice answered the call. "This is Brenda. How may I assist you today?"

Clara took a deep breath, inhaling a cautious optimism. "Hello, Brenda. My name is Clara Khoury. I'm a journalist with *Christian Living*, and I was wondering if I could get some information about a former student?"

"Hmm, what kind of information? Are you looking to verify attendance? If so, there's a form online you can fill out. You'll need the student's name, years of attendance, and student ID."

"Student ID?"

"Yes, usually, it's the social security number. And the student will need to sign it to release the information. Unless the student already signed a blanket release form."

"What if I don't have the student ID?" Clara held her breath during the pause.

"Then I don't think we can locate the student's records."

"Even if I was the student in question?"

"And you don't know your social?"

"I know it, but I believe I didn't use it to register back then."

"Oh yes. That happens. If you didn't provide your social, the university would have assigned you a student number. However, without it, it would be difficult to locate your records."

"Would a name be enough?"

"What you can do is submit a form online with your full name, the address at the time of your attendance, the years of attendance, and the pertinent information like the degree and college you were in."

Clara thanked her and ended the call, but she wasn't about to surrender. She dialed Professor Evans who'd recognized her on campus. His warm voice was welcoming, but his memory of names, as he had admitted, wasn't great.

"Oh, Clara, I'm sorry, but I can't remember her name. I do remember her being from Hong Kong. She was a bright student, full of enthusiasm and curiosity."

Clara listened, her heart pounding.

"I thought she worked as a part-time staff writer somewhere. Some big foundation, as far as I remember."

"Do you happen to remember the name?"

"No—oh, wait, I do. It was the Beaumont Foundation. She was in their public relations or publicity department. Every year, the foundation gives the college several scholarships. And I've just seen an application floating around."

"Thank you so much, Professor."

She hung up, her mind racing.

If she couldn't do anything about the Linda Boroski case, maybe she could uncover Michael's cash withdrawals. Her husband wouldn't harm her, but with the detective focused on him, they'd never find who did hurt her. Since Michael had gone to work, she could survey his desk.

First, she logged in to their joint bank accounts. Nothing seemed out of the ordinary. There were no large withdrawals. They each had their separate accounts in addition, though their savings account and various investment accounts were jointly held. She hovered the cursor over two partial liquidations of an investment account. Sometimes, depending on the market, they might sell off an asset and reinvest. However, she wasn't seeing any reinvestment or deposit into their joint accounts. "Hmm, I'll have to ask him about it."

She pushed back her chair and padded across the hall to Michael's desk in the study/guest room. So different from her organized chaos, he kept the surface clean with only his laptop and pens. As she ran a hand along the well-polished surface, she smiled over her fastidious husband.

But she'd come here for a purpose. She pulled out the drawers one by one. Flicking past the life insurance policies she'd known about, she paused at a legal-size envelope with a private detective's return address on it. He'd never said anything about a PI. When would they need a PI? He couldn't have been checking up on Faith's ex-boyfriend. They were comfortable, but they weren't wealthy enough to have to worry about gold-diggers for their daughter.

She opened the envelope, frowning at the contents.

Nothing except for a receipt of payment.

And then her laptop across the hall chimed with the notification that it was time for her session. Well, for now, any question could wait.

The late morning sunlight glinted off her screen as she adjusted her laptop camera against the glare to bring her therapist, Dr. Harris, into view. The psychiatrist's warm smile spread across the screen, her calm demeanor inviting as always.

"Good morning, Clara." Dr. Harris settled back in her chair.

"Hello, Dr. Harris." Clara sat up straight, her nerves on edge.

After discussing Clara's general state and the recent social changes, Dr. Harris broached Clara's recurring feelings of familiarity and unease. "You mentioned a strange connection with the name Linda Boroski and a sense of discomfort around Dr. Miller. Could you elaborate?"

Clara relayed her unsettling sensations. "I can't pinpoint any specific memories, but the vague sense of knowing is there. I've read about hypnotherapy. Do you think it'll work?"

"I'm not sure that's the best approach." Dr. Harris tapped against her armrests. "I hesitate to suggest that because it hasn't been proven completely effective. At best, it would allow deeper access to your subconscious mind."

"But it doesn't hurt to try it, right?"

Dr. Harris's fingers stilled. "If this is really what you want to do, then yes. The technique uses guided relaxation and intense concentration to achieve a heightened state of awareness."

Clara bit her lower lip. "I can't deny the idea of delving deeper into my mind is intimidating, but I've yearned for answers for so long. Do you think it could help me understand why I have these feelings?"

A small smile curved the doctor's lips. "Again, it's not been proven effective. But it's a possibility. Hypnotherapy can often reveal suppressed memories. Of course, we need to approach it with care and professionalism, and it's important you feel safe and comfortable during the sessions."

Clara let out her held breath, some of her long-held hopes rushing free as well. "If there's even a slight chance I can regain my memories, I'd like to give it a try."

"Then we'll do this. As always, you have full control, and we'll move at your pace."

Clara finished her session, then sank back. Rocking in her chair, she twisted it to face the bay window, sunlight now pooling on the hardwood floor. Maybe hypnotherapy could unravel the mystery of her mind.

She got some leftover salad out of the fridge and took it to her desk so she could go back to the Linda Boroski case without losing momentum.

Headquartered in Texas, the Beaumont Foundation maintained a local office in town. After frustrating transfers, Clara got hold of a live person only to discover the PR department wasn't part of the foundation but was a PR firm under the umbrella of Beaumont Inc., its for-profit counterpart.

At last, she secured the name of the PR department's key person during the time Clara might have worked there, Stella Beckett. Beckett had since moved on, but Clara found her on LinkedIn, then dialed the number on the profile. The phone trilled before a crisp, professional voice echoed through the line. It was a small victory, but a step closer to the truth.

"Hello, this is Clara Khoury—"

"Clara?!" The woman gasped. "Oh my! Is that you, Clara Wu? I thought I'd never hear your voice again. I recognize your ever-so-subtle accent. Where have you been all these years?"

Stunned, Clara played along. "Yeah, I, uh, had an accident."

"I knew it! I told those cops you wouldn't run away. You

were going to write a story that would launch your career—you had such big plans, too big to disappear in the middle of them. We did check with the hospitals ourselves, but you weren't in any of them. Anyway, are you in town?"

Stella was in Texas. "No, I'm in Orlando. What story was I working on?"

"Hang on. Let me get to the archives."

Keys tapped. Then Stella said, "Here we go. The notes only said you had a source—a reliable source. Something about a human trafficker. Once you had something solid, you'd let me know everything."

That didn't help. So, she was working on a story involving a human trafficker. Could this be real? Was she Clara Wu? "All right. Was I going somewhere to chase the lead?"

"Not that I know of. You were taking the weekend off first. Um, why are you asking me? Did you not write the story?"

"It's a long story. The accident messed up my memories." That was the closest to the truth, right?

"Oh, how terrible. You know what, I have a meeting to go to. But is this your number? Let's catch up soon, okay? We'll video chat."

Clara thanked her and hung up. If she'd been working on the story, how did she end up in the Outer Banks? Was this finally leading somewhere? Clara Wu. Maybe that's who she was. Could Stella help her find Clara Wu's family?

Surprisingly, the hypnotherapist Dr. Harris recommended had a last-minute cancellation and scheduled Clara that afternoon. Soft music in the background, the reception offered a calm oasis amid the bustling city.

Extending her hand in the waiting room, Joanna, the

hypnotherapist, greeted her. "Clara, I've reviewed your medical history. Now let's talk about your expectations for this session."

Despite the soothing ambiance, Clara hugged her purse to her stomach, pressing it against a twinge of anxiety. This was nothing like the hypnosis sessions portrayed on TV. There was no pendant swinging back and forth, no robotic voice commanding her to sleep.

Joanna touched Clara's arm as she led her into the office. "Remember, hypnosis isn't always a quick fix. It might take a few sessions before we see progress. But what matters most is that you feel safe and comfortable."

Clara nodded, released the death grip on her purse, and surrendered it to the chair by the door before settling on the leather couch. As Joanna guided her into a trancelike state, it was almost as if she were floating, her thoughts adrift.

"I'm taking you back to a safe time and place. You're in school. What do you see?"

At first, the only schools she saw were Faith's and Jason's. But Joanna's soothing voice guided her back further. "I see uniforms. Chinese girls."

"Can you describe the uniform? Teachers? The buildings?"

"Light-blue ties, full white dress. A playground. It was recess, I think. A small kid ran into me. It hurt. The classroom. I see the clock and a crucifix on the wall. A board with drawings and other writings pinned to it."

"Very good." Joanna then coaxed her to her college days.

Clara tried, but it was a blank.

"You're getting agitated. I'm bringing you out."

The session ended, leaving her with a hint of dejection. Though a few memories had floated to the surface, she'd discovered nothing significant. It was like trying to make her teenage boy tell her about his day.

Joanna scooted onto the couch beside her and gripped her

hand. "Don't worry. These things take time. Let's see what the next session brings."

Clara forced a smile. Maybe the next session would produce the missing pieces of her past.

CHAPTER 23

RON & MICHAEL

After the meeting, his team members began to filter out, their conversations fading into the distance, leaving a contemplative silence. Ron massaged his temple. So many items on the agenda.

Ana lingered, her brow scrunched and lips pressed tight the way she did when holding back information. She moved to his desk and pulled a flash drive from her pocket. "We've retrieved the footage from the prison."

When he plugged it into his computer, their version of Adam O'Shea sprung to life, encapsulated in pixels.

Ana braced her hands on his desk, steady against the quiet hum of office machinery. "I've run it through facial recognition. Scanned every available database, but there's nothing."

Ron enlarged the image. The contours, the way he held his jaw... "There's something about him, but I can't quite place it."

Ana pushed away from the desk, her palms leaving steamy handprints on the scarred wooden surface. "He's due for another visit to the Ghost soon—tomorrow, if the pattern holds. We could put a tail on him."

Ron's eyebrows shot up. "If this guy's as good as we think he is, he'll spot a tail faster than we can say 'surveillance.' We need something more covert, something he won't expect."

Ana smirked, her eyes sparkling. "What about spy toys? Olivia could lend us some."

A chuckle slipped loose as he ran a hand through his hair. "Spy toys, huh? Who would've thought I'd consider it one day? Let's see what that girl has in her bag of tricks."

"I'll ask her."

After Ana left, Tanner and Hernandez came in.

"Boss?" Tanner stood at attention, his gravity drawing Ron's attention. He'd known Tanner long enough to understand the man's nonverbal cues. This was serious. "We've finished our deep dive into everyone with even a peripheral connection to Olivia."

Ron sat up straight. "Yes?"

"Nothing, absolutely nothing, stands out as suspicious."

Tanner glanced toward Hernandez, hesitating.

Hernandez gave a subtle nod, his expression firm. "Except for one person. Eva."

Ron's head snapped up. He tried to suppress the quick jolt at her name. He wanted to vouch for her, but personal feelings couldn't cloud his judgment. This was about Olivia, and they had to exhaust every possibility, no matter how unlikely. He cleared his throat and kept his voice steady. "What's the issue?"

Hernandez raised the file in his hands a fraction. "During one of her interviews, she mentioned an Uncle Bill. According to her, this person was her inspiration to pursue a career in law enforcement."

"I thought I was her inspiration?" Ron leaned back, lacing his hands across his middle. Eva once told him he'd inspired her to seek out the FBI.

Hernandez smirked. "You were, boss. You're the reason she ended up in the Bureau. But according to her, this 'Uncle Bill' sparked her interest in law enforcement."

Ron tapped his thumbs together. "And you didn't find the guy in her records?"

"We thoroughly examined her family tree. No male relative matches the description."

Ron moved his hands to his desk, thumbs still tapping. If—a big *if*—Eva was the leak, he refused to believe she had done it intentionally. He'd known that girl since she was a kid. Plus, she was already in the field. He'd have to ask Olivia to be extra diligent in monitoring her reporting. "I'll update Olivia."

In his hospital office, Michael kicked back behind his big oak desk, Majid across from him. Outside, the hospital was doing its usual noisy dance—announcements over the speakers, people hustling around or chattering, and that ever-present hum of machines. But him? He zoned out from all that, zeroed in on this plain manila folder hanging out among the clutter of medical files and articles on his desk. That called out to him or something.

The folder held a secret, a deeply held truth he'd carried close to his heart for days. A secret about Clara, his wife, a woman who bore scars on her mind. Yet now, as she began to pierce the veil, the truth could send ripples into their world.

"Let me get this straight." Majid massaged his temples. "Her real name is Clara Wu. She emigrated from Hong Kong in her early teens, sponsored by her uncle, a US resident. She lived a life entirely different from what she knows now, yet she has no recollection of it?"

Michael let out a heavy breath, his fingers tracing the manila folder's soft edges. "Yes. The private investigator I hired months ago pieced this together. The police couldn't because Clara's fingerprints didn't match any existing records, perhaps due to inefficient information sharing between the states—or so the PI suspects. Or they didn't check against the federal database. Her prints should be on record with immigration."

The office door creaked open, and a young nurse poked her head in. "Dr. Khoury, I'm sorry to interrupt, but there's an urgent message for you from the ICU."

He gestured for her to come in. The hospital's pace offered no pause for personal predicaments.

"No need to apologize, Lisa." He slipped into his doctor's façade, read the message, scribbled a response, then handed it back. "Get this to Dr. Thompson in the ICU. And thank you."

As Lisa left, Dr. Kim stepped around her. "Sorry for the interruption. Would you like to do the rounds?"

Michael waved him off. "You can do it. Let me know if you run into any problems."

"Yes, sir."

Once Kim had left, Majid laid down the magazine he was reading. "Amir, why didn't you tell her as soon as you got it?"

"I've only received the report a week ago. After I read it, I was going to, but then she got drugged and started having nightmares. I thought I'd wait for a better time."

Majid scowled at the diplomas displayed on the wall. "As much as I hate to say this, she has a right to know. And there's never a better time when it comes to something so significant." Then he rubbed his hands on his thighs. "In other news, I put down a deposit."

Michael replayed the words in his mind. Oh, Majid must be referring to the hair salon he was opening. "Well, that's great. The location is good. I went by it the other day."

"All thanks to you, big bro."

"That's what family is for."
Would Clara's family have been there for her? And would they now?

CHAPTER 24

LILY & CLARA

Lily followed Dylan up a rock pathway to the Khourys' elegant residence bordered by groomed gardens, the upscale neighborhood reminiscent of her father's house. Michael Khoury swung the front door open. Clara stood at his side, her captivating blend of features suggesting Chinese heritage. Lily, being half-Chinese herself, noted the familiarity but refrained from asking about Clara's origins.

"Welcome," Michael greeted them, then gestured toward his wife. "You met my wife, Clara."

"Well, wish it was under better circumstances." Dylan shook hands with Michael.

"Nice to meet you, Mrs. Khoury." Lily clasped Clara's hand.

Clara tilted her head, tightening her hold on Lily's hand, studying her. "You look familiar. And, please, call me Clara."

Lily studied the woman. "You do too, but I don't know. I've only recently moved to the States. Perhaps we might have seen each other in Hong Kong at the Marino Hotel? I worked at the Business Center."

"No, we haven't visited Hong Kong." Clara furrowed her brow, then laughed. "Oh well. Do come, sit. Dinner should be ready soon." She showed them to an immaculate living room where cream-toned accent chairs offset the brown leather couch.

In the before-dinner conversation, Clara settled onto the couch beside Lily. While she spoke, Lily scooted closer, fascinated by the woman's resilience. "You speak Cantonese. Are you from Hong Kong? Almost every Cantonese speaker I know is from Hong Kong or second-generation with parents insisting on speaking Cantonese at home."

Clara fluttered her fingers by her face, perhaps to wave off the question, but a quiver seemed to go through them as she lowered them to her lap. "I wish I could tell you for sure. I had a traumatic head injury years ago, and I lost most of my memories."

"Oh, wow. That sucks. You don't remember anything?" Dylan braced his elbows on his knees, hands locked by his chin, frown fixed on Clara. "I don't know how I'd have survived."

Clara reached across the oak coffee table to squeeze her husband's hand. "I often doubt I would have if not for him."

"Clara and I met during that challenging time." Michael clasped hands with Clara. "I was a neurosurgery fellow then. It was a serendipitous meeting, but one I am grateful for every day."

As Dylan observed them, his eyes soft, Lily tried to imagine him in a similar scenario. Would he be as supportive and loving? Then again, she hoped she would never have to find out.

"So, you were her doctor?" Dylan asked.

"Initially. Then I withdrew from her care team." Michael brought her hand to his lips. "We moved to Chicago after my fellowship when I was offered a position there. Clara was still recovering. We returned to Florida only when I was offered the role of chief of surgery."

"That's quite a journey." Lily draped her arm over the side of the leather couch. "It must've been hard, though, especially for you, Clara."

"It was," Clara admitted. "But having Michael there made it bearable. He was—and still is—my rock. And over time, our bond evolved, leading to us getting married. But fragments of the past are still hazy for me."

Touched by their story and the bond it forged between them, Lily glanced at Dylan, hoping he would feel the same. Their friendship was built on their shared ordeal.

"Well, I'd better check on dinner." Clara pushed to her feet and crossed to the kitchen, stepping around the island, her bearing displaying a woman who knew who she was—even if she didn't. Minutes later, she gave them a wave. "Dinner's ready."

"All right then." Michael rose and gestured to the dining table. "Follow me, folks."

Faith and Jason, Clara and Dr. Khoury's teenagers, joined them. And Dr. Khoury presented a toned-down version of Clara's near-accident, casting Dylan as the hero of the day while leaving out the disturbing undertones.

While Dylan and Jason bonded over sports and video games, the more reserved Faith showed a keen interest in Lily's stories about life in Hong Kong.

They lingered after dinner. Then Lily fell quiet during the ride back, and Dylan didn't try to engage her. He seemed to understand her need to "decompress" after some social activities.

With him, everything felt easy and natural. His infectious laughter and earnest gaze made her heart flutter, and she couldn't deny the connection. Yet when she was with Kyle, the charming FBI agent, a different but potent chemistry fizzed. The two separate connections tugged at her heartstrings, and though no one was declaring relationships or exclusivity, she'd soon need to untangle her affection. For now, she'd revel in the ambiguity, basking in this moment between friendship and possibilities.

What am I going to do? How am I going to choose?

After Lily and Dylan left and the children retreated to their rooms, Clara, nestled into the leather couch across from Michael, who was watching TV in his favorite armchair. The sun had set, and the evening wind rustled the leaves.

"Michael?" She put her cup of tea on the coffee table. "Please turn off the TV. I need to tell you something."

Shifting to face her, he muted it. "Yes?"

"I called the registrar, no luck. But Professor Evans said the student he thought was me worked at the Beaumont Foundation. So, I tracked down the editor who was the student's boss. You won't believe what she said. She said I'm Clara Wu. But that can't be right, can it? You found me in the Outer Banks."

His face paled, his eyes widening. He said nothing, his mouth opening and closing as if he wanted to speak but couldn't find the words.

"Michael?" The breath hissed from her lungs. Going light-headed, she leaned forward, a chill settling over her. "What's going on? Why are you looking at me like that?"

"I–I—" Michael stammered, his voice low. "I didn't expect you to find out this way."

"Find out what way?" Her eyebrows came together. Her pulse quickened. Her whole body tensed. Did he know? "Please don't tell me you knew." Her voice came out louder than usual.

"I hired a PI not long ago. I got his report last week. Really, just a few days ago. I was going to tell you, but, well, you were drugged, then the nightmares. I, uh, I was waiting for a better time."

The envelope she'd seen earlier… "I'm not following." This

was not happening. How could he not have told her if he had known? "What did you hire the PI to investigate?"

"You, your background." He sprang from his chair and settled onto the couch beside her, taking her hands into his overly hot ones. Or perhaps her hands were overly cold. All of her felt abnormally chill. Holding fast to her, he told her what was in the report.

She pried free, her heart thudding so hard her chest felt ready to explode. He'd known—for days—and he hadn't bothered telling her! *Oh, Lord! Give me the grace to forgive.*

"I'm sorry. I should have told you sooner, but—"

"Right, the incident." Her temples thrummed. Any minute now, the headache would return. But whatever she was feeling now, it could wait. "So, I am Clara Wu? It makes some sense. But how did I end up in the Outer Banks?"

"That, I don't know."

Family. She had family. "Did the PI find my family?"

"No, not in the report. You can read it yourself. The report said your uncle sponsored you." He captured one of her hands, perhaps oblivious to how hard she was trying to forgive him, how hard it was to let him touch her in this moment, how very hot and clammy his hands were. "But if you want to, I can ask him to track down your family."

She didn't remember her family, so that wasn't a priority now. It sounded cold, but what she needed—aside from an aspirin—was to know what happened to her back then. She hugged her arms around herself so he couldn't try to grab them again. Shivers were starting in her core. Had she ever felt so cold? So lost. Alone.

Yes, probably.

Before Michael found her.

"Not now. Maybe later. I need to find out what happened to me first."

And Michael. She needed him. She blinked at him, and his

worried expression softened. Then his arms were around her, cradling her, supporting her. Yes, she needed him. She forgave him. "What happened to me?"

CHAPTER 25

CLARA

The morning ritual was always the same. Clara was an early riser like her husband. Years ago, she would've been getting the kids ready for the day. Not too long ago, she'd also have been chauffeuring them to school. Now that they had bought a new car, Faith was driving Michael's old sedan and taking over driving Jason to and from school, except when they had after-school activities.

Faith should be up now, yelling for her brother to hurry. Had she overslept?

Jason was fidgeting, his gaze darted around the kitchen, refusing to meet hers. Something was off.

"Where's Faith?" When her son ducked his head, Clara's heart rate picked up.

His silence was answer enough. She hurried to the front window. Faith normally parked on the curb since they only had a two-car garage. Her car wasn't there. "Michael, go check if Faith is upstairs."

Michael stopped in the middle of buttoning his coat to leave. "What do you mean? Of course, she is in her room."

He headed upstairs to check for himself. He knocked, calling for Faith, before returning. "I went in her room. She's not here."

"I knew it." Clara stopped in front of her son. "Do you know where your sister is?"

Jason's head jerked back. He gulped, then blurted out, "She went to a party. I didn't think she'd stay out all night."

For once, he uttered two sentences. Unfortunately, these weren't the words she wanted to hear.

Michael dialed the office, notifying them he'd be late. Then they took Jason to school, expecting to find Faith there.

Instead, a knot tightened in Clara's stomach as the principal echoed their fears. "She's not here. Nobody has seen her today."

They tasked Jason to question Faith's friends while Clara and Michael spoke with the principal. Josie's name kept popping up alongside a new name—Chase.

Mr. Lock, the principal, called Chase and Josie into his office. Clara had met Josie, but not Chase, a tall young man with an air of innocence.

"Dr. Khoury, Mrs. Khoury," Josie greeted them after Mr. Lock waved them into the office. At least she had manners.

The principal introduced the young man and asked the two teens if they had heard from Faith and about the party the previous night.

"Faith left early. I stayed." Josie waved to Chase. "Didn't you leave with her?"

"Yeah, I walked her to her car and said goodbye. That was it." He shrugged. "Then I went to my car."

Michael asked a few more questions, but when the teens had nothing more to add, Clara had him call the police.

Mr. Lock dismissed the students before the police arrived. After the preliminary questions, Officer Lopez tucked his pen and pad back into his vest pocket. "We'd like to talk to Jason. You can be present."

Clara grasped Michael's hand. "Sure."

"I'll summon him here." Mr. Lock buzzed his secretary. Then, when Jason walked in, wide-eyed, Mr. Lock stood up. "You may use my office. And if you need anything, let me know. I'll be in the front office."

"Jason, you're not in trouble." Officer Simmons gestured to the free chair before the principal's desk. "Why don't you sit by your mom?"

The chair legs rasped on the cheap carpet as Jason sat.

"Would you tell us about last night? Your sister was supposed to be in bed. But she went to a party. Tell us about that." Officer Simmons poised her pen over her little notebook.

Jason ducked his head, his sneaker scraping back and forth over the mottled gray carpet.

"Son?" Michael stepped in front of him. "You need to help us find your sister."

Jason's head jerked up, his wide eyes growing bigger. "There was this party, see? Some cool dude was going to be there. Said she'd be back by midnight. I was going to wait up but fell asleep."

"You mentioned a cool dude." Simmons tapped her pen. "Who is he? Do you know?"

His right leg shook. Clara refrained from touching his thigh to stop the shaking. "The girls she hangs out with would know. Yeah, definitely Josie."

"Are you sure you don't know who this cool dude is?"

Michael clamped a hand on Jason's shoulder. "If you know anything, you need to tell the officer."

"Chase," Jason mumbled.

The officers asked Jason a few more questions. They sounded like the same questions just asked differently. Then they said he could go.

"Mr. Lock had Chase come in, and he said he only walked Faith to the car," added Clara after Jason left.

"Thank you, ma'am." Officer Lopez summoned Mr. Lock back. "We need to talk to all the students who were at the party, especially Josie and Chase. We'll need their contact information, addresses, everything."

Mr. Lock was already on it, providing information from the school records. "I'll request the teachers report any suspicious behavior they might have noticed. Uh, I would also need to notify the parents or guardians."

"Absolutely." Officer Lopez spread some forms out. "Mr. Khoury, what is your occupation?"

"It's doctor. I'm the chief of surgery at Orlando Hospital."

Clara rubbed her forehead. "Faith is only seventeen."

Officer Lopez tucked the forms aside. "That changes things. With her age and your position, Dr. Khoury, this case could be more complicated than we thought."

Clara clung to Michael's arm. "What do you mean?"

"We'll need to treat this as a potential kidnapping case. We'll alert the Feds."

"Kidnapping?" Clara swallowed hard and pushed the word out a second time since no one had heard her first hoarse whisper.

"We'll do everything we can to find Faith," Officer Lopez promised, but it did little to assuage her growing panic. Her daughter was missing, and their world was spiraling out of control.

Disoriented by the transformation of her cozy living room into an FBI command center, Clara lingered behind Michael at the heart of this whirlwind. Hours after they visited the school, he clutched a phone in his trembling hand, agents moving in a coordinated dance around him. His palpable fear amplified her dread.

They'd received a call from an anonymous caller. Now, a raspy voice demanded, "A million dollars. Unmarked bills. Twenty-four hours."

An agent, his seasoned gaze sharp, signaled to Michael, his finger making a keep-it-going circle in the air.

Michael complied. "H–how do I know Faith is all right?"

A silence. Then a whimper, a gasp, and Faith's terrified voice. "Daddy—"

Clara's grip on Michael's arm tightened, her breath hitching in her chest. The call ended, leaving a heavy silence that seemed to echo with Faith's scared voice.

Michael's hands shook as he put down the phone. Fear of losing Faith must be consuming him too.

Agent Price, the special agent from something called the CARD team—Child Abduction Rapid Deployment—approached. "We're going to get her back, Dr. Khoury."

Clara found her voice, barely above a whisper. "Do we have that much cash?" Her mind raced, recalling Detective Jordan's mention of Michael's frequent, large withdrawals recently. Did they have enough?

"We have insurance."

"For kidnapping?" Seriously?

Michael nodded. "When we came to visit the hospital before I accepted the offer, Dr. Jenkins mentioned it as an option. I mean we pay for the premium. And seeing that Rick's son was kidnapped some time ago, I thought it prudent."

Right. Their friend, a chief medical officer at the hospital in Chicago had to pay a hefty ransom to get him back. "But... didn't that happen in Mexico?"

"I gather you will have the ransom?" Agent Price spoke over her question.

"I just need to call the insurance guy, and he should take care of it."

"Wait." Clara held up her hand. "You want Michael to take the money to the exchange?"

"Mrs. Khoury, your husband will be safe. We'll catch this guy and bring Faith home."

A fine layer of sweat coated Michael's forehead as he spoke with the insurance company and arranged for the cash delivery, his usual composed demeanor replaced by an undercurrent of anxiety that matched hers.

The doorbell chimed.

Agent Price turned toward the door. "Expecting someone?" When Clara and Michael shook their heads, the agent signaled for them to stay back, pulled his gun out, and yelled, "Who is it?"

"Detective Clive Jordan," came the response.

The agent opened the door upon seeing the badge and ID. "Do you have some new information?"

Jordan's brows furrowed. "Who are you?"

"Special Agent Dennis Price." The agent showed him his credential pack.

"CARD. Who's abducted?" Jordan asked.

"Faith, the daughter. You haven't said why you're here."

Jordan folded his arms across his chest. "I'm here to ask a few questions about the insurance—"

"Insurance?" Clara stomped to him. "I already told you. I knew about the life insurance policy."

Detective Jordan's tight features softened. "Yes, but did you know about the kidnapping clause?"

"I do now. What about it?"

Before Jordan could answer, Michael interrupted. "This is not the time, Detective. We're trying to save our daughter's life here."

Agent Price stepped forward. "I agree with Dr. Khoury. This is not the time or place for your questions, Detective."

The detective nodded, his gaze lingering. "I understand. I'll return another time."

As the door closed behind Jordan, Clara hugged her arms around herself to still their trembling. With their daughter's life in jeopardy, her questions would have to wait.

CHAPTER 26

OLIVIA & RON

Olivia sat back on the hard-back chair. Today's visit was nothing more than an excuse to come to the Federal Detention Center and chat with the guards, trying to figure out this Adam O'Shea. Ron had mentioned Eva might be a possible "leak," however unintentional her slip. As a young agent, Eva might not be as vigilant as veteran agents. And who was this Uncle Bill?

Well, Olivia couldn't do much about it now with Eva undercover. Unless Eva was working for the trafficker—totally unfathomable—she couldn't leak anything while undercover.

"So, nothing to add?" Olivia asked the Ghost. "You want us to capture Ray Ho, don't you?"

"I already told you everything you need to know."

Hands pressed against the cold steel table, Olivia waited a beat. "You know your deal would be off if you're holding out on us."

The Ghost tilted her head. "I understand. You have all you need to catch him. Now, is there anything else?"

She stood up. "Until next time."

Olivia left the meeting with the sense of a veiled chess game, each move masked with ambiguity. The Ghost had proven to be an adversary who was not to be underestimated. In her car, Olivia dialed Ron's number. "Get ready," she stated. "We have a game to win."

"The feed is live."

At Ana's announcement, Ron leaned back in his desk chair, hands laced in his lap, eyes drawn to the screen now projecting the video feed from the Federal Detention Center where the fake Adam O'Shea was set to arrive.

His phone buzzed.

"He's here," Olivia reported.

"Copy that," he responded.

The man checked in at the entrance, entered the visiting room, and emerged shortly later. Olivia brushed against him as they both walked out to the parking lot. They both bent down for something, and he picked it up for her.

Minutes later, she called again. "He's no lawyer. He's an operative. Trained. And he's good."

A sense of grim understanding passed between Ron and Ana. "I had a hunch," he admitted. "Olivia, can you—"

"Already done. Tracker's on him and his vehicle. Let's see where our Mr. O'Shea leads us."

"She's still got it," Ana murmured. She'd always had a bit of hero worship toward Olivia, aka Phoenix, a legend in the intelligence community.

Ron tapped his thumbs together. "Any chance the Ghost sensed anything off with your visit?"

"I just asked about the case," Olivia answered. "There's no reason for her to think I'd wait for him here. And I don't think he knows me. When I bumped into him, I let my phone drop, and he picked it up for me. There's a good chance we can lift a fingerprint."

Ron's tense shoulders relaxed. "Good work. We'll see if Deanna can pull a print."

Olivia headed straight to the lab to see Deanna as soon as she got back to the office.

"Thank you." Deanna's fingers twitched reaching for the phone, obviously ready to work their magic. She moved to her station. "Will let you know if I find anything."

Olivia went back to the squad room where Hernandez was speaking. "Nothing out of the ordinary. Just the usual stuff. Went to a Starbucks, picked up groceries. You wouldn't think twice if you saw him."

She shook her head. "That's what makes him so dangerous."

Deanna hurried in from the lab. "So, there's good news and bad news. The good news is we have prints. Clear ones. The bad news?" She gulped. "They're classified."

"Classified?" Olivia repeated, her heartbeat stuttering. "What about the picture I snapped of him?"

"No hits. Looks like the data has been scrubbed if it ever existed."

Silence descended, the implication sinking in. Olivia and Ron shared a glance. This classification was reserved for a select few, Phoenix being one of them, and its presence spelled nothing but trouble. She firmed her chin, stepping forward. "Let me try."

Deanna went to a station and opened the file. Olivia plugged in her credentials, and she was in. However, the file was heavily redacted.

"So, he's a spook," Ron said.

"I'd say so." Olivia clicked more keys. "I'm going to reach

out to my former handler. He should know. You do know what that means if this O'Shea was a Company man?"

Ron nodded.

"Either it's a covert mission or he's been turned."

"With regards to the Ghost, I feel confident the Company has no other asset as deep as I was." She shrugged. "Then again, you never know." Would Jay, her mentor and former handler, hide this from her?

CHAPTER 27

THE GHOST

No sooner had Marge Beaumont, aka the Ghost, been led out of the room, than another guard called her to an adjacent room. Another visitor. A guard, probably bored out of his mind, just grunted and jerked his thumb toward the table in the tiny room where a man sat, looking about as thrilled to be there as she was.

"I'll be right outside. If she gives you any trouble, just holler, sir." The guard then stepped out.

This was no lawyer visit. Rook, her code name for him, was here to report. Before they nabbed her, she'd been after this asset for years. Due to a personal loss Rook attributed to Uncle Sam, he became an easy mark. Now, he worked for her.

"Rook." She took the seat across from him, her tone and expression neutral. Decades in the business taught her how to mask her emotions. "Report."

"Yes, ma'am. I've got eyes on the task force. They're looking for John Liu and Ray Ho. Peters and his team are gearing up for some kind of sting."

She nodded. "Good." Ray Ho was the reason her lover, Rifkin, had died, even though Ho didn't pull the trigger or order the hit. "And what about Phoenix? Any developments there?"

His sensual lips pressed into a thin line. He waved, wafting a cheap cologne her way. "Still no concrete leads on Phoenix. If he exists, he's as elusive as the legend says."

Phoenix was real, but nothing concrete proved it. "Find out if Phoenix is an urban myth or a real threat."

"I'm on it." Rook flattened his thick hands on the tabletop and pushed to his feet. "If Phoenix is out there, I'll find him."

"Keep me posted."

"Yes, ma'am." He headed to the door.

She scowled at the steamy handprints now fading on the cold metal surface, slipping away like the Phoenix. *Fifteen years, I've been looking for you. Do you exist? Are you real, Phoenix?*

Fifteen years ago

French Renaissance furniture and an ostentatious large mantelpiece boasted of power and affluence in Roger Rifkin's great room. The high ceilings accentuated the mansion's grandeur. A bottle of Château Lafite was opened, and the smooth, deep red wine breathed in two crystal glasses. It was just another ordinary evening for Marge and Rifkin, or at least it appeared so.

She'd controlled him for years, a tool she wielded with finesse. Their relationship was a fusion of power and obligation. He had been a fresh senator when they'd met, and she had been his guiding force ever since. The intimate relationship that developed was merely a byproduct, but she never let it affect their power dynamic.

A blazing fire crackled in the fireplace. The dancing flames reflecting on his profile seemed to glaze the lines of aristocracy in his features and demeanor as she raised her glass to him. "There's a rumor about a deep-cover asset, Phoenix, in my network. You must have heard something."

He set his glass down, swiveling his gaze from the wine to her. "I've heard of Phoenix, but—Marge, I'm privy to many secrets, but not all, and this happens to be one of them."

"Well, isn't it time you learn about this one?" She sipped her wine, savoring the rich cassis, the hint of tobacco, truffle, and earthy notes. "I need answers."

His laugh was dry, more resigned than amused. "There are echelons in the Senate, levels even I can't reach. Certain things are so classified only a handful of people have access to them. I'm not one of them."

She didn't respond, letting the silence stretch, heavy and demanding. She sipped her wine, her gaze steady on him. Rarely was she outmaneuvered, and she didn't like the sensation.

"Can't or won't?" she pressed.

"Both."

She just stared at him, the silence humming with tension and unspoken words. Then she set her glass down and rose from the antique love seat.

"Very well." She moved to the grand French window, looking beyond her reflection on the glass into the night. "I'll have to find out on my own. It won't be the first time."

And as the fire continued to crackle in the hearth, she plotted her next move. She wasn't the type to let uncertainties linger. And she wouldn't stop until she found her answers.

CHAPTER 28

RAY HO

Ray Ho's reclined position in the plush patio chair belied the tension in his muscles, a tension that began to knot when his encrypted cell phone buzzed. The soft murmur of waves caressing the sandy shore should be erasing that tension like they erased any footprints on the beach of his private Bahamian island.

The phone call had been terse, unexpected. As he listened, his gaze flicked to the photos sent to him. "Impossible."

But the evidence was there, undeniable, on the screen.

"There you go. Problem solved," he said a moment later, looking at another photo, this one of a teen girl. "Okay, wait for my text."

Now, phone set aside, he stared out at the ocean, its tranquil beauty doing nothing to ease his turmoil. The sun was dipping toward the horizon, casting a golden path on the water, his path forward just as clear.

How many years ago? Twenty? Twenty-five? He didn't

remember. But he remembered he hadn't had time to check his handiwork. Now, he might regret it. If he only had a few more minutes, he'd have made sure there was no body.

He glanced again at the first photo, the face haunting. Returning to the States would be a big risk. "It may be worth it."

CHAPTER 29

CLARA & FAITH

Clara hugged her arms around herself in the back of the FBI surveillance van, trying to breathe with the air so thick. She focused on Michael standing in the parking garage and holding onto a bag containing a million dollars in cash—courtesy of their insurance company. Agents ready to spring into action at a moment's notice.

Agent Price gave Michael a nod, his voice echoing through Clara's earpiece. "Remember, Dr. Khoury, don't release the bag until you see Faith."

Michael nodded, his knuckles white on its handle.

Tires screeched in the vast space as a van pulled into the garage. The side door slid open to reveal Faith, looking as terrified as Clara felt.

"My baby," Clara whispered, her spine jellying.

Michael stepped forward, about to follow through on their end of the deal.

But then… The kidnapper snatched the bag, and the van shot forward.

"No!" Michael shouted, lunging in a futile attempt to stop them.

"Go, go, go!" Agent Price yelled, his voice crackling through Clara's earpiece.

In organized chaos, Agents surged from their hidden positions, guns blazing. The sharp echo of gunfire reverberated off the concrete walls as they gave chase. The van swerved, trying to escape, but not before an agent's bullet found its mark. One of the kidnappers slumped, a dark patch blooming on his shirt.

The screech of tires and the flurry of action seemed to blur together as Clara froze in place, only her blood moving in a deafening rush. The world somehow spun around her as reality sank in. Faith was gone.

The thick air inside the kidnapper's van smelled of sweat and rust. Every bump on the road sent fear shivering down Faith's spine, her body tensing. With her hands bound behind her back and her legs tied together, her freedom seemed nothing more than a distant memory.

Through the grimy window, she glimpsed her father. He stood there, rigid, holding a bag—the ransom. Her heart hammered her chest, a cacophony of hope and terror. This was it, the moment she had been waiting for.

Just as she was about to breathe out relief, the driver slammed his foot down on the accelerator, jolting her back against the hard metal wall. A cry escaped her lips, drowned out by the engine roaring and tires squealing.

Then the distinctive pop of gunfire echoed in the confined space, followed by the screech of rubber meeting asphalt. The van swerved, and she tumbled around. The men shouted, their panic palpable.

One man, the one who'd been holding the ransom money,

screamed, and then fell silent. An instant later, his body tumbled from the opened passenger side door, disappearing from her sight, their speed warning her against trying to follow.

The driver only pressed harder on the accelerator. The van rocketed forward, the world outside becoming a blurred mess of lights and colors. The remaining kidnapper was getting away with her, farther and farther from her father, from safety.

Faith steeled herself, grinding her teeth. She would do everything she could to survive. *Lord, help! Help Daddy save me, please.*

The van's abrupt halt jostled her. The side door was yanked open, and strong hands hauled her out and pulled her through a maze of alleyways that smelled of stale food and other things she didn't want to think about.

"Where are you taking m–me?" Her voice shook despite her attempt to sound confident. There was no response, only a rough push forward. She stumbled but righted herself, the cold in her belly spreading outward.

Soon, they were descending a set of steep stairs, a single bulb barely cutting through the oppressive darkness. Then a heavy door was opened, revealing a cavernous space reeking of damp and mold.

Rough actions cut her bindings, stinging her raw wrists and ankles. Before she could react, the door was slammed shut and locked behind her. She pounded on it, calling for help, but the only response was the echo of her desperate voice.

So she stopped and turned around in a basement of sorts, the grimy concrete walls cold and uninviting. Several other kids eyed her, girls mostly. All young, their eyes wide and haunted like pictures in her history textbooks of people caught in wars and disasters, people who had lost all hope.

Many looked Chinese, like her mom. They didn't say anything, only watched her with those wary eyes.

Faith gasped in quick breaths, hyperventilating now. *Please, help! Somebody, help!*

Cocooned by steel and glass within the FBI building, Clara felt a million miles away from the cozy comfort of home. If only she could be back there with her kids, safe and sound. Although the agents advised them to return home, she and Michael wanted to hear what this guy had to say about where Faith might be.

They were now stuck behind a one-way mirror as Agent Price and a younger, bigger, serious-looking agent grilled the injured kidnapper. She never thought she'd be part of such a scene. She brought cold fingers to her throbbing temples and slumped against Michael's side. "I just want Faith home and all this over."

Michael draped his arm over her shoulders, his body shaking beside her.

The man had been Mirandized and hadn't asked for representation. He now sat hunched over, his face paling under the harsh interrogation room lights.

Agent Price braced both hands on the table, standing over the culprit. "Who's the man in charge?"

The man grimaced, then sneered, and a cold shiver ran down Clara's spine. "Our boss ain't gonna let that girl go."

A sharp pang hit Clara's stomach. Michael squeezed her shoulders, the strength in his grip grounding her.

"Why?"

A smirk twisted the man's face. "He has another plan for her."

"And what is that?"

The man hesitated. "An auction."

Clara gasped, the breath knocked out of her. She threaded her arm around Michael, absorbing his strength to keep herself steady.

Agent Price leaned in closer. "Who is your boss? What's his name?"

The injured man grimaced. "John Liu."

A murmur went through the agents in the room with Clara and Michael. In the adjacent room, Price pulled out his phone, tapped it a few times, then showed it to the younger agent. The younger agent exited, pulling out his phone and dialing a number.

"Task force." The urgency in his voice echoed her panic. The name had set off some alarms. But had it brought them closer to finding Faith?

CHAPTER 30

R*ON*

Ron sat at his desk, engrossed in yet another report. His eyes had started to glaze when his phone vibrated. The unfamiliar number offering a welcome but worrying interruption, he pressed the answer button. "Special Agent Peters."

"Special Agent Peters, this is Special Agent Jameson. We're working on a kidnapping case and a name came up—John Liu."

Ron straightened, a knot tightening in his stomach. "Liu? As in the one we believe is running the trafficking operation?"

"That's the one. We've got a seventeen-year-old girl we believe might be in the auction Liu facilitated."

An icy grip seized Ron's heart. Eva was already deep in the field, making communication risky. But they needed to act—and fast.

He summoned his team, briefing them. Then he clapped once and rubbed his hands together, ready to get at it. "Tanner, take over sifting through the information from the human trafficking unit and their CIs. Hernandez, start reviewing any camera footage from the abduction and subsequent failed exchange. Ana, come with me to talk to the parents and the suspect." He shifted, nodding at his top agent. "Olivia, maintain your focus on preparing Simon as a bidder and Kyle as his bodyguard."

His team peered back, ready.

"Remember, folks, every minute counts. Now more than ever, our mission's clear—save the innocent girl, expose Liu's operation, and bring them all to justice."

Olivia touched Simon's shoulder. "And this might lead them to Ray Ho, the one responsible for Lily's and Dylan's abduction."

Wouldn't that be perfect?

A flickering fluorescent light gave the dull-gray room a weird, cold vibe—like being in a tiny, boxed-in crypt, surrounded by concrete walls and a one-way mirror that exhibited their unhappy faces. Ron sat with Ana at a beat-up old metal table, facing the tough guy named Craig, whose emotionless eyes stared right through them. He must've been around the block a few times in the criminal world, and he wasn't going to be easy to crack.

"I told you already," Craig grumbled, slouched in his chair, handcuffs rattling against the metal table. "We just wanted the money."

Ana set her jaw. "You said your boss was John Liu. My question remains. If you worked for him, you'd have turned the girl over right away. You wouldn't have asked for ransom." Her brow furrowed, her lips forming a thin line. "So, we don't think it makes any sense, Craig. Why ask for ransom money, go through all the trouble of a drop-off, only to put the girl up for auction?"

The man shrugged. "My partner thought we could make some money. That's all."

Ron leaned forward. "Let me help you understand something. Right now, you're being charged with kidnapping. That's a first-degree felony. In Florida, it's punishable by up to life in prison. If you help us, we may put in a good word for you."

Craig's smirk faded. His shoulders tensed, his demeanor shifting. "Look—this wasn't the plan."

"Really?" Ana scoffed. "So, what was the plan?"

Craig hesitated, his gaze shifting toward the mirror. He seemed to deflate, his bravado ebbing away. "Before the boss got involved, we, uh, do side gigs from time to time. Someone paid us to kidnap the girl."

"Who?"

"I don't know. My partner dealt with the guy."

"What are you supposed to do once you have the girl?"

The kidnapper kept his gaze on the mirror. "He would contact us."

"How would he know when you have the girl?" Ana leaned forward.

"He told us when and where to snatch her."

Ron caught Ana's eye. She had to be thinking it was an inside job. Someone close to Faith or at least someone who knew of her activities orchestrated this.

"Okay, why didn't you hand her over then? Why wait?" Ron asked.

"My partner got greedy. Thought we could make some money out of it. We held onto her for a couple days. Whoever hired us somehow notified the boss. He called and demanded we hand the girl over to him. His order was to take the girl. Didn't care about the ransom."

"The boss would be John Liu?" Ron needed to confirm.

"Yes."

"Who's your partner?" Ana asked.

"Ricky."

"Last name?"

"Herman."

Ana leaned forward. "And you're sure you don't know who offered the money for the abduction?"

"Ricky came back one day and started yammering about how much money we'd get. Said he had a great offer to snatch the girl." He held up both hands, the handcuff chains clinking. "That's all I know."

Ron glanced at the one-way mirror behind him. Surely, the agents would follow up on this Ricky fellow. Meanwhile, he and Ana exchanged a glance. A new player. Someone with money and motive.

CHAPTER 31

CLARA

When Clara and Michael got back, their place was as quiet with a heavy worry. They had sent Jason to spend the night with Michael's folks. Although she was wiped out from the morning's activities, worrying about Faith kept her going.

Michael too. He moved toward the kitchen. "I'll make coffee."

Then the doorbell rang, and he stilled.

They both stood frozen, eyeing each other.

"Check the door cam," he whispered.

She brought it up on her phone. "It's Dylan and Lily."

"Okay, let them in." He reanimated. "I'll get the coffee."

"Hello, guys," Clara greeted them. "I didn't expect to see you."

"Agent Peters asked us to come and be with you," Dylan said.

"It's good that it's you two." Michael emerged from the kitchen. "I've got coffee on if you need any. I daresay we had enough of strangers. But I didn't know you worked for the FBI."

Hmm. An agent at the FBI office had told them they didn't want them alone and would be sending someone over soon.

"We don't." Lily waved, her pink fingernails and matching silk blouse somehow insensitive against the dark mood, like wearing pink to a funeral. What was Clara thinking? This wasn't a funeral. Faith would come home. She had to believe that. "Long story short, Agent Peters heard about how we already know you and asked if we wouldn't mind coming over."

"But you should know, we've had recent experiences with the FBI," Dylan added.

"Where are our manners? Please come in." Clara opened the door wide and led them to the living room.

Michael crossed from the kitchen with fresh coffees on a tray. "Agent Price is in charge of the kidnapping. And now, there are two others from some task force, Peters and Ana. Wait, you did say Agent Peters sent you."

"He knows what he's doing." Dylan accepted his coffee.

Clara folded her cold hands around the warm mug, needing the comfort pressed to her palms more than she needed the caffeine. "He's the one who helped you?"

"Yes, his team and others," Lily said.

Clara drew in a shaky breath. "The man exuded a reassuring calm when we met earlier. I must say hearing you two had prior favorable experience with him offers a sliver of comfort."

Dylan swirled the coffee in his cup. "They're the best, the agents. They saved Lily and me when we were in a tight spot. They'll find Faith."

Clara exhaled, not even knowing she'd been holding her breath. What Dylan and Lily said felt like a big, warm hug in the middle of this crazy, scary mess. Michael must feel it too, a light sparking in his eyes. They were going to find Faith.

Lily sipped her steaming coffee, the heat fogging her face seeming to carry a whirlwind of thoughts, when Clara mumbled about a headache coming on and began searching in her purse.

"Ah, here it is," Clara muttered and downed a pill with a swig of coffee. Then her face turned ghostly pale. Her hand gripped the couch arm as if she were bracing for impact, and she started making gurgling sounds.

"Clara!" Lily gasped out.

The woman swayed, her eyes taking on a glazed, unfocused look, and fear jolted through Lily.

Michael was on his feet, his expression morphing from shock to sharp focus. "Dylan, get my medical bag from my office upstairs, first door on the left. Lily, call 911."

Dylan jumped to his feet, nearly knocking over his coffee.

While she talked to the dispatcher, Michael's hands moved over Clara with practiced ease, checking her pulse. Dylan returned to the room, a black bag in his hand.

Michael rummaged through it and pulled out a vial and a syringe. He prepared the injection with a steady hand, his gaze never leaving Clara.

"He's giving her Narcan," Lily informed dispatch. "She's overdosing. I hope it's not fentanyl. Heard it was really deadly."

"Grab the bottle. The pills need to be tested," Michael ordered to no one in particular.

Dylan picked up a bottle of store-bought ibuprofen. It couldn't be contaminated, could it? Or was it some new terrorist scheme to lace over-the-counter medicine with opioids to harm innocent people?

"Come on, Clara. Come on," muttered Michael.

The whispered plea broke into their silence. Lily's breath hitched in her chest, mirroring the anxious rhythm of the room.

"She's gonna be okay, isn't she?" she whispered, even as she started praying in her heart.

CHAPTER 32

RON, DYLAN, & MICHAEL

The Miller residence dominated its hill lot overlooking the city. "Posh place." Ron let out a low whistle as Ana parked their black sedan in the cobblestone circular driveway. Then he led her up the steps, badges in hand.

Chase's mother, or rather, stepmother, welcomed them with guarded hostility. After introducing themselves and explaining their intention, they requested to speak to Chase alone.

"But he already told the police everything."

"Yes, ma'am. We have some follow-up questions." Ana stepped forward. "It shouldn't take long."

"Very well." The woman acquiesced and left them in the vast living room while she fetched Chase.

Soon, the typical high school senior, tall with a lanky build, lumbered in and slouched into a seat across from them, fidgeting.

"Chase." Ron kept his tone nonthreatening. "We need you to tell us about the party again. What time you left, what time Faith left. If you saw her after that. Everything."

His head down, unruly light-brown hair flopping into his

eyes, Chase picked at a thread on his jeans. "We left around midnight. I walked her to the car. That was it."

His answers remained consistent with his previous statements, too consistent, and something about his demeanor felt off.

"You didn't see anybody around?" Ana asked.

After a pause, he shook his head. "No."

Ana caught Ron's eye and nodded, signaling her agreement with his assessment. So he pushed further. "Chase, we need you to be honest with us. This is important. Is there anything else you remember?"

Chase shifted in his seat, and his eyes flickered with something akin to fear. Yep, Chase was hiding something.

"In case you didn't know, lying to a federal agent is a crime," Ana said. "What did you see?"

The ambulance's wild siren still rang in Dylan's ears as he navigated the city's mazelike streets, gripping the steering wheel tightly. Lily sat next to him, not saying a word, looking as freaked out as he felt. The way Clara had been convulsing, the terror on Michael's face—those images were stuck in his head like a bad dream, just playing over and over. How downright haunting.

Clara Khoury, a casualty of an opioid overdose? It didn't make sense. Could she be a high-functioning addict? He couldn't deny how out of it she'd been when he met her, but still. That hadn't been her doing, had it? And if she were a user, why would she take something while she had guests?

He cleared his throat. Too bad he couldn't clear his mind as easily. "You texted Kyle?"

"Yeah, he's going to tell his dad."

He pulled into the hospital parking lot, his gaze catching the flicker of Lily's eyes in the dim light. Her face was drawn tight, a stark contrast to her usual vibrant expression. "You're coming in, right?"

"For sure." She unclicked her belt, and he hurried to catch up. The hospital welcomed them, a symphony of urgency underplaying the quiet atmosphere. But the world felt oddly still as they found Michael, his face ghostly under the sterile lights.

Dylan hung back. Michael was cornering a nurse. "She took an over-the-counter painkiller. That's all. I don't understand how…" He palmed his face, seeming to choke up on the event's severity. He took out the bottle Dylan had given him at the house. "Notify the police. Have them test the pills."

"He has no idea how she could have overdosed." Lily's voice was a soft murmur beside him. "Something doesn't fit, Dylan. She doesn't look like a drug abuser. I mean I know how we met her and all, but that wasn't *her*."

"I don't think so either." Dylan narrowed his gaze. "The puzzle pieces aren't aligning. It's as if we're caught in some dark, twisted version of reality."

As Michael walked away, swallowed by the medical personnel rushing around, two men entered the ER, their attire as sharp as their keen gazes—suits that screamed authority and badges that confirmed their identity as detectives.

"Something's up." Dylan nudged her.

Lily gripped his arm. "What do you think they want with Michael?"

Dylan shook his head. The detectives spoke to Michael in hushed, urgent tones. Michael's face blanched, his gaze darting toward where he'd last seen Clara.

Then the detectives led him away. No handcuffs, but the firm grasp on his arm was clear enough. A chill trickled down Dylan's spine. "Did you hear any of that? I tried, but the incessant hum of the hospital drowned out their words."

"No, I didn't catch it. What is happening?" Lily's grip tightened, her clenched fingers strangling his wrist.

Dylan ran his free hand through his hair, grabbing a fistful and pulling. "I wish I knew," he admitted, his voice grim. "I wish I knew."

"You don't think he…?"

"No, I strongly doubt it. Michael was there to save her. If he wasn't there with that can of thing—I don't wanna think about it."

"And he looked so worried. I mean, unless he's a great actor, he was frantic about her."

A nurse, her eyes shadowed with the weight of her profession, approached and spoke just above a whisper. "Mrs. Khoury is asking for her husband. He's not available, but she indicated she'd like to see you both."

They trailed the nurse, winding through plain, hospital-smelling hallways to Clara's room. Amid beeping machines and the steady sound of the ventilators, Clara looked way too pale—nothing like the lively woman they'd become used to seeing. Lily's fingers slid down his hand to mesh with his, her hold saying this was as hard for her to take in as it was for him.

Clara blinked at them, her eyes a whirlpool of emotions. "Where's Michael?"

As her voice floated over the hum of medical machinery, Dylan shared a glance with Lily. The unspoken question growing in weight with every second.

"He, um, had to step out," Lily responded. "He went with the police."

The monitors beside Clara's bed erupted with frantic beeps, mirroring the panic flashing across her face. A nurse rushed in, reaching for the equipment. But Clara dismissed her with a weak wave.

"Please," she whispered, her eyes desperate. "I need your help."

Dylan stepped closer. "What do you need?"

"Detective Jordan… thinks Michael is trying to harm me,"

Clara managed to say, her voice strained. "But Michael… would never… hurt me. You need to find out what happened. You need to prove him innocent."

Lily's hand shook in his grip. After their ordeal months ago, they were grateful to go back to their ordinary lives. Granted, he still wanted to find out about the treasure on his family property, but that only involved research, not danger. They weren't investigators.

Before he could say anything, Lily squeezed his hand. "We'll do everything we can to figure this out. We promise."

Dylan gawked at her. *Really? We will?*

Wrapped in the oppressive chill of the police interrogation room, Michael stared across the stark metal table at Detective Jordan. His partner, Detective Hayes, leaned against the wall, her hawkish eyes scrutinizing him.

"Dr. Khoury," Jordan initiated, his voice holding a taut edge, "where were you when the first attempt on Clara's life was made?"

Michael's heart thumped against his rib cage, concern for Clara and worry about Faith superseding the anxiety of the interrogation. Yet, he had to cooperate to hasten this process. "I was at the hospital. In the middle of surgery. You can check with the hospital staff. I have many witnesses."

Jordan scribbled something in his notebook. "True, but that doesn't rule out the possibility that you administered the dose beforehand."

Whoa. Wait a minute. He almost slapped the table. "What are you insinuating?"

Hayes pushed off the wall, crossing her arms. "Let's talk about the missing drugs at the hospital pharmacy."

The accusation hit Michael like a gut punch. "What missing

drugs? I'm new at the hospital. I haven't even been to the pharmacy yet."

His protests didn't soften the detectives' determination. Their questions continued.

"Can't we do this later? I'd like to know how my wife is doing. And I'd like to check with the agents for any news on locating my daughter. Let me call the hospital and Agent Peters." He let out a whoosh of breath, his lungs and body deflating. "And I have to tell my son what's going on."

"Speaking of your wife's overdose, you have access to the painkillers at home," Jordan pressed. "Why don't you tell us why you did it? Money? We know you've withdrawn significant sums recently. Gambling debts?"

"I don't gamble." He ground his teeth against the welling frustration, but it still clenched his stomach in a cold grip. He needed to call the hospital or the agents.

"Well then, what did you do with the money?"

"I loaned it to my brother."

"And that would be Majid Khoury?" Jordan asked.

"Yes, he's my only brother. Here's his number."

While Hayes jotted down the information, Jordan surveyed his paperwork. "Seems your brother has a juvie record."

Michael frowned. His brother's record was sealed. "Yes, so?"

Her blue eyes probed him. "Why doesn't your wife know about it?"

"Says who?" He'd mentioned it to Clara, but she hadn't been concerned. And it was years ago. She might have forgotten.

"Perhaps your ex-con brother is scheming with you?"

That was going too far. He threw up his hands and stood. "You guys are out of your mind! Now, are you arresting me?"

The detectives exchanged a glance but said nothing.

"No? Then I'm free to go. Next time, talk to my lawyer." Without waiting for their response, he walked out.

As Michael stepped out into the cool night, he couldn't shake off the icy dread clawing deep in his bones. The police station's fluorescent lights receded behind him, the haunting echo of interrogations lingering. He held up his phone and summoned an Uber, his fingers trembling as he keyed in the hospital's address.

On the lonely ride, the city's lights streamed past in a blur. He needed to make sure Jason was okay, but he couldn't force the calm his son would need now, not with his thoughts in turmoil, a maelstrom over Clara, Faith, and the surreal nightmare his life had become overnight. He needed a lawyer, a good one, but he barely knew anyone in the legal field.

Wait. During a scholarship award ceremony years ago, he'd shaken hands with a lawyer. Townsend, right? The gentleman had offered him assistance, should he ever need it. What was his name? He ran the name in his mind to recall his first name.

With a sense of urgency, he typed Charles Townsend into the search bar. Great. Townsend had passed away.

Closing his eyes, Michael rested his head against the car seat. The scholarship—he had received the Marino Scholarship. A lady presented him with the certificate and the check. Perhaps she could help or refer him to a competent attorney. He'd look into it after checking on Clara, receiving an update on Faith, and verifying Jason was safe.

"Sir?" The driver leaned over the console. "We're here, sir."

Oh. With his mind a whirlwind, he hadn't noticed the car pull up to the hospital's entrance. "Thanks."

He stepped out into cold, harsh reality once again.

CHAPTER 33

CLARA & MICHAEL

Clara woke to the steady beep of hospital machines and rubbed her eyes as the bright lights overhead stung. She tipped her head, and her heart beat faster. Michael sat next to her bed, looking like he'd been through worse than she had.

"Michael," she managed to whisper.

He grasped her hand, his thumb drawing soothing circles on her skin. "You're awake. I talked to the attending. Barring any unexpected development, you can go home tomorrow. How do you feel?"

"Any news on Faith?" Her already fast heartbeat pounded in her chest, the fear chilling her.

He squeezed her fingers. "Agent Peters said they were working on it. They have a lead and promise to keep us updated."

Becoming more alert, she threaded her fingers through his. New worry lines etched his face. "What about the detectives?"

Michael exhaled, his gaze dropping to their entwined hands. "They asked a lot of questions."

"You're holding back. Michael, what aren't you telling me?"

His sigh was a heavy one, filled with a tiredness he rarely displayed. "They believe I poisoned and drugged you."

The chill expanding from her core, she shivered. "I told him he was barking up the wrong tree."

Michael's head jerked up. "What do you mean?"

"He asked me all kinds of questions during his visits and intimated you were a suspect. With your medical knowledge and access to drugs and all. But I told him it was absurd."

"I know." He raked his free hand through his disheveled hair, then kneaded the back of his neck, his stiff-set shoulders displaying an unconquerable tension. "But he's… relentless."

"We need to find an attorney before this escalates any further. We need someone who can stand up for us."

"I agree. I'll start searching."

"And Jason? You need to pick him up from practice."

"I've asked Mom to pick him up. She'll take care of him until we, well, until we figure things out."

Clara reached out, her fingers tracing the hard planes of his face, the new creases around his eyes and mouth. "We'll get through this, Michael. We must… for Faith, for Jason."

"Yes, we will."

Michael stepped out of Clara's room and into the busy hallway, the hustle around him nothing compared to his chaotic world. He pulled his cell phone from his pocket and brought up his mom's number, his finger hovering over the call button before tapping it.

The phone rang once before she answered in Arabic. "Amir, how's Clara?" His parents always spoke Arabic at home and accented English with his children, which was a big concession.

"She's awake and doing better." How could he say that as if delivering patient updates?

"That's good." A rush of her breath whistled through the tinny speaker. "Jason is here doing homework, I think. Sitting in front of his laptop with earbuds in his ears."

Michael ran a hand through his hair and stepped aside as a nurse rolled a gurney toward an elevator. "How is he doing?"

"I don't know. He's a teenage boy. Doesn't talk much. He must be scared and worried, but he'll be fine."

Michael swallowed, his throat feeling dry. "I–I'm sorry you're caught in this."

"Nonsense. We are family."

Appreciating her strength, he nodded, even though she couldn't see it. "Mom, there's something else."

She fell silent, waiting. When he didn't speak, she asked, "Amir, tell me what's going on. And don't lie."

"I—Clara took some bad medicine. She's okay now." No reason to go into detail. Neither she nor Jason needed to hear it all. "The police—they're looking into it."

The pause on the other end lasted long enough for him to fear the call had dropped. Then her soft murmur came through. "What do you mean? It wasn't an accident?"

"No." He hadn't told her about the other incident. "But the police are investigating."

"All right, that's it. Jason will stay here for as long as necessary. We can stop by to pick up some stuff. You just take care of Clara and yourself."

He knew that tone. Knew when he wouldn't win an argument. But this time, he didn't want to try. He couldn't allow Jason to be hurt too.

His folks would keep Jason safe, wouldn't they?

CHAPTER 34

CAROL & MICHAEL

Carol Marino settled in a plush armchair in her grand library, lost in a novel. The lingering scent of leather-bound books mingled with the faint aroma of old wood, lulling her with its tranquility until a soft knock on the doorjamb interrupted.

Max, her loyal majordomo, stood on the threshold, a phone in his hand. Since Eva had taken a leave of absence, Max had stepped in. "Do you remember Amir Khoury, ma'am? He was a Marino Scholarship recipient about twenty-five, thirty years ago."

"Amir, Amir?" Repeating it didn't jog her memory. Over the years, she awarded many scholarships to worthy recipients. Even after the orphanage closed, the scholarship continued, catering to her special preference for the underprivileged, refugees, immigrants, and the like. Amir Khoury was one such individual with glowing eyes, infectious enthusiasm about the intricacies of the human body, and eager dreams of becoming a doctor. The scene played back in her mind.

"Yes, I remember him, the first Arab boy who won the scholarship." She spoke softly, lost in memories, then waved Max closer. "Bright boy. Wanted to be a doctor."

Max nodded, his posture straightening slightly. "He's now Dr. Michael Khoury, a successful neurosurgeon."

Her eyes widened, her lips relaxing with a satisfied smile. "I'm glad to hear it. He's realized his dream."

Max cleared his throat. "Dr. Khoury is on the line. He said Mr. Charles had promised any assistance he would need. Specifically, he'd like recommendations for criminal attorneys."

She furrowed her brows. "Is he in any trouble?"

"He did not elaborate, ma'am."

"All right. Refer him to Zimmerman, Charles' partner, now the Marino family attorney. He's a brilliant criminal attorney. And call Zimmerman to give him a heads-up."

"Yes, ma'am." He turned to leave.

"Let Amir—Dr. Khoury—know he's welcome here anytime. I'd like to get to know the man he's become." She reopened her book, then closed it, a finger holding her place. "Wait, invite him here. Tell him I'll give him the recommendation personally."

Nestled in the heart of the town of Marian, the Mirror Estate stood as a testament to old wealth and power. Michael stepped out of his vehicle, visiting for the first time. Lush greenery and pristine walkways surrounded a breathtaking structure of Indiana limestone.

He followed Max through the grand entrance to the great room, the high ceilings, intricate murals, and regal elegance unsettling him.

Ms. Marino waited for him in an elaborate chair, her elegant dress in keeping with the room's grandeur.

"Ms. Marino, thank you for seeing me," Michael began, his voice steady.

She waved away his words. "No need for formalities, Amir. Or do you prefer Michael? I heard you've done well for yourself since the scholarship."

"I go by Michael these days." He provided a brief overview of his life since receiving the scholarship.

She nodded at the right intervals, her face lighting up beneath feathery gray hair. "I am pleased with your accomplishments, Michael."

Taking a deep breath, he then broached his current predicament. "When I received the scholarship, Mr. Townsend promised me help anytime. I find myself in need of that help now."

"I am more than happy to assist." She reached over and patted his hand, making him feel at once five years old and cared for. "Just after your call earlier, my grandson Dylan asked me the same thing after explaining the situation. Todd Zimmerman is an exceptional criminal attorney. I've reached out to him on your behalf, so he'll be expecting your call."

"Dylan Roche is your grandson?" Michael smacked his forehead. "Of course! I went to meet him at M&M Enterprises."

"Yes, small world."

He then grasped her delicate hand. "I cannot tell you how grateful I am for your assistance. I felt, well, *lost*, having never needed such services before. Now, this visit has provided a lifeline."

But even if the lawyer cleared his name, he needed so much more. He needed Faith home and Clara safe. Would that ever happen?

CHAPTER 35

E*VA & FAITH*
Eva's muscles ached, adding to the weariness dragging down her mind as she stood in line with the others, waiting to be driven back to the Chinese restaurant. Four days undercover, and still, no signs of an auction. No whisper, no hint. Nothing. But she'd gotten word she needed to be on the lookout for a teenage girl, Faith.

The days blended in a monotonous blur: the clang of the alarm before dawn, the grueling work at the fish market, the meager meals. She'd adapted to her role, posing as another trafficked victim, hiding her determination behind a submissive mask.

She glanced at her reflection in the van's window. Her face was smudged, her eyes hollow. But behind those tired eyes, the fire of resolve still burned.

Inside the van, the conversations were minimal, the air thick with the smell of fish and fear. She'd sat next to Ling, the young girl she'd befriended on her first day.

"Do you"—Ling darted her gaze around—"do you know what's going to happen to us?"

"I don't know." Eva fisted her hands, her soul aching. Her team would help these girls—surely. But what of the others, so many others around the world they would never find, never reach? "But we'll get through this together. Just stay strong and follow the routine."

"The routine." Ling shivered. "Wake up, work, eat a little, sleep, repeat."

"That's right." Eva reached out to squeeze the girl's skeletal hand. "But add to that list two things—keep your head down and do what they say. We'll find a way out."

Ling's eyes flashed before they dulled. "I want to believe that. I really do. But every day feels the same. I'm scared, Mei-Yee."

Eva's throat tightened. So was she. Imagine how the others here felt, not knowing what she knew. And the others no one was coming for? It was too much to comprehend. "But we can't give up. We have to believe something will change—someone will find us."

They spent the rest of the ride in silence, the engine humming a constant, droning tune that echoed the repetition of their days.

At the restaurant, Eva's mind was still on their conversation. She had to find something, some clue to give to her contacts. Time was running out, and the desperation was growing.

As they filed out, she glimpsed a new girl. Blood whooshed in her head, her pulse too fast in her ears. The routine had become her prison, but it might also be the key to unraveling the mystery. She had to hold on, stay strong, and keep believing.

Was this the girl they were now looking for? The teenager's features suggest Indian or Middle Eastern heritage. All the others were Chinese. Where did they find this girl? If they got another "shipment" of victims, shouldn't there have been more of them? Perhaps this was the one abducted.

Summoning a smile, Eva approached the girl huddled in a corner. "Hi, I'm Mei-Yee."

The girl merely blinked, giving a slight nod, her lips pressed into a tight line.

"Are you okay?" Eva hushed her voice, kneeling beside the girl to bridge the distance in this squalid room.

The girl shook her head, tears welling up again. The echo of distant footsteps overplayed her whispered response. "I wanna go home."

The girl spoke perfect American English. She couldn't be one of the undocumented. Now Eva just needed her name to confirm. She reached out, touching the girl's trembling hand. "What's your name?"

"Faith," she answered Mei-Yee.

In the oppressive basement, encircled by unfamiliar faces, dread engulfed Faith. Her heart pounded against her chest, each thud echoing the fear that saturated her being.

Cornered in this dismal space, she retreated inward, seeking refuge in her thoughts. Words had abandoned her, stolen away by the fear now dominating her senses. All that remained was a haunting silence, punctuated by her quickened breaths.

She glanced around, sizing up the others. Mostly teenagers, mostly looking Asian. Maybe Chinese from the way they were whispering in broken, scared tones. Mei-Yee appeared older than the others and mixed-race. Why was Mei-Yee here with them? Why was Faith, for that matter?

"You'll be okay." Mei-Yee's words cut through the haze, her tone strangely assured, soothing. She sat next to Faith, her touch a light pat on Faith's shoulder, both reassuring and startling.

"How can you say that? How can anyone be okay in this situation?" Yet, even as she questioned her, the certainty in Mei-

Yee's words nudged at Faith, and an unspoken bond began to form.

"What do you… think they'll do to us?"

Mei-Yee hesitated, her vital brown eyes darkening. "Whatever happens, we're stronger together. We need to stick together, understand?"

Faith nodded, the heat of fresh tears swelling in her eyes. "I'm scared. They were going to release me, but then they reneged. I saw Daddy with the bag, but then they just snatched the bag and took off."

"I'm scared too," Mei-Yee admitted in a voice barely a whisper. "But we have to be brave. We'll find a way out of this, okay?"

Faith drew a shaky breath, nodding again. "Okay."

CHAPTER 36

OLIVIA

Fu Gardens Restaurant offered a sensory overload—the rich aroma of Chinese food, the bustle of clattering dishes, and the chatter of patrons in various languages. Olivia and Detective Annie Kwok sat opposite each other at a table, scanning the room. Detective Kwok worked in the human trafficking division and provided the task force with useful intel.

Today, they were scoping out the place and checking in with the CI. As a young waiter approached, Olivia recognized Kwok's confidential informant, David Chun, from his file.

"What would you recommend today?" Kwok asked.

Olivia knew it was their script. She had repeated many scripts before in her past life.

"Our chef has prepared a special seafood dish today, fresh catch from the sea." His English was accented, but understandable, and his words meant he understood and was ready to share information.

As he handed Kwok a menu, a paper slipped from between its pages, dropping into her waiting hand. She opened the note in her lap and studied the coded observations. "I believe it's for you."

Olivia took the paper Eva must've written on, her eyes drawn to one entry—a symbol representing Middle Eastern heritage followed by a series of numerals. The numbers decoded to mean Faith. Olivia's pulse quickened.

Kwok lowered her teacup, catching the subtle change in Olivia's demeanor. "What is it?"

"We have a lead." Olivia slid the paper back to Kwok, keeping it concealed.

"All Greek to me."

"It means she's here. We've found Faith."

Kwok's eyes sparkled. "You want dim sum? Or are you ordering from the menu?"

"Dim sum is fine." Olivia mentally compiled her response to Eva. Too bad, Olivia couldn't go to the kitchen without arousing suspicion. She shifted in her seat, pent-up energy making it hard to sit still. "We found her. Now we need to get her out."

In the meantime, they had lunch. The restaurant was like most authentic Chinese restaurants. Noisy. Cantonese, Mandarin, and English drifting from the other tables.

"Do you know if there's a banquet room here?" she asked Kwok.

"I don't think so. They just close the restaurant, I think, for special events."

So where would they hold the banquet/auction? Was there a basement? A back room they couldn't see?

Before they left, Olivia scribbled a series of instructions on a new piece of paper, using the same code. She handed it back to David with the check, their eyes meeting in silent understanding. This operation was far from over.

CHAPTER 37

DYLAN

In downtown Orlando, the M&M Enterprises office tower rose above the surrounding glass and steel structures, a testament to the Marino family's enduring influence. Dylan occupied a spacious corner office that balanced old and new, a reflection of his lineage and his modern aesthetic. While walnut bookshelves lined one wall with hardbound books and mementos from his family's storied past, glass framed the view beyond, juxtaposing history with the ever-evolving cityscape.

This afternoon, he sat at the sleek, glass-topped table across from Lily. She had just gotten off from her front office shift— this being her last week on that rotation. She'd be up in the office next.

Lily tucked her glossy hair behind her ears, her eyes big in the perfect heart of her face. "I hear you're no longer a management trainee. Nice office."

"Just a title change. But thanks." He appreciated the view. "Tell me again why you agreed to clear Michael's name. We're not detectives. And if you need reminding, we've met our quota for danger this lifetime."

"What makes you think it'll be dangerous? We're just going to find out what happened to Clara."

A lock of hair slipped free again. His fingers twitched to brush it back, to check if it were as silky as it looked. "And how do you suggest we do that? We're not investigators or detectives."

She simply looked at him with those bright brown eyes. "That's right. I should get Kyle to help. He's a special agent, a trained investigator."

"Fine." Dylan took a deep breath. Man, she knew what to say. "I hope your mom has taught you a few tricks."

Lily had been practicing kung fu with Olivia and learning basic hand-to-hand combat. "We've been training."

"Okay, so where do we start?"

"A tip from Kyle. Investigation 101. We start from the beginning. Where Clara was. What she was doing. Who she was with."

The little green monster edged its way up Dylan's belly. He swallowed to taper down the feeling. Nothing wrong with her asking for advice and maintaining friendship with whoever she wanted.

"I guess we revisit where I found Clara."

Her eyes alight, she tipped her head to one side. Her sleek hair cascaded over one shoulder, strands catching on the fluttery pink ruffles sprouting where her sleeves should be. "That'd be where we start. Maybe something'll point us in the right direction."

Dylan nodded, running a hand through his hair. He could still picture Clara, totally dazed, on the way to the roof. "I think you're right." He stood and reached for Lily's hand to help her up. "Let's go."

They left the cool, air-conditioning and stepped into the

vibrant Orlando afternoon, crossing the street and entering the building facing theirs. On their way to the penthouse, he recounted the encounter.

Lily headed toward the stairs. "Let's go up there and take a look."

When nothing there stood out, he shifted his focus to the stairs. "Maybe we ought to retrace her steps. She came up here. But from where?"

"That's right. We need to go downstairs."

They then walked around the perimeter. The building was sandwiched between two establishments—a local drugstore and a free clinic.

"You see those?" Lily pointed at the exterior security cameras on the clinic and drugstore. "Those could provide the evidence we need."

Dylan let out a low whistle. "You're right. They would have a clear view of this area. Maybe they captured something."

"Let's start with the free clinic." Lily strode ahead.

The free clinic offered a muted atmosphere far different from the bustling streets. The disinfectant scented the waiting room where patients flicked through magazines or swiped their phones. The worn linoleum and pale green walls spoke of a place that functioned on limited resources and unlimited dedication.

At the front desk, a middle-aged woman managed the patient flow.

Dylan pulled up a picture of Clara on his phone and held it out to her. "We're looking for any information about this woman. Her name is Clara Khoury. She was found in a bad state near here." He named the day and time. "Did anyone see her in here that day?"

"We're not allowed to give out client information." The woman handed back the phone. "However, I can say I didn't see her that day. And I don't remember anyone mentioning her."

"I know her." A man in a white lab coat stepped forward, his face lined with the toll of long hours, but his eyes alert and compassionate. "She's Dr. Khoury's wife."

Lily turned around. "You know Dr. Khoury?"

"Yes. He used to volunteer at the free clinic in Chicago. I caught some nasty bug when I visited my family last year, and he fixed me up real good. Just heard he moved down here recently. A good doctor. Do you have any news about the missus? Is she okay?"

"She's getting better." Dylan reassured the man. "We're trying to piece together what happened."

"Well, I wish I could help you more." The man gripped his coat lapels, rocking back on his heels. "If I hear anything or remember something, I'll get in touch."

"Thank you." Dylan handed over his card. "My cell and office number are on there. Please don't hesitate to call at any hour."

Next, Dylan followed Lily into the pharmacy. Air carrying a medley of sterile antiseptic and mild fragrances wafted from the cosmetics section, contributing to a calming atmosphere.

Behind the counter, a woman with spectacles precariously perched on her nose scrutinized a stack of prescription forms. As he approached, he brought out his phone and presented Clara's photo to the pharmacist.

"We're looking for information about this woman," Dylan started, trying to keep his tone even and professional. "She might have been in here on December 8. Do you remember seeing her?"

The pharmacist nodded. "She was here with another woman. They didn't fill a prescription, but the other woman did buy some over-the-counter pain pills. I believe they were both drinking something, but I'm not sure."

Dylan exchanged a glance with Lily. Was this a potential lead? "Did you mention this to the police?"

"No, but I had heard the police were in here while I was on personal leave a few days ago. Was this what that was about?"

Lily edged up closer, placing her hands on the counter below the prescription pick-up sign. "Do you have surveillance cameras here? How long do you keep the footage?"

The pharmacist pointed to a nondescript device tucked away in a corner. "Since we have drugs on site, we're at high risk for theft. Our insurance requires cameras. We keep the footage for about a month."

"Can we—"

"That's wonderful news," Dylan interrupted Lily. "I understand you won't be able to show us the recordings, but we will return soon with the authorities to secure the footage."

Outside, Lily called Kyle, putting it on speakerphone, and explained to him what they'd found. She huffed out a breath, those fluttery sleeves floating like wings as she jittered in place. "So, who do we contact to get a warrant? That's what we need to look at the security tape, right?"

"Slow down, girl." Kyle chuckled. "You're not law enforcement. You can report it to the detective in charge of the case. Then he or she will do their due diligence and investigate. But since you're trying to help the suspect, you have two choices."

"And they are?"

"Tell your mom. Let her do her magic and get you the footage. However, that won't be admissible in court."

"And the other option?"

"Does your friend have an attorney? If so, let the defense attorney know what you found out. He or she will take it from there."

She thanked him, hung up, and eyed Dylan. "So?"

"We'll ask Michael if he's retained an attorney yet. Grandma referred him to ours."

Lily goggled at him. "I didn't know Michael knew your grandmother."

"I didn't either." He placed a hand on the small of her back to guide her across the street toward his car in underground parking. "I'll drive you home. And, apparently, he was a Marino Scholarship winner way back when."

"My car's here, so I don't need a ride." Lily stopped abruptly. "I bet Faith's friends know something."

"Yeah, I'm sure the cops talked to them." He pivoted to where she normally parked her car.

"You know how kids are. They aren't always open to adults." She pointed her key fob to her Toyota to unlock it.

Weren't there rules about messing with an active investigation? But this was Lily. "So what? We go to the school?"

"Yes, I have a late shift. You don't have any early morning meetings tomorrow, do you?"

Should he tell her yes and let her deal with the consequences? Nah, he couldn't let her do this alone. "Let's go together."

CHAPTER 38

LILY & CLARA

The next day, Lily stood beside Dylan in the school office, peering through the glass partition at the crammed high school hallways. "Wow," she whispered as kids flowed past chatting, laughing, and bumping into each other in their hurry to their next class. "I went to an American school in Hong Kong, but it was nothing like this."

When Clara told them about Chase, Lily thought the teen might be more forthcoming with young adults closer to his age.

She nudged Dylan. "There he is."

The kid stood taller than those around him, with sun-kissed hair that caught the light. Waves and shouts directed his way displayed his popularity as he strolled past.

Dylan nodded, his gaze trailing the young man who entered the office.

As he approached, Lily offered a friendly smile. "Chase, hi. We're Dylan and Lily, friends of the Khourys. We wanted to talk to you about Faith and the party. Is that okay?"

Chase thrust his hands into his hoodie pouch, his shoulders

inching higher before he offered a slight nod and took a seat across from them.

Dylan cleared his throat. "I've heard you're quite a force on the soccer field. Central midfield, right? That's a challenging position. How's the season going?"

Chase's eyes lit up, and he launched into his recent matches, his upcoming tournament, and his favorite soccer stars, the initial stiffness in his shoulders easing. Dylan made comments, bonding with the teen while Lily waited. The only thing she knew about soccer was the team that scores the most goals wins.

After they had exhausted the topic, Dylan brought the conversation back. "Chase, we understand it might be uncomfortable to discuss, but anything you remember about that night —anything at all—might help us find Faith."

Chase's enthusiastic demeanor dimmed. He shifted in his chair, flexing his hands on its arms.

"Well, there was one thing. My dad"—he swallowed—"he was asking about Faith. He was interested in the party, about when we'd be leaving. He wanted me to text him when we were about to leave."

"Your dad?" As something squeezed her throat, Lily managed to keep her tone neutral. "Did he say why he was so interested?"

"No." Chase twisted his grip on the armrests, then started picking at the cracked faux leather covering. "I thought it was strange. He doesn't care about my dating life."

Keep calm. Don't look at Dylan. Don't tip the kid off or scare him. Lily could almost hear her mom's voice coaching her. "Thank you for sharing this with us. We know it's not easy, but you've been a great help."

Chase's head jerked up, one golden brow rising on tanned skin. "I can go now?"

"You bet." Dylan fist-bumped the teen. "And best of luck on your next match."

As they watched him leave the office, Lily gripped Dylan's arm, too tense to dare to say something. He just covered her hand with his, then stood and helped her up. They didn't talk on the drive back to his office, but once she sank into the chair facing his desk, she broke the silence. "Why would Chase's dad be so interested in when Faith was leaving the party? It doesn't make sense."

"I agree." Dylan rubbed his brow. "I mean, my mom used to ask me about my plans for the night. She might ask when I planned to leave, but never my date."

"I thought you said you weren't popular," she teased.

"Not popular doesn't mean never going on any date." He kept massaging his temples, his hand shadowing his eyes. "But getting back to his dad, why do you think he was so interested in Faith's plan?"

She shrugged. "Don't know."

Minutes passed before Dylan lowered his hand, his shielded expression stark. "What if his dad had some... ulterior motive?"

Lily jolted in her chair as he voiced what she'd been trying not to think. "What? You mean like he, um, could be involved in Faith's disappearance? Isn't he a doctor? Michael must know him. Why would he do that?"

"I don't know. I'm just throwing it out there." Dylan held up a hand. "It's—well, I can't make sense of it any other way. Why else would he need to know when Faith was leaving?"

"Okay, amateur hour is over." Lily pulled out her phone and called Kyle. The phone rang twice before he picked up.

"Lily. What's up?"

"I'm putting you on speaker again. You got me and Dylan. We met with Chase today... at his school. We had a talk about the night Faith disappeared."

"What did he say?"

"It was strange."

In the long silence after she finished, she tried to imagine his posture on the other end. When he spoke again, his voice was low, measured. "So, you're saying Chase's dad asked for the specifics of Faith's movements that night?"

"Yeah," Dylan chimed in. "Seriously, Kyle. It was weird. Chase seemed to think it was weird too."

Another beat of silence. A heavy breath. Then a rush of movement. "Did he mention anything else? Any other interactions with his father that seemed off?"

Lily and Dylan exchanged a glance. "No, nothing that he mentioned." Lily tightened her grip on the slim piece of technology, the edges cutting into her fingers. "But we just thought… you should know."

An exhale rattled the speakers. "Yeah, this could be important. Good job, both of you. I'll pass this on to my dad. He'll know what to do next."

Lily ended the call, sinking into a heavy silence. "It feels… significant, doesn't it?"

"Yeah, a piece of the puzzle." Dylan pushed to his feet and paced to the window, then stood there, one hand braced on the glass twenty-some stories above the city. "But I'm unsure of what it could mean."

She crossed to the kitchenette in the corner and grabbed two flavored sparkling waters from the minifridge. "I guess we'd better call Clara." She handed Dylan one before unscrewing the top on hers. "Any chance I can bribe you with this?"

"Not a chance, my friend." He saluted her with his. "That's so not a task I'm looking forward too, and you didn't even offer something with caffeine or sugar to pump me up."

Right. But Clara deserved to know, needed to know, even if it added another layer of worry. As she dialed Clara's number, Lily took a sip, cool liquid sluicing over her dry mouth and throat.

The phone barely rang once before Clara picked up. "Lily? Any news?"

Dylan raised his bottled water, winking at Lily, then updated

Clara on what they had found at the pharmacy. "If Michael's retained an attorney, you need to give this information to him or her."

"I'll have Michael tell him. Thank you both."

"You're welcome. Lily is going to talk about what we found at the school."

"We spoke with Chase today."

Clara's breath hitched. "Oh? Wh–what did he say?"

Dylan bowed, gesturing Lily on, his dramatics helping her overcome her nerves. As she recounted Chase's strange conversation with his father, the heavy silence on the other end weighed on her.

When Lily finished, Clara remained quiet. Then she whispered, "His dad is Dr. Ben Miller."

Lily eyed Dylan, who shrugged. "I'm sorry, but we don't know him."

"Hmm..." Clara murmured, seeming lost in thought. "Ben and Michael... work together. But... I knew it. Thank you, both of you. I need to talk to Michael." And she hung up.

Lily frowned at the dormant screen as Clara's number vanished from it. "Was that strange?"

After hanging up, Clara looked up to find Michael standing in the doorway, a cup of tea in his hand. They had come home from the hospital no more than thirty minutes ago.

"What is it?" He crossed to her side, one hand on her shoulder.

She recounted the conversation. "It's Dr. Miller. He might have something to do with Faith's abduction."

His eyes widened. "Ben? No. He's a renowned doctor, a respected man in the community."

"I know, Michael. I know." Tears blurred her vision, her

voice catching in her throat. "But something feels off. Remember the dinner the other night? He acted so strange. And then he asked me about some project. Something you'd never heard of. And now, with what Chase said, we can't ignore it."

Michael sank into the chair beside her, the cup of forgotten tea clattering to the end table. "Let's tell Agent Peters."

"They must've already alerted him. But there's something else. They went to the pharmacy next to the building where *it* happened. The pharmacist recalled seeing me and a woman, and they have a camera. If you let your attorney know about it, we might be able to see the footage."

His brows knitting and his hands clenching the armrest, he didn't seem to be listening. He kept muttering. She leaned closer to catch whatever he was saying. Something about—confronting him?

She gasped. "No, Michael! That detective is already after you. Don't give him any excuse to lock you up. Let the agents do their job." She scooted across the couch and grasped his hands. "Let the Lord take care of it."

Please, God, please. Speak to him, help him—stop him.

She held her breath, waiting.

At last, she sensed him relax a bit. She patted his back. "Now, you need to call your attorney and let him know about the pharmacy."

Who was that woman?

CHAPTER 39

LILY

Soon after Lily hung up with Clara, Agent Peters called. Lily put him on speaker.

"His father is Dr. Ben Miller," Ron said after they recounted their talk with Chase. "We don't know how he's involved in the abduction or if he is. But that's a good tip. I heard you two were snooping around trying to clear the good doc's name."

"We didn't do much." Lily sipped her water, the peach flavor washing some of the sourness from her tongue. "Just asked some questions. We told Clara what we found out at the pharmacy. Michael should be able to get the footage legally."

"Why do you need the tape?"

"Oh, didn't I say?" She capped her water. "Seems I've told the story so many times it's hard to remember who knows what. But the pharmacist remembers Clara was there with another woman. The other woman bought some over-the-counter medicine, and they were drinking something."

Dylan spoke up. "We're hoping the other woman saw something or knew something."

"Or maybe she drugged her," Ron said. "You did the right thing. The defense attorney should be all over it now."

With that, they said goodbye. Lily stretched, holding her arms high above her head before tipping her neck side to side. "I wonder if I can nap before my shift tonight."

"You okay?"

"Yeah, just tired." She rubbed the back of her neck. Man, that kink was brutal. How stiff must she have been all day for it to get so bad? "I should get going. I have my last shift tonight."

"Is this your last rotation? What are you going to do next?"

"I don't know." She stood and carried her empty water bottle to the recycling bin in the kitchenette. "Back-office work, I hope. I'm done with guest services."

"Yeah, I found it brutal when they had me on it." Dylan nodded, his expression understanding. "I'll see you."

After her shift, as she headed to a grocery store and navigated the deserted aisles, she couldn't shake off the undercurrent of unease. She gathered her items, the silence echoing around her. The sense of dread didn't fade as she stepped into the deserted parking lot, the harsh glow of the overhead lights scarcely penetrating the corners.

The sudden appearance of the masked man jolted her. Then the cold steel of a gun pressed against her. Fear surged, but she suppressed it, forcing herself to focus. Her mom's training kicked in.

She grabbed his wrist, twisted, and pushed, leveraging her body weight to send him sprawling. She wrestled the gun away, her heart pounding.

"Someone, help!" she screamed, her voice shrilling across the empty lot, a desperate plea she hoped would be answered.

Sirens wailed in the distance, the sound growing louder. Her attacker scrambled up, lunging for her, but she was ready. She kicked out. Her foot connected with his chest, sending him sprawling onto the asphalt.

As she trained the gun on him, her chest heaved, and her hands shook. Fear and power zinged through her, at once chilling and exhilarating her. The hand-to-hand combat training had paid off. Mom would be proud.

An hour later, Lily wanted nothing more than to flop down on her bed and sleep. It was after midnight. She had to stay and give her statement to the police. Now her mom regarded her, arms crossed as she leaned against Dad's study doorway. "We need to determine if you were targeted or if it was a random mugging."

"Why would I be targeted?" Lily swallowed a yawn.

Mom scowled. "You know about my past and your dad's connection to the Ghost's organization. We can't be too careful."

"And you fought this guy?" Dad exited the room and gripped her shoulder. "Are you okay?"

"I'm fine. I want to go to bed." The yawn breaking free, Lily eased away from his heavy hand. Heavy? How tired was she? She headed upstairs to her room.

Her father's voice followed her. "I'm sure it's nothing."

"Maybe, but…"

Lily closed her bedroom door on her mom's response, too tired to hear a but.

CHAPTER 40

EVA & CLARA

Eva's body ached as she trudged back to the basement. The stench of fish clung to her, a pungent reminder of the grim operation. Each fish she had cut open, each packet of drugs she had retrieved, led to a world she hadn't understood until now.

She needed to report this, but first, she had to find out about the auction and get Faith out of there. No, not just Faith. All of them. They were all victims, all trapped in this nightmarish existence.

The poor girl, Faith, was terrified. Eva kept telling her everything would be okay. They would get out of this. But to the teenager, they were empty words.

The basement door opened. A guard strolled in, scanned the packed room, and pointed to Eva.

"Get up."

She rose, her eyes meeting his before she averted them, portraying a terrified victim.

As she stood, he stretched out his hand, sliding a folded piece of paper into hers. Her fingers closed around it, concealing it within her clenched fist. "Understand?" he asked, loud enough for everyone to hear.

She nodded meekly, stepping back, retreating into her corner, her heart pounding.

After what felt like an eternity, she rose to her feet again. "Bathroom," she mumbled, nodding toward the door in the corner. The guard grunted his approval, eyeing her till she disappeared behind the door.

Inside the claustrophobic space, she unfolded the note. The scribbled words made her heart leap to her throat. Olivia got her message and responded that the auction would be the next evening. She also outlined the plan to capture Ray Ho and rescue the victim. Eva read it again to ensure she hadn't misinterpreted the coded message. Then she destroyed the note, flushing the remnants down the grimy toilet.

Back in the room, she took her spot again, preparing for the plan.

When the door opened again, the manager walked in, seemingly pointing to random boys and girls, including Faith and Eva, but not Ling. Eva panicked for a second, then relaxed. It didn't matter. They would all be free when her team stormed the place. Then, hands on his hips, the manager faced the group he'd picked. "Tomorrow, you'll have the day off. I need you cleaned up and presentable."

After the manager left, Faith whispered, "What's happening tomorrow?"

"Whatever it is"—Eva hugged her young friend—"I think we'll be free afterward."

Clara's heart pounded as she hung up the phone, Agent Peters's voice still ringing in her ears. Faith was alive. Safe, for now. The palpable relief lifted a weight from her shoulders, and the same relief animated Michael's eyes.

"They have a plan." She crossed to her husband and stopped inches in front of him. "They should get Faith back by tomorrow evening."

His face broke into a smile, his dark eyes glistening. He pulled Clara into a hug and rested his chin atop her head, his days-old beard snagging against her hair. As she clung to him, his chest rising and falling beneath her cheek, his warm whisper rushed over her. "Thank God."

They stood together, savoring the reignited hope. Then they said a quick prayer, their voices united in their plea for their daughter's safe return.

He then called his attorney, updating him on the discoveries Lily and Dylan made. Clara checked her emails, still reeling.

An email from Stella caught her attention. Her eyes narrowed as she opened it, memories of the Linda Boroski case flooding back. She'd been no closer to finding out what had happened to Linda. Instead, the case uncovered more of her own past.

She skimmed the message. It would have to wait. Faith's safety was paramount, and they needed to clear Michael's name. Everything else could be put on hold.

"Anything important?" Michael stepped back into the room.

Closing her laptop, she shook her head. "No. Just something I'll need to look into later. How did it go with the attorney?"

"He's hopeful." He jammed his hands into his pockets, his shoulders square again after days of pressure slumping them. "Things are looking up."

Clara reached out, taking his hand, feeling the strength and determination in his grip. "We're getting there. We'll have Faith back soon, and we'll clear your name."

He nodded. "I know we will."

The doorbell rang.

She jolted. "Who could that be?"

Michael shrugged and brought up the door cam on his phone. "It's Majid."

She sank into the couch as Michael greeted his brother and let him in.

"Amir, Clara." Majid stepped inside. "Any news about Faith? Is she…?"

When Majid's voice trailed off, unable to utter the worst-case scenario, Michael relayed the latest information, the words *human trafficking* hanging in the air.

A growl rumbled in Majid's throat, and his fists clenched. "Those useless cops. They are doing nothing. They have to find her!"

Michael placed a steady hand on Majid's shoulder. "Calm down," Michael urged. "Did you not hear? The agent said they'd get her back by tomorrow evening. She's alive and safe."

After a few moments, a worried frown replaced Maid's heated glare. "Is it true, Michael? I heard you were talking to a criminal attorney."

Although Michael tried to downplay it, Majid wasn't having it. "You think I don't know how they see us? They always see us as suspects because of our background, where we're from! I'll tell them what the money was for."

"Whoa. Hold up." Michael raised a hand. "I don't think that's a good idea."

But Majid ground his teeth, his jaw set in stubborn lines. "I know what they think. I have a record, a juvie record."

"You were only sixteen. Your record is sealed."

"But all they see is an ex-con. Add to the fact where we're from, they'll do everything to nail you."

Clara shifted on the leather couch, the cushion confining. Now she remembered that Michael had told her about Majid's juvie record a long time ago. But she was more curious about the money. "What money, Majid?"

In the unsettling silence, only the ticking clock dared speak up. Finally, Michael exhaled. "Majid has been working as a hairstylist for years. You know that. His dream was always to have his own salon, but he never had the finances for it." Michael palmed his face, grinding his hand against his eyes. "When the opportunity presented itself—his boss wanted to sell the salon—I offered to help him out. Well, it's not a loan. I'm treating it as an investment. You know, a silent partner."

Clara blinked. "That's fantastic! But why keep it a secret? Why not tell me?"

Majid's lips fluttered as he huffed air. "I didn't want you to know, Clara."

But why? She eyed them.

The brothers exchanged a glance. Then Michael rolled his eyes. "His pride."

Now she got it. Both their cultures valued male dominance. She got up and went to her brother-in-law. "Majid. I'm so happy for you. You're a talented stylist. Faith always likes the way you do her hair. Now, you'll be doing my hair and her hair for free from now on."

Majid chuckled. "I wouldn't charge you anyway. And thank you." Then he clamped a hand on Michael's shoulder. "Seriously, I should tell the cops. They have no more reason to suspect you."

"I gave them your number. If they haven't called, then I don't know." Michael shrugged. "But I'm gonna let my attorney know."

The younger man opened his mouth and closed it a couple of times. "When you mentioned *human trafficking* earlier, I, uh, I heard something. A client, uh, blabbered on the phone."

"What did you hear?"

CHAPTER 41

DYLAN

In Dylan's room at the Mirror Estate, his computer's persistent hum contrasted the yellowed paper cluttering his workspace. The perplexing piece of history had been monopolizing his attention. After the recent hullabaloo, he found a chance to dive back into the cryptic mystery.

Under the glow of the dim desk lamp, the worn-out map still wouldn't spill its secrets. Beside it, Tommy, his "Dr. Watson," leaned over the desk, squinting at the map. A fresh pair of eyes always helped. Tommy broke the prolonged silence. "Did you find anything on the internet?"

Dylan threaded his fingers through his hair. "Nothing. I've searched everywhere I could think of, from obscure history forums to deep diving into digital libraries of old cartography. But there's nothing remotely similar out there. It's… unique."

Tommy tapped on the desk. "Maybe we should bring Lily into this. She's bilingual. Haven't you heard bilingual people are smarter? They can think in two different languages."

"I don't want anyone else to know about this discovery. Not

yet. I know she's smart—if you count Mandarin, she speaks three languages. But she's got enough going on. Plus, she's helping plan her parents' wedding."

"Okay, whatever you say." Tommy waved him off. "It's weird to be planning your parents' wedding. Normally, you wouldn't be born yet when your parents got married."

"Theirs is a little different."

"I know. It's kind of romantic." He started humming the song, "Reunited."

Dylan shot him a look. "Who've you been dating now? Didn't know you were into love songs."

Clapping a hand to his heart, Tommy sighed dramatically, then sobered up. "What about Fr. Phil? You said you didn't want anyone else to know about this."

"He's a priest. He's used to keeping secrets."

"Okay, your call. The plans are drawn, and they're starting construction soon. What happens if we can't break this before your 'evil' aunt moves here?"

"Don't say it like that. She really is evil." Dylan braced his hands alongside the map. Why wouldn't it speak to him? He pushed away from the table. "I don't know. Let's hope the security is secured enough. Besides, I'd like to think that if we can't decipher the map and find the location of any supposedly buried treasures, she won't be able to either."

Yeah, a guy could hope. But she was the Ghost. She'd nearly bested him once, and who knew what she was up to now?

CHAPTER 42

SIMON & OLIVIA

Tonight, Simon stepped into the serpent's nest. He'd been extended a private invitation to the auction at Fu Gardens, thanks to his status as a former US senator. Beside him, Kyle maintained a watchful stance, exuding the lethal presence only a trained bodyguard could.

Upon presenting his e-invitation, Simon was escorted through a crowd of ordinary patrons to a nondescript wall where a section swung open to reveal a back room. A shiver ran down his spine as he walked through. He'd been in this place with Olivia and Lily and hadn't had an inkling about what lurked behind this façade. There, he was given a tablet along with bidding instructions.

Inside, they'd set up the room like an auditorium, complete with a podium before a large screen front and center and rows of chairs. He ignored the buzz of hushed conversations to survey the crowd. Aha, a high-profile lawyer known for his ruthless litigation skills, a charismatic TV personality who commanded millions of followers, and a foreign dignitary whose presence could ignite an international firestorm. Too bad, the man's diplomatic immunity would likely shield him from any fallout.

Recognition flickered in a few eyes as they identified the former senator. However, no one rushed to engage him in conversation, just gave discreet nods of acknowledgment. This wasn't a venue for socialization. It was a marketplace where lives were traded like commodities.

Simon chose a seat toward the rear, ensuring his button camera had an optimum vantage point.

Behind him, Kyle remained standing, his muscular frame imposing against the luxurious decor. Similarly built men revealed their roles as bodyguards.

Simon tried to relax, act natural in keeping with the mélange of nonchalant expectancy, a bizarre juxtaposition considering the dark undercurrents. Still, his gut churned. What a glimpse of the underbelly of society, a place where the rich and powerful came to play. How had he gotten thrust right into its midst, ready to expose their wicked games?

Seated inside an unmarked FBI van, Olivia fixed her gaze on the monitor before her. The feed from Simon's button camera provided a live stream, each pixelated image adding to her rising tension. Beside her, Ron was squinting at the screen, his brows furrowed.

Meanwhile, a thrum of anticipation kept their team alert. Simon had provided a panorama of the room, capturing the attendees before focusing on the podium where a Chinese man announced the auction's commencement. Electronic bidding began.

Images began to flicker on the screen, photos of teenagers,

their faces marked by a fear that made Olivia's heart clench. She scanned the faces closely, but neither Faith nor Eva was among the displayed.

Ron muttered under his breath. "We can't be too late. The doc said his brother's client mentioned the auction was this evening."

The radio crackled to life, Tanner's voice cutting through the static. "Ana and I could go in, do a quick recon, see if we spot them."

For a brief pause, everyone considered the suggestion. The risk of blowing their cover was high, but so were the stakes.

"No," Olivia replied, raising her chin, steady and resolute. "We can't risk tipping them off. If Eva and Faith aren't in the room, they might be held somewhere else in the vicinity."

Ron, the one in charge, flashed her a thumbs-up. "Olivia is right."

She nodded a silent thank you in his direction.

"But we can't just sit here doing nothing," Ana chimed in, her frustration crackling over the radio waves.

"No, we won't," he responded.

Simon subtly adjusted the angle of his button camera, providing them with another sweep of the room. The faces of the unsuspecting criminals were displayed in stark clarity.

It was a risk, but it was one they had to take. Every second wasted was another second Faith and Eva were in danger. They had to act now.

"I suggest we raid now," Olivia said. Would Ron agree?

Agonizing seconds ticked by. Finally, he raised a hand. "Let's do it."

"Did you say now?" Simon echoed.

His gaze swept the room again, hoping to see Eva and Faith.

But they weren't here, and their photos weren't on display. Leaning back in his chair, he shifted slightly, his gaze meeting Kyle's. The young agent stood behind him, his stern face betraying no emotion. However, Eva was a good friend of his. Kyle had to be worried.

Swallowing a surge of concern, Simon faced the screen. He wasn't supposed to know about Eva and Faith, and he couldn't ask about them. He needed to keep his cover intact for future use.

His earpiece crackled to life then. The faint hum of the hidden microphone relayed Olivia's low voice, meant only for his ears, her urgency unmistakable. "Bid as planned, but stay alert. Ron just green-lit it. Kyle will get you out."

This was it. He tapped his mike once, signaling acknowledgment. With one last glance at Kyle, he braced for the coming chaos.

The night came alive as Olivia, flanked by Ron and a team of skilled agents, stood outside the restaurant. Behind the unassuming front was a dangerous world they were about to infiltrate.

"On my mark," Ron said into his earpiece, his voice steady and commanding. Their backup held positions at other entrances, ready to flood the building at the signal.

Olivia was to lead a team to rescue the victims and search for Eva and Faith while Ron rounded up the auction host and participants.

When the command came, the agents surged forward and kicked the doors open.

"Everybody, get down and stay down!" Olivia called out in English, Cantonese, and Mandarin, her tone brooking no argument. The patrons, gasping and shrieking, did as instructed.

With a synchronized nod, she and her team moved in a coordinated surge, carving a path through the crowd toward the back. The hidden door leading to the basement might as well have had a neon sign above it, and they used this to their advantage.

"Hands! Let me see your hands!" Agents shouted everywhere they cornered a suspect.

As they approached the concealed entryway, the unmistakable crack of a gunshot tore through the air, as jarring as a lightning bolt. Agents dove behind overturned tables, crouched low to the ground behind pillars, and scrambled behind the bar.

"Cover! Take cover!" Olivia shouted.

Her agents responded, their guns drawn and fingers squeezing triggers as they sent bullets toward the unseen attackers. Amid the cacophony, Ron focused on detaining the auction host and attendees. Even from here, she could tell the auction room erupted in pandemonium. The bodyguards would do their jobs, and some patrons would slip through while others would fight or surrender.

As shouts, commands, and gunfire electrified the atmosphere, she wove through the restaurant, scanning for victims and latent threats. Here and there, agents sported scrapes and minor gunshot wounds, but nobody faltered. The mission was too critical.

Bursting into the basement, they were met with a harrowing sight—huddled, terrified victims, their faces the embodiment of human suffering. Her heart sank, a rush of empathy threatening to break her focus. She shoved it aside, locking it away for later contemplation.

"Secure them! Now!" Her voice left no room for question. "And get them out of here!"

With military precision, half the agents surrounded the traumatized victims, forming a protective human shield as they guided them up the stairs and out into the chilly night air. The other half of her team squared off with the remaining threats, their weapons singing a loud, deadly song as they engaged.

In organized chaos, the high-octane dance between law enforcement and criminals played out, Olivia at its center, the eye of a hurricane, resolute and unwavering.

They secured the back room while Ron's team handcuffed the auction attendees. But Eva and Faith weren't in the building.

CHAPTER 43

EVA & OLIVIA

E arlier that day, as promised by the manager, Eva, Faith, and several others didn't have to go to work. They were taken to some gym and given clean clothes, soap, and toothbrushes. After bathing and changing, they were returned to the restaurant basement where, instead of meager portions of fried rice, they were treated to a real lunch. Somehow, it made Eva think of the last meal for the condemned. It better not be a bad omen.

She was still waiting for the signal that the raid was going to happen when a burly guard hauled Faith to her feet. At the unexpected development, Eva rose, kept her head low, and began to follow them.

But the guard was leading Faith to a waiting van, so Eva needed to act. Now.

She lunged at the guard, catching him off guard. A scuffle ensued, her training kicking in and giving her the upper hand. But as she disarmed him, another man emerged and pressed a gun barrel against Faith's head.

Eva froze, the triumphant fire in her veins doused. Disarmed and overpowered, she was pushed toward a black van parked nearby, its doors open ominously. The icy grip of defeat clenched her heart, but she didn't let it show.

She met Faith's terrified gaze with a firm nod. "It's going to be okay."

Faith nodded back, but the terror didn't leave her eyes.

Then they were tossed into the van, the doors slamming shut.

The van took an endless series of turns. From the back, Eva could make out only blurred houses and indistinct street signs. Her sense of direction seemed to spin, but she still kept a count of the turns. Soon, the van stopped. As the doors swung open, she squinted into the blinding daylight.

The house before them appeared like any other suburban neighborhood. Just a spacious structure, displaying no overt signs of sinister activities. Faith was pulled out of the van, a goon holding a gun to her head. Another pointed at Eva, his eyes telling her to follow.

They were made to march up the steps, past flower beds and a bright front porch. As they reached the top, the front door opened with an eerily silent, mechanical ease. They stepped inside, the cool air-conditioning a stark contrast to the muggy heat outside.

Beyond a spacious foyer, stairs led up to the second floor. To their left was a room, a door ajar revealing a glimpse of a home office. To their right was a front room, likely the living room, cozy and inviting with its plush furniture and warm hues. Everything appeared immaculately kept—clean, polished, and tasteful.

The men led them up the stairs, the wood beneath their feet creaking. They were directed down the hallway to a door at the far end. An opulent master bedroom with plush carpeting, an expansive bed, and a sitting area.

After a cursory look around, the men left them with the final click of the door, and the key turned.

Eva took a deep breath, glancing at the petrified Faith. She wanted to comfort her, but what she needed to do was to think of a way to call for help. And she had to think fast.

Olivia stalked into the task force office, followed by Simon, Ron, Kyle, and Ana. While the raid had been successful, the letdown of failing to rescue Faith and extract Eva eclipsed the triumph. As Eva's handler, Olivia felt responsible. "I better not regret picking such an inexperienced agent," she muttered. Then she spun to Ron. "I want to question Liu."

He shook his head. "You know you can't. You're not a field agent."

She scoffed. "But I'm an operative."

"We'll do our best." Ana patted Olivia's shoulder in passing. "Don't worry."

When Ron and Ana left to question John Liu, Olivia's frustration mounted. She paced.

Simon cleared his throat. "They'll get something out of him. Just give it time."

"I don't have time," she snapped. "We need to find out who's behind this. Now. It's not good. Eva found Faith. So, they were together. They couldn't have vanished. She might have blown her cover."

They waited. The minutes dragged on. Tension tautened her muscles.

Then Ron and Ana returned, their faces grim.

"Nothing." Ana waved in front of her face, her short-cropped brown hair bouncing with her frustrated movements. "He's not talking."

As Olivia's heart sank, Ron held up a hand. "We did recover a burner phone on him, though."

She perked up. "Anything on it?"

"Just one number." Kyle shrugged. "Traces back to another burner."

Seriously? Olivia stomped to a desk and back. "So, we're back to square one."

"Not entirely." Simon touched her arm. "Why don't you talk to the victims? Maybe they know something."

The hard knots in her relaxed a fraction. "That's a good idea."

She left the room, raced to the FBI office where they were holding them, and found herself face-to-face with a frightened young victim.

"What can you tell me?" Olivia asked in Cantonese.

Tears glazed the girl's eyes. "Mei-Yee and another girl were with our group. We got cleaned up and fed. Then a guard took the other girl, and Mei-Yee followed her."

Olivia reached out and almost grabbed the girl. A calming breath helped her maintain her gentle questioning. "Did you see where they went?"

The girl's stringy hair swayed with her headshake. "No."

Had she hit another wall?

Her phone rang.

"Olivia." Ron spoke fast when she answered. "Deanna had found a surveillance camera from the establishment across the street. It captured the whole thing—Eva's fight and Faith and Eva being loaded up in the van. Now, Deanna's tracking the van."

"Finally, some progress. I'm on my way."

CHAPTER 44

EVA, RON, & FAITH

The cold gray morning light seeping through the blinds failed to comfort Eva. She'd spent the night in this unfamiliar room, with its windows bolted shut, thinking, hoping to find a way to get help.

She had no phone and could find no landline. She had no gun or other weapon. All she had was Faith to protect.

What was she going to do? How would she get out of this?

Heavy footsteps clomping to their door alerted her to move in front of Faith, her protective instincts kicking in as the door creaked open. A man walked in, a handgun resting in his grasp, his face hard. He slid a tray of food across the floor, the clattering sound screeching in the tense silence. His cold gaze darted between them, a subtle threat in it.

"Behave," he warned. "The big boss is coming."

"Who? John Liu?"

The man fixed her with an angry stare. "Shut up! You're the reason he got caught. Wait till the big boss gets here." He pivoted and left. The locks clicked into place.

It's got to be Ray Ho.

Faith had no appetite, but Eva convinced her to eat. They'd need the strength. After what seemed like forever, the door lock clicked, and a notable Chinese man entered. His deep-set eyes narrowed, his gaze pausing a moment longer on Faith.

Eva had seen him in photographs at the office. Ray Ho often glared from the front of case files. He was not a man to trifle with, but no way would she let him harm Faith.

Sneering, Ho instructed his underlings. "I'll be ready in a few minutes. Have the younger girl ready."

Before Eva could react, they separated her from Faith.

As one man escorted her to a different room, another took Faith in the opposite direction. Faith's frightened gaze locked with Eva's before she was forced away.

This was her moment—their only chance at survival. Eva stumbled into the man escorting her, the action seeming accidental. Her hand slipped into his pocket, stealing his phone.

She dialed 911, turned the speaker way down, and slipped it back into her pocket. Once she was inside the room and the goon left, she whispered, "This is FBI Special Agent Eva Higgins."

Footsteps paused outside.

She stopped and kept the call active. Every second counted now. Surely, their silent call for help would be heard before it was too late.

With his team back in the unmarked FBI van, Ron reviewed the footage. Local law enforcement had been canvassing for leads. Deanna tracked the van to the freeway, then lost it.

"Sir." A police officer approached, his face taut. "The 911 dispatch center received a call a few minutes ago. The supervisor said it seemed suspicious and thought we should know."

Ron frowned and leaned forward. "What did the caller say?"

"Nothing clear, sir, but it's worth a listen. I can forward the recording to you."

A moment later, Ron received the message with the recording attached. The others in the van huddled around when he pressed play. The small space seemed to shrink even further as the recording started. "This is FBI Special Agent Eva Higgins." Then muffled voices, yelling, scuffles.

When the recording ended, he eyed the police officer. "You traced this?"

"Yes, sir." The officer pointed to a location on the digital map projected on one of the screens. "The call was made from here."

Ron slapped his hands together. "Okay. Let's move, people."

Faith's heart pounded as the guard dragged her into a dimly lit room. The slam of the door reverberated through the space, and she stumbled, catching herself before she fell.

"On the bed." The guard jerked his thumb toward a piece of lingerie thrown across the covers. "Change into that. And hurry."

Terror squeezed her throat, stopping her breath. Her body froze, unable to obey.

"I said hurry!" The guard stomped from the room. The lock clicked behind him.

Faith gasped as the flimsy lingerie went in and out of focus. She hugged her arms around herself and backed away until she thudded into a wall. No way would she change. She couldn't.

She began to search the room, her hands trembling. Barely above a whisper, she muttered prayers, imploring God to help her, to give her strength.

The bare room offered no escape, no way out. Her shoulders sank.

There had to be a way out. There had to be!

Then the distant voices sounded. Banging, grunting, screaming. Her body went rigid, every bit of her straining to make sense of the chaos.

The door burst open, and Mei-Yee charged in, her face scraped and bruised, her nose bleeding, and her left eye closing where a dark mark formed.

"Run!" Mei-Yee commanded, her voice ragged. "Now!"

What was going on?

As Faith struggled to comprehend, the Chinese man, the one the guard called the big boss, sprinted into the room, his eyes wild, his gun waving.

Mei-Yee pushed Faith out of the way, her body shielding her as the man raised that gun.

Time seemed to slow. Faith's eyes locked on the weapon. Panic surged through her, and she grabbed the only thing within reach—a lamp with a heavy base—and swung it with all her might.

The man crumpled to the floor, and she stood, momentarily paralyzed. Did she just kill him?

"Come on!" Mei-Yee clutched Faith's arm and yanked her out of the room as the distant wail of sirens grew louder.

Her mind a whirlwind, her body operating on adrenaline, she followed Mei-Yee, the reality not yet sinking in.

They ran, their breath ragged, their footsteps echoing through the corridors. Behind them, the chaotic sounds continued. They stepped out of the house into the flurry. Agents sprinted from a van nearby, guns at the ready, movements displaying practiced efficiency.

CHAPTER 45

CLARA

The phone call Clara and Michael had been awaiting came. Michael answered, Clara clinging to his side.

Was Faith safe? Clara held her breath. She had begged the Lord at morning Mass to save Faith.

"Yes?" The word croaked from Michael. He cleared his throat and tried again, louder. "Yes? Tell us."

"Faith is safe," Agent Peters said, the same relief loosening Clara's knees also thick in his voice. "She's been taken to the hospital for a checkup, but she's safe."

Clara pulled the phone away from her husband. "Can we see her?" she nearly screeched.

"We're sending a car right now, Mrs. Khoury. It'll be there in five minutes."

The car ride was a haze, drizzling rain smearing the view into a watery tapestry of hues, while Michael called his mom to give her the news. She would meet them at the hospital with Jason.

Once their family gathered, an officer led them to Faith's

room. Michael gestured Clara in first, but she paused in the doorway, gripping the doorjamb as her knees wobbled, the sight of their daughter lying in the hospital bed almost undoing her. But Faith's lips curving as she saw them was worth everything. And in that moment, laughter and tears, a cacophony of relief, erupted.

"Mom!" Faith half sat up, reaching out and smiling.

And Clara rushed over to gather her baby girl into her arms. The familiar peachiness of Faith's shampoo was absent, replaced by something caustic, and Clara swallowed hard, not wanting to imagine everything Faith had been through these last—Clara spun to Michael. "Was it only four days?"

But, with a doctor's precision, he was checking Faith's vitals. Then he conferred with the attending physician. Clara watched him, taking comfort in his calm, methodical demeanor. He was silent until he smiled at her and Jason. "She's fine." He crossed the room and hugged Clara. "She's been through a traumatic event, but physically, she's fine."

A sob escaped Clara. The past few days began to recede, replaced by a bone-deep gratitude. Their daughter was safe and, by some miracle, largely unharmed. *Thank you, God!*

After the family had some time alone, Jason went home with his grandmother, leaving Michael and Clara in the hospital with Faith. Soon afterward, Agent Peters stepped in with a woman of delicate Asian beauty. Her high cheekbones and almond-shaped eyes bore an uncanny resemblance to Lily, imprinting on Clara an immediate recognition.

The woman hesitated at the threshold, her gaze riveted on Clara, her eyes wide and questioning. After that flicker of uncertainty, she broke the silence in a voice as soft as the rustling of silk. "Clara?"

Caught off guard, Clara blinked. "Yes?"

The woman then offered a radiant smile. "I thought Eva said you were missing. I'm Olivia. It's been forever."

Olivia's declaration threw Clara into deeper confusion. "Eva? Who's Eva?" she asked, the knot of her brows deepening.

Before Olivia could respond, Faith's voice cut through the room. "How's Mei-Yee?"

"Mei-Yee is actually Special Agent Eva Higgins," Olivia said, maintaining focus on Clara.

"It makes total sense." Faith's lips curved up in a big grin. "She saved me."

"Eva will be fine." Agent Peters's gaze traveled from Olivia to Clara and back to Olivia, lingering. "I'll leave you now, but you can expect another agent to stop by for Faith's statement."

As the door closed behind him, Olivia touched Clara's arm. "You don't remember me?"

Michael stepped forward, extending his hand toward Olivia. "Olivia, is it? I'm Michael Khoury, Clara's husband, and Faith's dad. Why don't we step outside for a chat?"

As the two of them exited the room, the hospital's harsh fluorescent lights outlined their silhouettes, marking the start of a conversation that might unravel the mysteries. Clara blinked several times, her head facing the door. She'd wanted this for so long, but was she ready?

CHAPTER 46

EVA

Eva's breath hitched as Lily's last sentence hung in the air, painting a new yet surreal picture of her life. Lying in the stark hospital room, the rhythmic quiet beeping of machines marking the passing seconds, she closed her eyes. "I scarcely know what to feel. I'm so relieved but still bewildered."

Opening her eyes, she pushed herself up on one elbow. "So Clara, Faith's mother, is my long-lost aunt?" Who could have foreseen such an ending? "But I–I thought—" She stopped as her throat closed over the words, her voice barely above a whisper. "I thought she was an abduction victim."

"Well, evidently, not." Lily bounced in the plastic bedside chair, her animated hands speeding up her tale. "Michael found her at the Outer Banks. Neither has any idea of how she got there. And she still doesn't remember anything."

Dylan, standing beside Lily, placed his hand on Lily's shoulder. "I had a weird feeling when we were at their house. The way Clara looked at you was strange. Now, I know why. She saw your mom in you. Subconsciously, she must remember your mom."

Eva shook her head. Ouch, that hurt. She pressed a hand to the bandage wrapping her skull. "I can't believe this. I wanted to become an agent because of her. Because I thought she was a trafficked victim."

Kyle stepped forward. "Your determination to find your aunt led to the capture of Ray Ho. That's a good thing."

"Yes, it is," she admitted. "I appreciate your perspective. I guess every cloud does have a silver lining."

"Just sayin'." He winked. "Sometimes, the path we think we're meant to walk isn't the one we're supposed to be on."

A contemplative silence followed those philosophical words.

"Wow, that's deep." Dylan finally exhaled. He scratched his head. "I usually hear that type of comment from Fr. Phil."

Kyle smirked. "I have my moments."

Eva let their banter fade. Her aunt Clara had suffered a gunshot wound. Now she couldn't remember her past. And she was Faith's mom. The girl Eva had fought to save the previous day. "So"—she drew out the word—"I've been spending time with my cousin these last days and haven't known it?"

Lily's nod jostled her slinky hair, fanning it around her shoulders. "Kinda cool, isn't it?"

"Come to think of it. Can we not do something about Clara?" Eva's twitchy fingers ironed the hospital blanket's hem. "Help her recover her memories?"

Lily reached out to offer a reassuring squeeze on Eva's knee. "Oh, they tried. They've done a lot. Michael has consulted multiple specialists. And Clara even tried some hypnotherapy. But memory recovery isn't something you can force. It happens on its own pace, if at all."

"But there must be something?" Eva shifted, not ready to accept Lily's answer. She was an FBI agent. She found solutions.

She'd escaped a trafficking ring and rescued an abducted girl, and she wouldn't be powerless in *this* situation.

"I've read something about memories." Dylan crossed his arms and rocked back on his heels. "Sometimes, the mind blocks out memories as a defense mechanism—you know, when the memory's so painful the person just doesn't want to remember."

A silent nod was Eva's only response, her gaze fixated on the sterile white floor tiles.

"But there is something else," Lily confessed, her fingers drumming a soft rhythm on Eva's knee. "There have been attempts on Clara's life. Dylan and I have discovered some leads and shared them with Kyle and the task force."

Eva's head snapped up, a cold knot twisting in her gut. Her hands clenched around the blanket. "Attempts on Clara's life? Who's trying to hurt her?"

"We don't know yet." Lily dragged the toe of her sneakers across the tiles, screeching out a horrible sound. "That's what we're trying to find out."

Kyle nudged Dylan. "Did you two give the defense attorney the information?"

"Not directly. We told Clara and Michael. They should alert his attorney," Lily responded.

Eva ground her teeth. She might not be able to help Clara recover her memories, but she could help protect her. "I want to help. Whatever it takes, I want to help Clara and her family."

CHAPTER 47

OLIVIA, FAITH, CLARA, & MICHAEL

Olivia pulled up to the Khoury residence, its impressive façade befitting Michael's status. The house defined what real estate agents would market as an executive home, and the manicured lawn offered the perfect backdrop for impeccable landscaping.

When Clara invited them in, Olivia strode ahead of Ana into a spacious living room. Soft, neutral beige adorned the walls, plush furniture invited one to settle in and carry on a conversation. The room ended at an open-concept kitchen with gleaming countertops and state-of-the-art appliances. An elegant archway farther to the right offered a glimpse of the dining room. The whole layout was both stylish and functional, luxurious and homey.

"Let's get comfortable in here." Clara led them to the leather couch. "Would you like anything to drink? Coffee? Soda?"

"Coffee would be wonderful." Olivia smoothed down her slacks, fatigue settling in as the leather couch cradled her. "It's been a long week."

"No doubt about that." Clara laughed. "And you?"

"None for me." Ana held up a hand. "I downed a whole pot this morning."

When Clara came back with the coffee, Olivia gestured to her companion. "Agent Ana Ruiz is here to talk to Faith. I understand she's back now and staying home from school today."

"She's upstairs in her room. Would you like me to get her?"

"No, that's all right." Ana stood. "Just point me in the right direction."

"Right. Just go up the stairs, second door to the right."

Clara sat with Olivia. Despite the decades, Olivia could still see the familiar features in Clara. They had both grown older, but the years couldn't diminish the bond they formed since childhood—*if* Clara could remember.

"Hey." Olivia moved to a seat across from Clara, folding her legs underneath her. "I wanted to share some stories with you. From when we were kids."

Clara dipped her head, her fingers trembling as she tucked her shoulder-length black hair behind her ears. She swallowed visibly, then raised her chin. "Please—thank you."

Olivia began telling her about when they met, recounting their childhood, their families, and their shared history from the annual New Year's Eve party to their joint misadventures with Marie. All tales of laughter, mischief, heartbreaks, and innocent dreams.

No recognition sparked in Clara's eyes. No sudden gasps of memory, no flash of realization. Clara listened, her eyes growing misty, but the girl Olivia once knew remained buried within the depths of her lost memories.

After a while, Clara cleared her throat. "When I met Lily, I thought she looked familiar. And now, I realize she looks a lot like you." She gestured between them. "Maybe somewhere in the back of my mind, I remember you."

"Well, regardless of your memories, Clara, I'm just glad you're safe. And we're here together now. Lily and I talked to Marie last night. She's delighted to hear about you. I don't know if you knew, but she's now Sr. Marie. Has been for many years. We'll need to FaceTime her soon. And she promised to pray for you."

Clara laughed. "I am glad I'm okay too. And I'd love to chat with Marie." She beamed, her warm smile spreading out her lips and curving up her high cheeks to leave crinkles beside bright eyes. "I love hearing these stories. Even if I can't remember them, they feel… right. So, don't stop sharing them, okay?"

Olivia's chest warmed. She reached across the chasm between them—not only the leather couch cushion but also the gulf of forgotten past—and grasped Clara's hand. "My dear friend, I promise I won't. I'll share all the stories, all the laughter, and all the memories so you know who you were. Our beloved, long-lost friend."

"Faith? I'm Ana Ruiz with the FBI. May I come in?"

The door was open, but the agent knocked anyway. Sitting at her corner desk and catching up on her homework assignment, Faith pivoted the chair to face the doorway. She was taking three AP classes and couldn't fall behind. She closed her laptop and waved the agent in. "Sure."

Ana sat on the bed—the only place available—and Faith's sunny yellow duvet billowed with the woman's movement, before settling back in place. "How are you feeling?"

"Good, thanks."

Ana bent forward, elbows braced on her knees, hands clasped before her. "Whatever you're feeling is okay. I understand you didn't suffer any physical injuries, but you went through a traumatic experience. Cut yourself some slack."

"Dad said I could talk to a counselor."

"That's good." She waited a beat. "Do you feel up telling me what happened?"

Faith nodded, a chill racing up her spine over her terrifying ordeal.

"There was a party. Chase was going to be there." Who was the girl so excited to see him? Could she ever be that girl again? A wistful twinge pinched her chest. "I thought it would be fun. I didn't know it would turn into a nightmare."

Ana held up a hand. "Take your time."

"I remember… leaving the party." Faith shivered, her arms sliding around her middle, holding her together, even as she raised her chin. "Then I was grabbed from behind. There was a cloth, a horrible smell… and then… darkness."

Heart pounding, she hugged her arms tighter, shakes starting deep inside her as she relived the terrifying experience.

"Go on."

Ana's voice grounded her. She was here. In her room. Not there. It was over. Faith took a deep breath. "I woke up in a room. I didn't know where I was, and… I was scared. A guy came in and told me to say something. I heard my dad's voice over the phone.… I called out for him."

Tears blurred her vision, but she blinked them away. She wasn't going to break down, not now. She'd gotten through *that* —she could get through *this*.

"I heard them talking, the guys who took me. One of them was arguing on the phone about money. He wanted more. I think he got it because he seemed satisfied later."

"And the other man?"

"He… he just went along with everything. He didn't say much." Faith shuddered at the memory of the silent, looming figure.

"And then?"

"I was put in a van. At the drop-off, I thought I would be

free… but…" She couldn't do it. Couldn't go there. The memory too fresh and too terrifying.

But Ana understood, nodding. She stretched forward, elbows still braced on her knees, clasped hands extended as if reaching to comfort, but promising no physical contact. "We're going to do everything we can to find these men. Did you see them? Do you think you'd recognize them?"

Faith closed her eyes and saw them again. "Yes."

"Good, because we caught them. You know we got the one at the drop-off. Did they tell you we caught the other one at the raid? We may need you to make a positive identification later."

She suppressed a shiver. She could do this. She'd do it to protect others. She stiffened her spine. "Okay."

"The driver took off with you. What happened after that? Where did he take you?"

"To some basement. I think it was a restaurant." She then shared how Eva befriended her and Eva thought something was going to happen and they would be free. "But then a guard grabbed me, and Eva followed and tried to free me but ended up being taken as well."

"What happened when they took you to that place?"

"We spent the night locked in a room. Then, the next day, this Chinese man, the big boss, showed up." Faith recounted how Eva burst through the door and fought with the man. Faith grabbed a lamp and hit the man.

Ana's eyebrows lifted. "You hit him with a lamp?"

"Yeah." Faith cringed and touched the back of her head, right where she'd hit the guy. "It was the only thing I could think of."

"And what happened next?"

"He went down. I panicked, but she led me out of the house. And we heard sirens then. When we were outside, you all were getting out of the vans and trucks."

Ana smiled, her gaze full of respect. "That was brave of you, Faith."

"I don't feel brave," Faith confessed, her voice quiet. "I was just… really scared."

"Being scared doesn't mean you're not brave. Sometimes, bravery is doing what needs to be done, even though we're terrified. And you did that. You helped save yourself and Eva. You should be proud."

Faith forced a smile. "Thank you."

"You're welcome. I think that's all for now."

A laugh burst out. "Do you know Eva is my cousin? I had no idea. It's wild!"

"Yes, I heard. I guess it's serendipity."

The trip down memory lane was supposed to help Clara, but even though her memory was still locked, it was nice to hear stories about her as a child. If she never recovered her memory, she'd treasure these as her "found" memories.

"As young as we were, we were quite a trio, you, Marie, and I." Olivia was smiling nostalgically. "Eva, your niece, never believed you just ran away like the police said."

Clara tucked her feet up beside her. "Even though I heard Eva was my niece yesterday, I still have a hard time processing it." Seriously, Eva, the agent who had rescued Faith, was her niece? She chewed on her lower lip. "So many pieces to my past I've yet to discover, so many connections I never knew I had."

"Yes," Olivia continued. "She's got into law enforcement, looking for answers—"

The doorbell rang. Clara checked her door cam app and frowned.

"Salesman?" Olivia asked.

"No, she's, uh, I forgot her name. She works with Michael at the hospital. A neurosurgical fellow. I wonder why she's here.

Oh!" Clara sprang from her seat. "You don't think something happened to Michael? Has he been arrested?"

"Go ahead and see what she wants. I'm going to the bathroom."

She padded to the front door. Her hand hesitated on the door handle. Then she pulled the door open. "Something happened to Michael?"

"I don't believe so, Clara," the woman said. "I'm here for you."

Clara's heartbeat jittered. A frown pinched her forehead. "I apologize, but your name escapes me." She stepped back to allow the woman entry, hoping her lapse in memory wouldn't betray her growing dread.

"It doesn't matter." The woman seized Clara's arm and pulled her forward toward the door. Then the woman stepped behind her. The chilling, metal touch of a gun pressed against Clara's back. Panic surged through her like a rogue wave, over-whelming her senses as the woman commanded, "Walk."

Clara had no choice but to obey, her steps mechanical.

As they stepped into the blinding daylight, the woman forced Clara to face her. The gun pointed at her head, an ominous threat that consumed her entire field of vision.

"Sorry. Nothing personal," the woman said.

Time seemed to stretch into infinity. The world shrunk. The distant, innocuous suburban neighborhood sounds drowned out by her heartbeat, a rapid, erratic drum in her chest, and the adrenaline coursing through her veins.

The world spun out of focus. Her knees wobbled, and the grass beneath her swayed. She was lightheaded, her mind spin-ning as if caught in a tornado. The gun appeared to grow and then shrink, grow and shrink, her vision contracting and expanding as fear threatened to consume her.

Then her mind yanked her back two decades. She was again facing danger, another gun pointed at her, another life hanging in the balance. The memory was visceral, its fear mingling with her current terror until she wasn't sure which was reality.

She didn't know how long she stood there, trapped between past and present. But then a rush of movement brought her back.

Olivia came out of the bathroom and frowned at the empty living room. Had something happened to Michael? She started to turn the corner to the front door and halted. Clara was outside the door with a woman behind her. The way they were standing gave her a bad vibe. Something was off, and Olivia, trained to trust her instincts, felt a knot twist in her stomach. As she edged closer, adrenaline coursed through her veins. Clara's expression morphed into raw fear. Olivia's heart clenched—she'd seen that look too often in her line of work.

Ana was coming down the stairs. Olivia put a finger on her lips as they made eye contact. Then she gestured her plan. She moved to the patio doors, slipping out into the backyard. As she rounded the front of the house, she ducked behind a decorative hedge, Ana on her heel.

There was Clara, her eyes wide and glassy, and the woman from the door, a gun in her hand. Of all the audacity and in broad daylight, no less. This wasn't an act of desperation, but the work of a lunatic—not a trained operative.

The woman widened her stance. "Sorry. Nothing personal."

Olivia's training kicked in. She nodded to Ana, conveying the unspoken plan, then emerged from behind the hedge, her gun aimed at the woman's temple.

"Drop it."

Ana executed a swift chop, and the gun fell from the assailant's hand.

"You're okay." The voice—Olivia's?—reached Clara through the haze. "Everything is okay."

Clara's vision swam, her body disconnected from the world around her. She was vaguely aware of Ana subduing the woman, of the clink of handcuffs in the quiet afternoon.

Still shaking, Clara allowed herself to be guided into the safety of Olivia's arms. Yet, even as her friend cradled her, the inner turmoil refused to settle, her mind awhirl with images— Olivia from their shared childhood in Hong Kong and Olivia from just minutes ago, recounting stories of Clara's forgotten past. The fragments of her memory, new and old, felt disjointed, confusing.

What's happening to me? The words were a whisper in the chaos, her reality blurring at the edges.

Michael exited the surgical suite, preparing to discuss the surgery with the patient's family. It would be a lengthy recovery, but the surgery was successful. First, he pulled his phone out of his pocket and turned it back on. It buzzed with messages. All from Olivia. Strange. She asked him to call as soon as possible.

He called back and started to apologize, but she cut him off.

"Michael, I'm at your house. Clara's been attacked. You need to come home. The police are here and taking statements."

His heart dropped to his stomach, his body frozen. "What?" Had he heard her correctly? "Is she all right? Who attacked her?"

"It was Dr. Hill. I don't know why, but you need to get here. Clara's disoriented and confused."

He let his assistant know he had a family emergency and requested the surgeon who assisted in the surgery now brief the family. Then he drove home, the car seeming to crawl despite his speeding.

He found Clara in the living room, her eyes wide and her

body trembling. Olivia sat with her, offering soothing words, but Clara seemed lost in her thoughts, mumbling incoherent fragments of memories.

"The police left except for a couple of officers." Olivia pushed from the couch and, with a firm grip on his coat sleeve, edged him into the kitchen. "Faith is in her room. She came down earlier because of the commotion. She was freaking out seeing her mom like this, so I sent her back upstairs. An officer is with her. I gave my statement. So did Ana. She had to go back to the office. And they agreed to wait till Clara was better before taking her statement. So, they'll be back." She let out a low breath and tipped her head toward the living room. "I think she's remembering something. Listen to her. It's something about the stories I was sharing with her, something from our childhood, but there are details I didn't tell her."

He then sat beside Clara, taking her hand. He rubbed her fingers, warming away their cold and clamminess. "Clara, it's me—Michael. Can you tell me what's happening? What are you remembering?"

Her eyes flickered.

As she shivered, he drew her closer, cradling her against his chest.

Then her soft breath warmed his neck. "Ben… Dr. Miller… something wrong… I saw him… Linda on the ground… the man, the Chinese man, Ray Ho… that voice."

Michael stiffened. The other night at the restaurant, Dr. Ben Miller must have recognized Clara, but her attack was—no, he didn't have time to dwell on the details. He only knew Ben was somehow connected.

"I need to call my lawyer and check on Faith." He slid Clara free, transferring her to nestle into the couch. She didn't seem to notice the difference. "Olivia, please stay with Clara."

CHAPTER 48

CLARA

Clara followed Linda into Ben Miller's party.

Linda slipped her arm through Clara's. "I'm so excited about our double date this coming weekend. It's going to be perfect. Thanks for coming along."

"Sure." Clara laughed. Linda had met a new guy and wanted to go on a boat ride with him. But because the boat belonged to a guy friend of his, she suggested a double date. "Sounds fun, and speaking of perfect, we're going to have perfect weather."

Ben, Linda's on-again, off-again boyfriend, stood by the pool, drink in hand, watching Linda. They were technically "off," but his possessiveness twisted Clara's stomach. He'd been watching Linda all night. Now, as the crowd began to dwindle, he stomped toward her. "What's this about you going off this weekend with another guy?"

Linda tossed her silky hair over her shoulders, her delicate chin high. "What it is, Ben, is none of your business. Besides, it's a double date, not some torrid overnight getaway."

Clara cringed. "I think I need to visit the restroom."

Before her roommate could respond, Clara stepped away from the conversation to give them the space they needed.

The marbled bathroom provided a temporary haven. She took her time touching up her makeup. When she emerged, heightened voices came from the pool deck. Two male voices—Ben's and a stranger's.

"What'd you do?" Ben asked.

"You saw. It was an accident," the other voice said.

"We need to call the cops," Ben swore. "Dad will have a fit."

"Don't worry. I'll have someone take care of it."

"Wait, wait!" Ben sounded panicky. "Clara is still here. She's gonna find out."

What were they talking about? And where was Linda?

Clara peeked around the corner. But no! She couldn't be seeing right.

Linda lay sprawled on the deck, her face pale against the dark teak. Ben was pacing by the pool, his face flushed. Clara didn't see the other fellow whose voice she heard. Rushing over, she kneeled beside her friend, her heart pounding. Linda wasn't breathing.

Panic seized Clara, an icy grip on her chest. "What happened, Ben?"

Pain slammed her head a second before her world spun into blackness.

Sometime later, Clara blinked, her senses sluggish and disoriented. Her hands were tied together, the coarse rope biting into her skin. The unyielding pressure of duct tape sealed her lips, reducing her protests to feeble mumbles. The room smelled of stale cigarettes and damp upholstery. Ben was nowhere in sight, but two men were, their faces as indecipherable as their language.

"We'll take care of it." One then spoke in English to someone on the phone, his accent rolling the words into unfamiliar territory.

Then they hoisted her up and shoved her into the back of a windowless van. Linda's sudden proximity was a gut punch. Her friend was unnaturally still, her face a mask of tranquility eerily similar to death. Tremors racked Clara, her mind spiraling with the worst of scenarios.

The only windows were on the back door, and they were smudged with grime and dust, allowing no glimpse of the world outside. The engine roared to life, and the van jolted into motion. Clara was left in the dark, each turn and bump heightening her fear.

What felt like an eternity later, her body pitched forward as the van parked. The door slid open, and a harsh sliver of light cut through the darkness. One man stepped inside and hauled Linda's body out. The door slammed shut, and Clara was plunged back into darkness, the reality of Linda's lifeless body leaving with the stranger settling in her stomach like lead.

The van lurched back into motion. Desperation soon replaced the fear, and Clara prayed fervently for salvation. Against her will, she dozed off.

And then the van stopped again. The mechanical screech of the doors protested what was coming before one of the men yanked Clara onto her unsteady feet. The scent of the sea filled her nostrils as she stumbled along a marina, bathed in the dim glow of distant streetlights.

Large vessels bobbed in the waters, but one caught her attention. The men were communicating with someone aboard in rapid Cantonese, and her proficiency in the language helped her piece together their cryptic conversation.

She held her breath, her whole body going as still as Linda's at the words *human cargo*. A cold rush sluiced over her, bringing on quaking shivers. They were trafficking people.

Grinding her teeth to stop their clattering, Clara steeled herself. She was not going to be another faceless victim lost to that sinister world.

As the men's chatter continued, indicating their imminent departure, she bolted. Her bound hands made her strides awkward, but she didn't care. She focused on one thing—escape.

One man shouted.

Her breath came in short bursts now.

Running footsteps echoed behind her, getting closer. Then light glinted on a gun in her peripheral vision.

"Stop!" a man yelled in Cantonese.

She stopped. Was that Ben? What was he doing there? How did he get here?

She couldn't clearly see the guy behind him, but the next one surprised her, the man with Ms. Beaumont, Ray Ho. Officer Bill's warning came to mind too late. She'd stumbled upon Ho's operation. But how was Ben connected to him?

Others shouted in Cantonese that they had to leave. Something about a coast guard vessel approaching.

Ho didn't seem to care. His expression changed when he saw her face and recognition hit. He muttered something to Ben. They talked briefly. Then a sudden force collided with her, sending her spiraling into darkness once more.

CHAPTER 49

CLARA, OLIVIA, & EVA

Clara shifted on her couch as Detective Williams surveyed her. Olivia had helped her call the information line and asked to speak with the detective in charge of the Linda Boroski case. Then with Olivia's help and Michael's support, Clara recounted the incredible tale. Now she wasn't sure whether the detective believed her.

"All right. Let me make sure I have everything clear." Williams flipped to the beginning of his notes. "You were present at the murder of Linda Boroski twenty years ago, but a gunshot wound to the head caused you to lose your memories until recently?"

"Yes." She shivered, wrapped her arms around her body. "It all came flooding back to me yesterday. I know it's a lot to take in—and it's been so long—but I had to tell someone."

Williams skimmed his notes. "We don't have much to go on other than the autopsy results. Ms. Boroski wasn't shot. Her skull was caved in. That fits with what you remember. You are positive the one voice was Ben Miller? But you don't know the other voice? So, we don't know who killed her."

"I'm sorry. It was so long ago. I don't think I knew that voice then. It sounded like it was an accident—"

"But they could have called the police instead of covering it up," Williams said.

"I imagined the other guy pushed her. Anyway, I didn't see what happened." But, even as she was saying it, she thought the voice sounded familiar. Where had she heard it before?

Michael gripped her hand. "So, what now?"

Williams closed his notebook, standing up. "Very well. We'll start verifying your statement and begin our investigation. Thank you for coming forward with this information. Hopefully, we'll be able to bring justice to Linda Boroski and you."

Clara spent the next few hours jotting down her old memories. Call it paranoia, she didn't want to lose those memories again. Faith went back to school, but Michael stayed home.

"You won't believe what Zimmerman found out." Michael clicked to disconnect his phone. He sat on his favorite recliner in the family room.

"What did your attorney say?" Clara sank back into the couch's supportive cushions.

"He got the pharmacy's feed. It was Dr. Hill. She was with you the day when you were drugged. She may be the one responsible. She has access to narcotics and the video shows her slipping something in your coffee. Unless you have a perceptive taste bud, you won't likely know it."

"But the pills I took the other night—oh!" Her hand pressed to her throat.

"What is it?" Michael sat upright.

"I think she put the bottle in my purse. When we came home from the hospital, the bottle was with my belongings. I didn't pay any attention to it then. Thought I must have brought it with me."

"But why?"

"That, I don't know."

Having heard the account yesterday, Olivia was still processing Clara's story as she waited for the gate to be opened at the Mirror Estate. The whole situation felt like a puzzle, but she was starting to see how the pieces fit.

She reached for her phone, tapping Ron's number into the screen. She needed to share this with him, to hear his thoughts.

"Ron," she said as soon as he answered. "You need to hear what Clara remembers. She's connected Miller to Ray Ho."

She waited through his pause, imagining this as hard for him to believe as it had been for her.

"How? What's the connection?"

Olivia's hands tightened on the steering wheel. "Miller was with Ray Ho and another guy when he shot her twenty years ago."

"Really? She knew Ray Ho?"

She snorted. "You're gonna love this. She worked as a junior staff writer for the Beaumont Foundation. And she saw Ray Ho with the Ghost."

"Back up. She knew the Ghost?"

The gate opened, and she drove up toward the guesthouse. "I doubt she met the real one. Wait, have I told you the Ghost has used a body double? Anyway, Clara remembers the Chinese man, Ray Ho, with Ms. Beaumont."

"I know about her body double. We picked her up when the Ghost was arrested. I'm not sure if any charges have been filed yet against her. And you're now saying Clara remembers Ray Ho mingling with the Ghost."

"That's right."

"Okay, but that was twenty years ago. How does that tie into Faith's case?"

"I don't know yet. Let me connect a few more dots."

"Okay, keep me posted."

"By the way it appears, everything is connected. Assaulting Clara, kidnapping and abducting Faith, even attempting murder twenty years ago. Any chance you can finagle your way into making it your team's case?"

"As if I don't have enough to do."

"Wait till you hear this. Clara has been researching Linda Boroski's case. She's been talking to people. Would it be too far-fetched to think she rattled some cages? And some people might want to silence her forever."

"What do you propose?"

"We caught Dr. Hill at the scene. I can discreetly see if she has any connection to the Ghost or Miller."

"By discreet, you mean—never mind. I don't want to know."

She took that to mean yes and ended the call. The connections were there. She just needed to tie the threads together. She exited the car, heading to see Eva so she could confirm a few things with her.

Olivia entered the guesthouse's spacious sitting room and approached Eva seated by a window overlooking the gardens. Eva seemed right at home in the luxury, her posture relaxed, her eyes bright.

"Olivia! It's good to see you. What brings you by?"

Olivia took a seat opposite Eva. "You look well, considering everything you've been through, but how are you recovering?"

Eva smiled. "I'm doing good, actually. I could have gone home, but Ms. Carol insisted I stay here. The guesthouse is nothing short of fancy, and I can't say I mind the pampering."

"That's good to hear." Olivia crossed her legs and rested her hands on her lap. "In case you haven't heard, Clara started remembering her past. But there's still something I need to understand. You first thought of the trafficking connection. What made you think of that? What led you there? Lily mentioned something about a journal."

Eva's smile faltered, and she ducked her head, her fingers playing with a linen napkin on the coffee table.

"Eva?" Olivia prompted, leaning forward. "What is it?"

After a silence, Eva exhaled. "Aunt Clara kept a journal. Mom went to her apartment to collect all her stuff. My grandparents couldn't bring themselves to do it. Anyway, when I was older and searching for clues, I found it. It has… information that makes the connection quite clear."

Olivia's eyebrows shot up. "What does it say? Why didn't you mention it?"

Her shoulders sagging, Eva picked up the napkin, laid it on her knee, and plied her fingers across it, ironing the linen flat, then creasing it. "I wasn't sure how to handle it. It's personal— her private thoughts, her fears, her pain. But it also has details and connections. I didn't say anything because I didn't think it was relevant."

Olivia scooted back. "Eva, it's relevant now. We need to see it. With Clara's consent, of course. It could be the key to this whole mystery."

Eva tossed the napkin back to the coffee table. "I'll talk to Clara, make sure she's comfortable with it. I just wanted to protect her, you know?"

"I understand." Olivia placed a reassuring hand on Eva's arm. "We'll handle it with care. But we need to follow this lead. We owe it to Clara and everyone involved."

Eva excused herself and sat alone in her room at the guesthouse. The journal, Clara's private thoughts and fears, lay hidden in a drawer, evidence that could change everything. As an FBI agent,

Eva knew its importance, the urgency of sharing it. But her promise to Uncle Bill, the trust she had with Clara—it all tangled up inside her.

She reached for her phone, her fingers hovering over Clara's contact. Uncle Bill's words echoed in her mind, his stern warning not to reveal anything about him. She wasn't going to, but the journal was different.

She dialed Clara's number.

"Hi, dear!" Clara's concerned voice came through. "I'm so sorry I didn't remember you."

"It's not your fault. I'm so glad your memories came back, but"—a deep breath helped her push the rest out—"I need to talk to you about something. I found your journal. The one you used to write in."

Clara gasped. "Oh! I remember I used to keep a journal. You have it?"

Eva caressed the journal cover, her heart pounding. "It's here with me. And it has information, connections pertinent to the case."

Silence settled, a moment stretching out.

"Well, it's best you share it with the police and the FBI."

Eva exhaled her relief. "I wanted to ask for your consent first. I understand it's personal, private. But it could be vital to finding the truth."

"I appreciate you checking with me. I'd like it back when they're finished with it. But I think they need to read it."

"Thank you."

They talked a little more, words of encouragement and love exchanged before they hung up. Eva felt lighter, the burden lifted, the path ahead clear.

She retrieved the journal from its hiding place, holding it reverently, understanding its significance. Then, journal in hand, she returned to the sitting room where Olivia was waiting.

Olivia looked up, her eyes widening. "Is that…?"

"It's Clara's journal. She gave her consent."

"Thank you, Eva. This could be what we need." Olivia took it carefully, then placed it in an evidence pouch.

It was the right thing to do. For Clara, for justice, for the truth.

In her mind's eye, she saw Clara's last journal entry.

Dear Journal,

Tonight, Linda and I are going to a party, but I find myself preoccupied with thoughts so distant from celebrations and social gatherings. Since the warning from Officer Bill, I've been on edge. It's a strange sensation, as if eyes are watching me, even when I'm alone. Perhaps I'm imagining it, but something deep inside keeps nagging me, insisting I'm not overthinking this.

I've dug into this Ray Ho character. Connections to criminal activities, reports of violence—I never thought I'd find myself tangled in something like this. Weeks ago, these were matters I'd only read about in newspapers or watched in movies. Now, they feel frighteningly close.

I can't help but wonder if I'll see Officer Bill again. He seemed concerned, and I trust his instincts. If I do see him, I'll turn over my notes to him. Perhaps he can make sense of them. But part of me can't understand why I'd be in danger. I only overheard a conversation between Ray Ho and Ms. Beaumont, just a fleeting moment in time, and yet it seems to have set something in motion I can't grasp.

As I write this, I glance at my reflection in the mirror, my makeup done, my dress chosen. I'm ready for the party—

on the outside. Inside, I'm a whirlwind of confusion and anxiety. Linda has been a true friend, standing by me, but I haven't told her everything. How could I? It all seems so surreal.

I need to put these thoughts aside for now. The party awaits, and Linda will be back soon. I'll try to enjoy the evening, to lose myself in laughter and music. But I know these questions will linger, shadows at the edge of my mind.

I'll write again when I can.
Clara

Soon after Olivia left, Kyle showed up, and Eva buzzed him through the gate. "Guess I'm popular today."

Moments later, he walked in carrying an object that made her heart skip a beat—her own phone, a tangible connection to her old life. He waved it. "I thought you'd want this back."

"Thanks, Kyle." She took it, her fingers navigating the familiar screen. An unread message caught her eye. Uncle Bill. She wouldn't read it while Kyle was visiting. "You didn't come here just to bring me this, did you?"

He shrugged. "Has Lily been by to visit?"

"No, but she called. She doesn't come unless Dylan is here." Oh. Oops. She touched his arm. "Have you told her how you feel?"

Closing his eyes, Kyle rubbed the bridge of his nose. "She works with him. And they've been sleuthing together."

"Has she put you in the friend zone?"

"Technically, we're all just friends."

"Well then, I suppose you can make a move. Christmas is coming. Have you shopped for her yet?"

"That's where I need your advice. What should I get her?"

They brainstormed before Kyle got a text alert and had to leave.

Then Eva read Uncle Bill's cryptic message, such classic Uncle Bill—veiled and filled with caution. His role in her life had always been shadowy, his presence a constant undercurrent. She hit the call button.

"How are you, kid?" he asked, his voice a distant echo from the past. The conversation flowed smoothly, filled with the coded language they perfected over the years. He implored her not to mention him to anyone, to keep him in the background, to ensure his safety.

"Clara wasn't trafficked," she blurted out. "We've found her. And Ray Ho? We've captured him!"

There was silence on the other end, then a deep sigh. "Even so, Eva. I need to stay off the radar. For your safety, for mine."

When she disconnected, confusion threaded through her thoughts. But she trusted Uncle Bill, and if he insisted, she'd comply.

They said that bad things came in threes. *Visitors come in threes for me.* Later in the afternoon, Agent Peters arrived.

"How are you feeling?" Ron asked.

"I'm doing much better. Thank you, sir." Although unease twinged her at his thoughtful expression.

"There's something I need to ask you." He leaned forward, his forearms resting on his knees. "I've heard you mention an Uncle Bill. Who is he?"

As the question hung in the air, Eva found herself caught between the truth and her recent pledge of secrecy. She took a deep breath. "Uncle Bill—he's a family friend. Someone I've known since I was a child."

"And his last name?"

"I–I'm not sure. At family gatherings, he was always just Uncle Bill."

They locked gazes. Then Ron rose. "All right, Eva. Rest up. I'll see you soon."

Alone with her thoughts, she shivered. Why couldn't she shake the feeling she somehow disappointed Agent Peters?

Didn't matter. No matter what, she couldn't betray Uncle Bill's trust.

Olivia settled across the table, having come to the Federal Detention Center to update the Ghost.

"Olivia," the Ghost drawled, her voice echoing in the cramped space. "So, how's the weather outside?"

The banality of the question seemed to amplify the seriousness of their impending conversation.

"Pretty clear skies," Olivia retorted, matching her humor. "In fact, we managed to get rid of a troublesome cloud."

"Oh?" The Ghost raised an eyebrow, playing along.

"We captured Ray Ho."

The Ghost's demeanor remained unchanged. "A troublesome cloud indeed. And what do you plan to do with him?"

"Well," Olivia shrugged, "you know, the usual. It's up to the attorneys. But we've got a lovely spot picked out for him. He'll be in a detention center until the powers that be decide where to send him. And you'll be going to the Mirror Estate grounds soon. I've told you they were checking into it, but now, they're drawing up plans to retrofit the old orphanage into a secure facility."

"That's good." A smile twisted the Ghost's usually flatlined lips. Just what was she up to?

After the meeting, Olivia headed back to the task force office. It was late in the day. Not many people were around. She settled into a chair at an empty desk to research Dr. Hill, the woman who tried to kill Clara. If the doctor were somehow connected to Miller or Ho, Olivia would find it.

Hmm… The woman had divorced and received a substantial settlement. She noted the attorney's name, Skip Hunter.

She glanced around, ensuring no one was paying any attention. Then she transitioned from the normal database queries to the internet's shadier corners, bypassing firewalls and slipping through security protocols.

"Find anything interesting?" Simon spoke from behind her, making her jump.

She switched the window. "I didn't know you were coming in. Thought you were going to check with the police about Lily's mugging the other night."

"I had a meeting with Cunningham's law firm. Just stopped by to see if you'd be here. And I did. It's nothing. The guy has a rap sheet. Sexual assault. I'm thinking that's what he was trying to do."

It very well could be random, but she'd make sure once this was over. "Well, hopefully, you feel better about her training with me."

His warm hand rested on her shoulder. "I guess so. It does come in handy. So, what are you doing?"

"Looking into Dr. Hill's background. Trying to make sense of what happened."

"What'd you find?"

"Nothing yet. Will let you know, though."

He squeezed her shoulder. "I'm heading out. See you later."

"Okay." She waited for a beat before clicking the hacked window. Dr. Hill's online "locked" diary now bared before her, the secret thoughts and musings of a woman spiraling into madness.

Delusions and an obsession with Michael Khoury crammed her last weeks. One entry detailed a series of misconstrued encounters to justify "getting rid" of Clara. She even chronicled how she "ran into" Clara that day and slipped something in her coffee. She then suggested to Clara she needed to jump off the building. When that failed, she put fentanyl-laced pills in a bottle of pain meds and slid it into Clara's purse.

"So that's it." The attacks were because of a woman's delusions and had nothing to do with the attempted murder twenty years ago or Ho or Miller. She'd let the detective in charge know. Then she sucked in a sharp breath. The dates on these entries. How odd. Their time stamps were much later than the posts were supposed to have been written.

CHAPTER 50

CLARA & OLIVIA

They'd canceled their planned Christmas party for the previous weekend. Was that her fault? Clara shifted on her desk chair. Ms. Marino invited them to Mirror Estate for a Christmas celebration. Michael's family didn't celebrate Christmas, but they always had a get-together during that time. Clara, Michael, and the children would always attend Mass as a family, then visit his folks. And then the big moment was tomorrow. She would go see her parents. Eva promised she hadn't revealed anything and made sure they weren't out of town. She'd go with them to lead the way since Clara's dad's health wasn't that good and something so shocking would need a little cushioning.

Clara's phone rang, jolting her out of her reverie. She glanced at the screen. Professor Evans.

"Hello, is this Clara? I'm sorry to—"

His voice brought a rush of memories, filling in yet another piece of the puzzle that was her past.

"Professor Evans! I remember you now." She laughed,

almost clapping. "Thank you for calling. And please, no apologies are necessary. How can I help you?"

"Uh, oh, well, Clara, my dear, you see, my wife insisted I finally clean out some of my 'junk,' as she calls it. And I came across a research paper by Clara Wu. I thought you might like to know the student I thought you resembled was indeed Clara Wu."

A chill ran down Clara's spine. Excitement or trepidation? Maybe both. "Yes, Professor, that's me. I'm Clara Wu. I lost my memories due to a brain trauma." No reason to mention the gunshot. "But I've since remembered. I remember you quite well."

After a stunned silence on his end, he exclaimed, "My goodness, Clara! This is astonishing news! I can't begin to express how pleased I am. But what a journey you must have been on."

They fell into a comfortable conversation, catching up on each other's lives and reminiscing about the university. With Professor Evans as engaging and insightful as she now remembered, she found herself relaxing in the conversation.

The professor's genuine interest in her well-being was a balm to her troubled soul. As they chatted, she savored a sense of connection to her past, a reminder of who she'd been and the path she'd taken to become who she was now.

Eventually, they wound down the conversation.

"Merry Christmas, Clara," Professor Evans said. "I'm grateful to have reconnected with you. Please don't hesitate to reach out if you ever need anything."

"Merry Christmas to you too, Professor, and thank you. This call has meant more to me than you can imagine."

Now would seeing her parents be as smooth as reconnecting with Professor Evans?

The low hum of conversation punctuated by the occasional clatter of a coffee mug or a ringing phone offered a steady constant in the task force office where a team of agents and consultants gathered.

Olivia cleared her throat, commanding attention. "Eva has turned over Clara Khoury nee Wu's journal. It appears there's a connection between Clara's assault case, Linda Boroski's murder, and Faith Khoury's recent abduction."

She clicked the remote, and Miller's picture popped up on the screen. "Ben Miller, our primary suspect, is believed to have either killed Linda Boroski or helped cover up her murder."

After Olivia shared the full details, Tanner took the remote and flipped to the whiteboard where everything was listed. "Are you thinking Ben contacted Ho to kidnap Faith? Because he feared Clara's digging into Linda's case would expose him? Seems convoluted. Faith wasn't even born yet. Why target her? Why not silence Clara instead?"

"Wait." Ana held up a hand. "Maybe he did. Didn't Clara have multiple attempts on her life? Maybe he orchestrated those."

Simon crossed the room to stand by Olivia, his presence warming her. "I thought the woman was deranged. I heard Clara and you talking last night."

Olivia stiffened to keep from leaning into him. When would they get some time alone, just the two of them and no cases on their minds? "Yes, but two things are still bugging me."

"Let's hear them," Ron said.

"First, the time stamps don't match up with the entries. Second, her divorce attorney."

Ana shuffled her notes, her bobbed hair curving into her tanned cheeks. "What about the lawyer?"

Before Olivia could answer, Tanner asked, "What's the lawyer's name?"

"Skip Hunter," Olivia said. "Well, the timing is suspicious.

According to Clara, as soon as she got permission to do the piece, Skip Hunter was her first interview. He was Linda's new boyfriend."

"Wow." Hernandez tapped the keyboard. "What a coincidence."

"I don't like coincidences," Olivia said, even as Ron said that he didn't believe in coincidences.

"Speaking of coincidences." Tanner grabbed the file he dropped on his desk. "Guess who is Ben Miller's attorney? I've been keeping tabs on that case since they all appear to be connected."

Everyone, including Hernandez and Simon, went quiet and looked at each other processing the implications.

Ron stepped back a few feet and sat on his desk. "Now, that's one too many coincidences."

"Okay, let's try this." Ana slapped her notebook down on her desk and paced. "According to Clara, Ben and another male were at the murder scene. And there was a third guy with Ben and Ray Ho during her shooting at the Outer Banks. Could this attorney be the other male?"

Olivia's pulse quickened. They were close to a breakthrough. She could feel it. "He could very well be—"

"But it's all conjecture right now. We need proof," Ron said.

"Right, so Hunter and the doc." She drummed her fingers on the giant monitor stand. "I think we follow the money. See if we can find anything there. Maybe he paid her to be the patsy or conned her to take the fall. And we need to find the connection between Hunter and Ben twenty years ago. Confirm if they knew each other then."

"I have an idea." Ron crossed his arms, lifting one foot off the ground as he adjusted his seat on the desk. "We'll send Dylan and Kyle to talk to Chase and see if the boy knows Hunter."

Kyle had been quiet until now. He cleared his throat. "Dylan is not an agent."

"Yeah, but he has a rapport with the boy." Ron's gaze softened on his son.

"Yes, sir."

"Ana, any update?" Ron asked.

She pointed her pen toward Hernandez. "I think he's got something to share."

The junior agent straightened as if at attention. "According to the trackers Olivia planted, there has been no movement from our O'Shea. Which doesn't add up."

"What if he found the trackers?" Kyle suggested.

Olivia shook her head. "If he found them, he'd have led us on a wild goose chase, put it on a different vehicle to throw us off. More likely, he's changed vehicles, maybe even clothes. It strengthens my suspicion he's a trained operative. He knows the game too well."

"It takes one to know one." Simon patted her shoulder. "Phoenix is a legend in the intelligence community, I heard."

"She is!"

Everyone in the room knew Olivia was Phoenix. And yes, not too long ago, she'd been in the thick of things. "Thanks for the confidence. Let's check the cameras around the area where he was last seen. I suspect we'll spot him in a different vehicle or on foot with different clothing."

"Let's get to work." Ron gathered up his papers.

CHAPTER 51

KYLE

Kyle leaned against Dylan's car in the high school parking lot. Eight years since he graduated high school, he already felt out of place. The teenage angst and euphoria couldn't be further from his adult world of criminal investigations.

Since they were hoping to talk to the teen without his parents hovering, they opted to wait here. With this being the last day of school before Christmas break, they wouldn't get another shot like this for weeks. Good thing the teen was eighteen, so legally they could talk to him without his parents present.

"Here he comes." Dylan nodded toward a tall teenager in the crowd. Chase, that was his name, and judging by his casual fist bump with Dylan, they were already buddies.

"Faith's back safe. So, what else do you need to know?" Chase frowned and only now seemed to notice Kyle. "And who's this?"

"This is my friend"—Dylan smirked—"*very* Special Agent Kyle Peters."

"Agent?" Chase crossed his arms and flicked his light-brown bangs out of his eyes. "What now?"

"Just a few questions." Kyle jerked a thumb toward the coffee shop across the street. "How about we continue this over some coffee?"

The teen rolled his eyes. "Sure."

Well, that didn't sound enthusiastic.

"Where's your girlfriend?"

At the teen's question, Dylan held up both hands. "Lily isn't technically my girlfriend. We just hang together."

"Oh, cool. I like her."

"We do too," Dylan said as they crossed the street. Soon enough, they were huddled in a cozy booth, inhaling air moist with the comforting aroma of freshly brewed coffee and baked goods.

Chase spread his arm across the empty chair beside him, his long legs splayed out. "What do you need to know now?"

"Don't you want to order something first?" Dylan stood beside the table. "I'm buying."

"In that case, I'll take two chocolate chip muffins and a latte, please."

Since Kyle didn't want anything, Dylan went to place the order. Were Dylan and Lily becoming a thing? They worked together. Whereas, Kyle could only see Lily once or twice a week *if* their schedules worked out. And then it was like a group outing. Come to think of it, he hadn't had a proper date with Lily. It was always a group thing, or they were running for their lives. Then again, she never said the dreaded "let's be friends." Yet.

Dylan returned with the muffins.

While they waited for their coffee, Kyle slid his phone across the table, displaying a photo. "Ever seen this guy?"

Chase tipped the screen against a glare, his eyes narrowing. "Yeah, that's Uncle Skip."

"Uncle Skip?" Kyle probed. "As in relative?"

"No, he's a close friend of my dad. They go way back. Why? What's this about?"

"Nothing that concerns you," Kyle said.

The teen looked from one to the other again. "Okay, give it to me straight. What's going on? Dad's been talking to Uncle Skip and other lawyers. Two cops showed up the other night."

"Your parents will explain when they're ready," Dylan said.

Chase shrugged, then scarfed his muffins. He pushed from his chair as he slugged his drink. "If there's nothing else, I have to go. Thanks for the snack, dude."

"Anytime." Dylan stood as well, then gestured to the empty table in front of Kyle. "You're done too, right?"

Kyle almost rolled his eyes like the teen. Sometimes Dylan drove a guy to it. He followed his friend back across the street. Dylan had insisted on driving. Kyle hopped in the passenger seat.

"You all right?" Dylan asked.

"Yeah. Now we've got the connection between Hunter and Miller."

"If you say so." Dylan started the car.

"I hear Lily is going to work in the office in the new year."

"That's what I heard too. Marketing, I think."

"You'll be working together."

"Not really. I'm in development. But we have lunch together with Tommy. Unless he's got a lunch date. Or unless I have a meeting. You should join us if your schedule allows."

Lunch every day? That'd be tough to compete with. "Maybe I will."

CHAPTER 52

CLARA, MICHAEL, & OLIVIA

lara stood in the kitchen, the sizzle of sautéing garlic and onions steaming the air. She was focused on chopping vegetables when the doorbell rang. Her movements stilled, her grip on the knife tightening. Since the attacks, she'd become cautious, even suspicious of unexpected visitors. She reached for her phone to check the doorbell camera feed. On the screen was an older man, well dressed in a tailored suit, his expression serious but benign.

Michael came in through the garage, setting down his bag and loosening his tie. He picked up the pace and moved to her side. "Hon? What's wrong?"

She passed over the phone, and he leaned in to kiss her hair. "All good." Then he moved off to let the gentleman in. "Clara, I'd like you to meet Todd Zimmerman, my attorney."

"Pleasure to meet you, Clara." Todd extended his hand with a warm smile.

"The pleasure is mine." She drew her hand back after a quick shake, still on edge. "Please sit. Anything to drink?"

"I'm good, thanks. I won't be long. I wanted to deliver the good news in person." Todd moved to the waterfall island separating the kitchen from the living and dining areas, pulled out a folder from his leather briefcase, and laid it on the marbled counter. "The police have decided not to charge you, Michael. It appears Dr. Hill is now their primary suspect for the recent attacks."

A loud exhale escaped Michael's lips as Clara's tension subsided. She switched off the burner and slid her arms around her husband's waist. "That—why, that's fantastic news."

"It is." Todd patted the folder. "I'm going to leave these documents with you. They're my investigator's reports. These are your copies."

After Zimmerman left, Michael went to get the mail. On his way back inside, he flicked through the usual junk mail, pausing at a legal-sized envelope addressed to him with no return address. It wasn't even stamped. Strange. He opened the flap and shook out the single item inside—a flash drive.

Clara was once again preparing dinner, so he sat, got his laptop out of his bag, plugged the drive in, and opened the audio files. The first one was dated December 12. Ben Miller spoke to an unfamiliar male voice.

"Whose phone is this? Where's your burner?" asked the stranger.

"It's a nurse's. I'm at the hospital," Ben said. "She's alive. It was like seeing a ghost last night. Crazy thing is she has no memory of what happened."

"That might change. And she's been digging."

"What do we do?"

"Nothing." Click.

The next file was dated December 13. The same two voices were on the recording.

"She keeps dodging my call and won't accept the trial invitation," Ben said.

"I thought you said there were no such trial."

"But I was going to—"

"Hush. Don't say that on an open line," the stranger paused. "But don't worry. Everything is under control."

"What do you mean?"

"Your girlfriend is our perfect patsy. I've prepared her. She thinks you want this—she's right too. She'll write these mad journal entries about Khoury, take care of the nosy wife... The cops will write her off as a loon. I'll plead insanity for her. Easy and over."

Michael's stomach churned at the plot against his wife. Dr. Hill must've been Ben's girlfriend. They were afraid of Clara's recovering her memory. So somehow, they'd been involved in Clara's getting shot so many years ago.

"Play that again," Clara said.

Caught off guard, he paused the audio. "Sorry, I didn't know you were listening. We don't know—"

"I need to hear the voice again. Just play it."

Michael replayed the section, letting that disembodied tone spill from the laptop speakers.

"I know who that is," Clara said.

"You do?" Maybe they would get some answers.

"We need to call Olivia. Right now. She'll know how to handle this."

Clara's call left Olivia's mind racing as she steered through the winding roads. "Call Simon," she ordered her hands-free device. "Hey, hon." She spoke when he answered. "I'll be home late. Why don't you and Lily grab dinner without me?"

Once Simon acknowledged, she called Ron. "I'm headed to the Khoury residence. Can you meet me there? Something's come up—big."

"I'm on it."

After she parked in the Khourys' well-manicured driveway, she almost sprinted to the front door. It swung open before she knocked, and Michael ushered her inside. Ron arrived minutes later and wasted no time.

"Okay." He clapped his hands together in his signature gesture. "Let's hear it."

After the audio, Ron let out a low whistle. "What do you know. Your hunch was right, Olivia."

"Sometimes I don't want to be right." Her shoulders slumped, heavy with the weight of the implications.

Apparently, Ron knew how that felt. He rubbed the back of his neck. "So, Michael, this is Ben Miller?"

"Definitely."

"And the other voice? Clara? Any ideas?" Ron prompted.

"It's Skip Hunter." An underlying layer of emotion Olivia couldn't quite place tinted Clara's flat voice. Perhaps it was triumph or perhaps fear. "I'm sure of it. I interviewed him for Linda's story. Listen for yourself." She tapped her phone, and the recordings played.

"Wow." Olivia nodded. "You've got a good ear, my friend— good memory too. I agree. The voices sounded alike."

"I'll have the lab do the voice comparison. If it's a match, we're good." Ron then held up a hand. "But where'd you get the recordings?"

"Um." Michael cleared his throat. "It was in the mailbox." He picked up the envelope and held it toward Ron. "This is the envelope."

Ron pulled out a pair of gloves and took the envelope.

"You're the only one who handled it? If so, maybe we'll get some prints. And we'll need the drive too."

"Wait. You have a doorbell camera, right?" Olivia asked. "Can you check?"

"Clara didn't touch the package or drive. As for a camera, I don't think it points to the mailbox." Michael fished out his phone. "Let me see."

They watched a replay of his car pulling into the garage and another car pulling into the driveway. Fast-forwarded to the attorney leaving. Michael was right. The mailbox was out of range.

Once outside after saying their goodbyes, Olivia stopped Ron with a hand on his sleeve. "The file is date stamped. You can pull the phone records and verify the call. I don't suppose either would be recording the conversation if they were using burners. Chances are one of them was on a landline."

"We get the voices verified. Then we can get a warrant for the records for their phones."

CHAPTER 53

THE GHOST & OLIVIA

Marge Beaumont, aka the Ghost, sat in the visiting room's sterilized bleakness, waiting for Olivia. Usually, she'd only be brought in when the visitor was already there. But Olivia had called ahead. Now the woman kept her waiting.

Other than Phoenix, Marge's obsession was to avenge Jade's death. Jade had been loyal. Apparently, two agents had been on the scene of her demise—Ron Peters and Ana Ruiz. Peters was an old nemesis. But Ruiz? She was a new name. Rook was now digging into Ruiz's past for any information to aid the quest for retribution.

What would be the best course for revenge? Swift and final or prolonged, a testament to the torment Marge endured from Jade's loss?

The soft grating of the door opening broke in.

"I apologize." Olivia crossed the room. "Got held up in traffic."

Marge shrugged. "As if I had a better place to be."

"Good news for you. The AG has signed off on the deal. So, it's now official. Plans are drawn. Work will begin soon."

This was nothing new. Koenig wouldn't dare defy her. Ah, the waiting!

Olivia slid some papers toward her. "Here's the signed agreement. Your copy. I want to point out the security clause. No exceptions will be made for the monitor. It will be mandatory."

An ankle monitor and other security measures didn't concern Marge. Arrangements were already in motion. She had people doing her bidding.

After a lengthy pause came the perfect time to say, "I'd like to see Dylan."

Olivia blinked, probably wondering why and what game she was playing. "Why?"

Yep. The woman was easy to read. "He's my nephew. Isn't that a good enough reason?"

"Whom you tried to kill."

Marge would never kill Dylan before he told her everything about the hidden treasures, if they existed, and where they were buried. But nobody needed to know that. "It was all a misunderstanding."

"I'm not sure if that's how Dylan sees it."

"Well, would you ask?"

"I'll see what I can do."

After her meeting, Olivia returned to the office to update the team. She stood near the main desk, her arms crossed as she faced Ron and his team. Tanner and Ana were on a video call while Hernandez was huddled over a computer.

"So, the Ghost wants to see Dylan," Ron repeated.

"Yeah." Olivia nodded. "And Dylan should consider it. Better to know what she's planning upfront."

"I doubt he'd want to see her. Remember she wanted to kill him. Pointed a gun at him."

"Maybe, but I have a feeling he'll do it. He can get a read on her. It's the best way to get inside her head."

"Boss, you're gonna want to hear this." Tanner beckoned, the video call evidently over.

"We've been in touch with our counterparts in Hong Kong and southern China." Ana rolled her chair back from her desk, her perky bob feathering her tanned cheeks. "They've been on a rampage seizing Ray Ho's properties, from residences to offices."

"And?" Ron asked.

Ana smiled. "And they've found something—"

"Big," Tanner finished.

"Miller has been supplying him with girls and boys for years."

Uncrossing her arms, Olivia clenched her fists, her pulse quickening. "What did they find?"

"Hernandez, beam it up," Tanner told the junior agent, also a tech wizard.

Documents lit up on the big screen. The first one looked like some sort of record.

Tanner pointed to a spot. "It appears this criminal keeps immaculate records of his suppliers and customers. Look here. Olivia, you'll need to confirm. But our contact said this one was the Chinese version of Ben Miller's name."

Olivia stepped closer. "The Chinese characters literally say 'American doctor.' We'll need stronger evidence to support that."

"Here's a case of the right hand not knowing what the left hand is doing. Our counterparts have a wiretap on all Ho's phones." Ana tucked her hair behind her ears. "And a phone call logged on the fourteenth is very interesting. Hernandez, please do the honor."

Voices from the audio file boomed over the speaker.

"Impossible." That must be Ray Ho's voice, given his accent.

"I saw her. She is alive. See for yourself. I took a photo of her." Ben Miller's voice. "She doesn't remember anything."

"There you go. Problem solved."

"But she's been digging in the past. We can take care of her once and for all, but we'd need your help." There was a pause. "She's got a daughter, though. Beautiful, Middle Eastern look. Do you have a market for her? I'm sending you a photo. If we can get her to you, will you mark us as even?"

"Okay, wait for my text."

She looked to the side. "It appears Miller was telling Ho Clara was alive. Does that mean he was asking him to get rid of her?"

"You know, he said 'if we can' and 'mark us.'" Ron tapped the speaker. "He might've been trying to pay his and Hunter's debt to Ho. Here's my take. He or Hunter asked Ho for help twenty years ago. And they've been in his debt all this time. Perhaps they pay by supplying young girls and boys to Ho. Then he does the dirty work for Hunter. And this time, Miller was hoping to give him Faith if Ho would wipe their debt clean."

"But it appears Miller has been supplying Ho with girls and boys all these years. You'd think their debt would be paid off." Olivia frowned. "Though, of course, once you're involved in that racket, you never get out, do you? It's always 'just one more' like blackmail. If all the kids he'd abducted in the past hadn't freed him from his debt, adding one more wouldn't. Seems we're still missing something."

"Maybe I can help. Maybe he truly had gotten free of that, and this debt had nothing to do with the other kids?" Hernandez tapped a key to send an image to the screen. "You're looking at the ledger. It appears Miller borrowed fifty grand from Ho some years ago. With their outrageous interest, he now owes him more than half a mil."

"Hmm, that might account for the debt he wanted wiped

out." Olivia drummed her fingers on Hernandez's desk, then held up a finger, raising her point. "There's still personal vendetta here—I mean, yes, they also wanted to keep Clara distracted until they figured out how to 'handle' her."

"So you're saying Miller and Hunter wanted to torture Clara for coming back into their lives."

She raised both hands now. "What better way than torturing her daughter? Miller getting his debt wiped out with Ho must've been a side benefit."

"Maybe." Ron rocked back in his chair. "All we can do is speculate at this point. Anyone know if Deanna found any prints from the envelope the Khourys received?"

"Nothing. Everything is clean. Even the drive." Tanner hung up the phone. "That was her on the line. You can always attribute it to an anonymous tip."

Yes, but it was probably the work of the attorney's investigator. However, due to ethical concerns, the attorney couldn't publicly give this kind of information to Michael without risking the Bar Association punishment. After all, it appeared right after the attorney left. But it was all circumstantial, and she could live with that.

Ana raised her hand like she was in school. "So, what about the Ghost wanting to meet with Dylan?"

"I'll ask him," Ron said.

Olivia stifled a yawn. "If there's nothing else, I'm heading home."

Just why would the Ghost want a face-to-face with Dylan?

CHAPTER 54

LILY

Lily sat at her new desk. Finally, the rotation was over, and the real job was beginning. This week, she was shadowing the person she would be replacing. She'd have next week off for Christmas. Then she'd start her new job after the new year. Marketing/sales wasn't like what she used to do back in Hong Kong as a glorified secretary. Here, she would be doing big-girl work.

Her phone buzzed, Kyle's contact flashing. She swiped to answer. "Hey, what's up?"

"Are you ready to leave yet? Do you want to grab dinner together?"

She opened her mouth to suggest getting Dylan to go along but then closed it. "Sure. Should we meet somewhere?"

"Want me to come pick you up?"

"Nah, I have my car here. No sense driving me back to get it."

Did she imagine he sounded disappointed? If he was, he recovered enough to make plans to meet her at an Italian restaurant close to her house. She started for the door, then paused to let her parents know in their group text that she wasn't going to be home for dinner.

Twenty minutes later, she parked and got out. Then the hair on her nape stood on end. After her ordeal months ago, she'd experienced PTSD—she couldn't go anywhere alone, and she needed people she was comfortable with. However, it had faded.

So, why was she feeling so strange? Like she was being watched. Dylan once told her he felt like that when he first got to the Mirror Estate. Was she getting paranoid?

She took a deep breath and turned around, ready to face anything, but there was nothing to see, just cars and trees. Maybe she needed another talk with Fr. Phil. He had helped her so much in coping with PTSD. And she thought she was over it. Could the incident at the convenience store stir up something?

"Lily." Kyle startled her. "What's the matter?"

She shook her head. "Nothing. Thought I heard something."

"Let's go in." He took her arm and led her into the restaurant. The hostess settled them at a table by the window and left them with menus.

When Lily looked up from her menu, she tensed. "Kyle, you see that man in the blue shirt? At the bar? I remember seeing him back at the hotel. He was sitting there in the lobby."

Kyle's body didn't move, but his eyes did. "You work at the concierge desk. You must have seen lots of people coming and going. Besides, it's not a crime to be at a hotel. He might have been waiting for someone and had time to kill. It's probably a coincidence."

"My mom doesn't like coincidences."

"Dad doesn't believe in coincidences either. For all we know, he's a tourist and likes Italian. Isn't this one of the restaurants you guys would recommend to tourists?"

She took another glance at the guy. She'd let it rest for now. However, she would keep an eye out for him. Her mom told her to trust her instincts. "Yes, it's in a lot of brochures."

"Let's enjoy our dinner and forget about the tourist."

CHAPTER 55

RON & EVA

Ron scratched a bug bite beside his jaw. Only a few days before Christmas. You'd think the buggers would let up for the holidays at least. Speaking of letting up for the holidays, could he actually tie up all loose ends and send his team home early this year? Ana complained about last-minute shopping. Tanner said his folks were coming into town. These people worked hard and deserved to celebrate the holidays.

"All right, people." Ron spoke to the group he'd once again gathered in the squad room, all stood in front of the big screen except Eva, still on medical leave, and Simon who didn't see a reason to be present. "Olivia, why don't you get us started on Ray Ho?"

"Sure." Olivia sauntered closer to the screen. "His case is wrapped up. We've got witnesses, we've got evidence seized from his properties in Hong Kong and southern China, and best of all, we've got John Liu ratting him out. Detective Kwok is happy. She's been trying to nab Liu and Ho for a long time."

When Faith's face appeared on the screen, Tanner picked up

the remote. "Let's start with Faith's abduction. Initially, it wasn't our case. But we picked it up once the kidnapping unit notified us of the Liu connection. Eva did a good job saving her and subduing Ho."

"Moving on." Olivia picked up the narrative. "When Clara began digging into Linda Boroski's murder, it brought her to Skip Hunter. Can you imagine that? A woman he thought dead came to see him, and he put on a great show. Didn't even blink. Of course, she didn't remember anything then."

Ana sat on the corner of a desk. "And Hunter started plotting her murder then?"

Ron's index finger twitched to the bite again. The anti-itch cream hadn't helped. He crossed his arms to keep from tearing into the welt.

"I think so." She took the remote from Tanner and flipped to show the slides in sequence. "Clara's first incident at the rooftop was right after she visited Hunter. As for Miller, he called Hunter after he saw Clara in real life. Now this is based on our discussion. When Hunter didn't seem that concerned or maybe he just didn't want to say it on the phone—that's based on the audio file —Miller figured he could kill two birds with one stone. You know, canceling his mounting debt and exacting vengeance on Clara. He might have even been hoping he could stop supplying girls and boys after cleaning up Ho's mess on this. Though I doubt Ho would ever let him out."

"There are some merits to that." Hernandez fiddled with the keyboard. "Payments to the kidnappers traced back to Miller. Those two idiots only received ten grand each for their trouble."

"Those guys aren't pro. If Miller had hired pros, it would have cost him a lot more."

Okay, things really were wrapping up. Maybe they would get to walk out of here today and for the holidays. Ron exhaled. "So far, we tied Miller and Hunter and, of course, the woman doc to

Clara's recent attacks. Miller and Ho? We have the audio files. Anything else?"

"Yeah." Ana shifted, bouncing the leg she'd dangled off the side of the desk. "Ho's records, financial and otherwise, all link Miller to Ho."

Ron scratched a square around the heated area of the bite. "Linda's case isn't our jurisdiction, but do we know if Hunter or Miller was the killer? And was Hunter the other male Clara recalled?"

Olivia took that one. "Now that Clara has had time to think about it, she believes it was Hunter. She says it sounded like it was an accident. They could have been fooling around or arguing, and Hunter pushed her. But Ho wanted to kill Clara because they recognized each other. He couldn't let her tell others his life in the underworld."

"Don't forget Chase told us his dad and Hunter are great friends." Kyle spoke for the first time.

Hernandez let out a low whistle. "That's right. What a web of plots."

Tanner cleared his throat. "The local police have decided not to charge Michael Khoury, and they're preparing charges against Skip Hunter and Ben Miller. Given the new evidence, they'll be charged with attempted murder on Clara and also for their involvement in Faith's case. They're also on the hook for Linda Boroski's murder."

"Good work, everyone." Ron dug at the bite itself. Maybe he'd try some cortisone on it. "Let's go home and get some rest."

"Wait." Olivia held up a hand in a stop motion. "Sorry, but we still haven't found the leak."

"Right, the fake Adam O'Shea." Ana, who'd pulled her hair free of her ponytail when Ron said they could go, now fingered through her released bob, then started texting someone. A shopping buddy? Or, perhaps she was going on a date? "Have you reached out to your contacts?"

Olivia looked up. "Yes, but I haven't heard back. I read Clara's journal. I suspect the Officer Bill Clara knew is Eva's so-called Uncle Bill. We need to get in touch with this guy."

"All right, I'll talk to Eva," Ron said. "Anything else?"

This time, nobody said anything.

Eva reclined on the plush guesthouse couch, her gaze drifting over the book she was pretending to read. She missed work. This sucked. She closed the book, giving up on her forced relaxation. Then her phone buzzed on the coffee table, flashing Agent Peters's contact.

"Sir?"

"Hey, Eva. I hope you're feeling better. Got a minute?"

"Sure." Her feet thudded to the floor as she sat up, suddenly alert.

"I've been trying to get a bead on Uncle Bill. Got some questions he might be able to answer. Any chance you can connect us?"

Her stomach tightened. Uncle Bill had always insisted on secrecy, and now her duty to her job clashed with her loyalty to him.

"Uncle Bill has always been the one to initiate contact with me." She pushed the words past her closed throat. "I've never reached out to him for anything."

"Are you sure you've never had to contact him in any way? Dead drop, maybe?"

Her heart skipped a beat. If Agent Peters used those terms, he suspected Uncle Bill was Intelligence.

"No, I've not had to give him anything. He calls if he needs something."

"Okay, let him know we'd like to talk to him."

"Will do." As she hung up, Eva sat in conflicted silence, wrestling between duty and trust.

CHAPTER 56

LILY

Adrenaline quickened Lily's pace through the corporate-chic lobby. Her heels clicked on the marble floor, echoing her determination. The man had been popping up too often. Time to confront him and end this.

Tess, the friendly receptionist with a penchant for oversized flower brooches, scrunched her nose when Lily asked about the man. "Sorry, don't know him. Do you want me to call security?"

Lily shook her head. "It's fine. Just curious."

When she refocused on her quarry, he rose from his stool at the lobby bar and abandoned his half-finished drink. He eyed her before he headed to the elevators.

"This is it," she muttered. She broke into a brisk walk, narrowing the gap between them. Her pulse quickened. Was he following her? Stalking her? And for what purpose?

She was a few paces away when the man pressed the elevator button. The doors slid open instantly, as if anticipating his retreat. Just as he stepped in, she reached the elevator and blurted out, "Excuse me!"

He hesitated, one foot in the elevator, the other out. Their eyes met. She had his attention, finally, and the elevator seemed to hold its breath, keeping its doors ajar as if awaiting drama.

"Do I know you?" She kept her voice smooth while her heart pounded.

The man avoided her gaze, blinked several times. "I don't believe so." White, light-brown hair, average height, in his forties, he'd dressed casually, a button-down shirt and pants.

She jammed her hands on her hips, stepping into his space. "Then why have I seen you multiple times, always watching me?"

He glanced left, then right, as if scanning for an escape route.

"The lady asked you a question."

Lily turned to Kyle's voice. "What are you doing here?"

Kyle whipped out his credentials. "FBI Special Agent Kyle Peters. Step out of the elevator, please."

The man did. "What have I done?"

"Stalking."

"I'm not stalking her. I'm a guest here. I'm just getting my card key." His hand started moving toward his pocket.

"Slowly," Kyle commanded.

Smirking, the man showed the key. "Do you guys treat all your guests like this?"

She gripped her hips tighter, bunching up her blazer. "Why were you at the Italian restaurant last night?"

"Because the front desk recommended it."

"Can I see some ID, please?" Kyle asked, then passed the card key to Lily. "Can you check this key to see who it's registered to?"

She checked at the nearest console, then returned the card key to Kyle. "The guest's name is Toby Filmore with an Ohio address."

"So, Mr. Filmore, what brings you here?" Kyle asked.

"Business."

Kyle handed the key and wallet back to the guest. "Sorry for the inconvenience."

His gaze on her, Filmore slid the items back into his pocket. "Can't be too careful these days. Good evening."

As the man left, Lily groaned. "I'm sorry, Kyle. I feel so dumb. It must've all been a coincidence. What if he complains?"

"I wouldn't worry. Dylan wouldn't fire you for this creep."

Probably not, but still. She smoothed the rumples from her blazer. "What are you doing here, anyway?"

People were waiting for the elevators. He guided her out of the way. "Just stopping by on my way to do some last-minute shopping. But, man, they're sure packed this time of year."

Retailers occupied several floors of the M&M Enterprises building which was connected to the hotel. She smirked. "I'm used to the crowd, having grown up in Hong Kong, though it's still a spectacle to see shoppers come out like this for Christmas shopping."

"Yeah, I imagine that part's a new experience for you. Christmas isn't celebrated the same way in Hong Kong, is it?"

"No. There's hardly any gift giving. This is pretty great, but the biggest holiday I miss is Chinese New Year." Anyway, this was her new life.

CHAPTER 57

OLIVIA

Olivia laughed getting ready to go to Midnight Mass. "It even smells like Christmas."

"Nothing like cinnamon and freshly cut pine mingling with the warmth radiating from the fireplace." Simon put on his suit jacket.

She tilted her face toward the colorful lights strung across their Christmas tree.

The lights flickered. Olivia stilled, instantly on alert. She checked her phone. Wi-Fi was still on. Their alarm wasn't triggered. And then the lights went off.

"Relax." He buttoned up. "It's probably just the wind."

Her Spidey sense tickled. In her former life, it saved her many times. She wasn't going to start ignoring it now. "Stay here." She told her fiancé and daughter. She took her gun out of her purse and shoved it to Lily. "Take this."

Good thing she'd taught Lily how to shoot. Simon had no intention of learning, and he wasn't the type anyway. Lily probably wouldn't shoot either, but after her ordeal, she'd wanted to do everything to protect herself. Olivia herself didn't like guns.

Her boots crunched softly on the gravel as she stepped out into the night. She breathed in slow, the air too thick to inhale—or perhaps it was just her heightened state, this gnawing feeling that something wasn't right. She almost reached for her flashlight, but no. Darkness was her ally now.

Her eyes had adjusted to the low light before she began to make her way around the perimeter. With each step, she strained her ears for any signs of movement, any indication her fears were grounded in reality.

As she rounded the first corner, she scanned the shadows beneath the trees and paused, letting the silence speak, listening for the whisper of leaves or the subtle creak of a shifting weight. Nothing. She crossed the backyard, damp earth muffling her footsteps.

She scrutinized the garden shed, the tree line beyond the property, and the secluded spots so inviting to someone with ill intent. Again, silence greeted her, but this time, it was reassuring rather than ominous.

Her circuit complete, she ended up back at her starting point. A final glance toward the street revealed only the familiar scene of parked cars and well-lit homes. She exhaled the breath she didn't realize she'd been holding. Maybe her instincts had been overly cautious this time, but she'd do it all over again. Trusting her gut had kept her alive this long.

As she reentered the house, the tension eased in her shoulders. Nothing was amiss—at least not tonight—and that sense of security, however temporary, was something she never took for granted. The lights had come back on.

"Okay, you're right. Just the wind." But she'd better beef up security soon.

"All right, let's go." Simon prodded Lily forward with a hand to the small of her back. "We don't want to have to stand."

As they buckled up in the car, he started the engine.

"Hey, Mom, did they arrest that doctor?" Lily asked.

"Ben Miller? Yes, that's what I heard," Olivia said. She'd heard more than that, but she wasn't about to discuss ongoing investigations with her daughter. Evidently, Miller had met Ray Ho at one of those high society functions—his father used to curry favor with the likes of governors, senators, CEOs. Of course, Ho had maintained a businessman persona, but somehow, he'd enticed the young Miller with cash and girls if he would lure young, unsuspecting girls and sometimes boys into Ho's network. Miller insisted he had no idea what Ho's operation was. Olivia snorted. Yeah, right. And Miller claimed that once he got sucked into the dragnet, he couldn't get out. At one point, Ho made Miller watch him execute someone who wanted out of the life.

"What's gonna happen now?"

"He already lawyered up." Simon turned into the almost-full parking lot. "Cunningham is representing him."

The reputable firm, Cunningham, Hoyt, and Powers, had extended an invitation to Simon to discuss a possible partnership. However, he didn't seem interested.

"Okay, go." He stopped at the entrance. "And I'll park."

CHAPTER 58

CLARA & RON

The day after Christmas, the Mirror Estate gleamed with lights and decorations. Clara and her family were invited to a gathering at the mansion. She craned her neck now, scarcely resisting lifting onto her toes for a better view as she whispered, "I've never seen anything so magnificent."

Michael introduced her and their children to Ms. Carol, the matriarch.

"I'm pleased to meet you, Clara." The woman spoke in a voice rich and kind as she clasped Clara's hand in her cold one. "I've heard so much about you from Eva."

"And I've heard so much about you, Ms. Carol." Clara kept her grip gentle, something quite delicate about the woman. "Thank you for having us."

The lady then tucked her hand through Clara's arm and guided her deeper into the room. She surveyed the other guests, some familiar and some new. "You've already met Dylan, I presume." The lady leaned in, her soft gray hair tickling Clara's cheek. "According to that boy, he saved your life?"

Heat spread to Clara's cheeks, even as a shiver stalked her spine.

"Well, never you mind." Ms. Carol patted Clara's arm. "I imagine you don't want to think about that day. But you should know some others here—Lily, Olivia, and Simon? Or have you not met Olivia's fiancé yet? And Eva? She's your niece, dear?"

Eva strode over, her face glowing with health and her eyes sparkling with mischief. "Perhaps I had better rescue you, Auntie, from Ms. Carol." Eva tugged her away. "Come along. You've met Agent Ron Peters, but have you met his son and my dear friend, Kyle?"

Then there was Fr. Phil, a priest with kind eyes and a gentle manner.

Olivia sidled up to them. "How's Faith doing?"

Clara glanced at her daughter chatting with Lily. "Physically, she's fine. Psychologically, it'll take a while. And you know, Lily has been a great help. I know she shares with Faith her struggle with PTSD. Hopefully, Faith will learn to cope with it."

Olivia made a soft sound. "I imagine she's having trouble sleeping—that's to be expected."

"Well, one thing I'm happy about is that she now wants to go to college here. Before, she said she wanted to go back to Chicago. Now, she's applied to my alma mater. And she might even commute initially."

"I think she needs to feel safe," Olivia said. "It took Lily a while to find ways to manage her PTSD. Her talking with Fr. Phil helped a lot."

After Olivia excused herself, Clara mingled and exchanged pleasantries, but her mind kept drifting back to the last weeks. How was it possible she now remembered her past? It all started with the name of Linda Boroski, a name key to unlocking memories she never knew she had.

Seems history repeats itself. Twenty years ago, she was investigating Ray Ho, and that led her to danger, a path that changed her life forever. This time around, she was investigating Linda's murder, and it led her to Ray Ho and danger again.

"I hope you're enjoying yourself," Michael whispered in her ear, his arm wrapped around her waist.

She smiled and leaned against him. "I am, but it's all a bit overwhelming."

"Your editor loved your article."

"Yes, and Stella wants to know if I'm an investigative journalist now." She tucked the back of her head against his chest. "I just want to go back to writing something mundane."

Toward the end of the party, the guests were beginning to relax to the soft strains of holiday music, and with his responsibilities momentarily lifted, Ron could enjoy himself.

"Excuse me." His son tapped his shoulder.

Ron excused himself to Michael and followed Kyle to a quiet corner.

Kyle's eyes were troubled. "I haven't been talking to Mom since she married the new guy. I know you haven't talked to her for years either, but... well, she called and asked where we'd be at Christmas. I told her our plans, but she has other ideas."

Ron's eyebrows shot up. He and Sheila had parted amicably, but the distance had grown over the years. "What do you mean?"

Kyle's phone buzzed, and he glanced at it, his face turning paler. "Dylan's app just alerted him of a guest at the gate. And Dylan wants to check with me if the woman is who she said she was."

"Who is it?" Ron asked, though he had a sinking feeling he knew.

"It's Mom." Kyle's voice dipped to barely above a whisper. "She's at the gate coming up here."

Why would Sheila come here? What did she want? Ron

pressed cold fingers to his churning temples. He needed to stay calm, for Kyle's sake and his own.

He gripped Kyle's shoulder, giving it a reassuring squeeze. "Okay. Let's go talk to her."

Together, they made their way to the front door and stood outside.

Sheila approached, her hand twisting around her clutch purse. "Ron." She ducked her head, and her soft lips quivered. "I know this is unexpected, but I need to talk to you. Both of you."

Ron exchanged a glance with Kyle, then nodded. "All right. Let's talk."

"I need help. I think my husband might be a spy."

Tangled Secrets, the next gripping installment in the Mirror Estate series, is available on Amazon and Kindle Unlimited. Grab it now!

In case you miss it, here's where you can download book 2, *Living Secrets*, or any previous books you've missed.

THANK YOU!

Thank you for diving into *Forgotten Secret*! Writing this story has been such a wild ride and knowing that you've spent time with the cast means the world to me.

I hope you loved reading it as much as I loved writing it. If you'd be so kind as to leave a review on Amazon and/or Goodreads to share your impressions with others, I would greatly appreciate it. Your insights will help other readers find the book.

BONUS SCENES

BONUS SCENE 1

MICHAEL

Michael and Majid Khoury had spent an unforgettable day boating with friends in the Outer Banks, their laughter echoing over the water as the sun dipped below the horizon. But the real world beckoned, and Michael had obligations the next morning. He and his brother bade their friends farewell at the dock and began walking toward the parking lot.

As they moved through the dimming light, a shape on the ground near the ramp caught Michael's eye. "Wait a second," he said, squinting to make out the form.

Majid frowned at it too. "Is that a person?"

Michael rushed over, his mind shifting into the focused, clinical gear that had seen him through countless medical emergencies. He knelt beside a young woman lying prone. She'd been shot, a bullet wound to the head visible through her matted hair.

"Check her pulse," Majid said, as if he needed to instruct the physician in Michael.

Michael's fingers found the woman's neck. "Pulse faint, but there." However, she wasn't breathing. "Majid, take your shirt off and press it against the wound. We need to stop the bleeding."

As Majid complied, Michael eased the woman to her back, then tilted her head back slightly and pinched her nose shut, beginning mouth-to-mouth resuscitation. Just as he felt the first slight stir of air from her lungs, the blare of sirens intruded, and paramedics rushed onto the scene.

Michael stood, allowing them to take over. "I'm Dr. Michael Khoury, a neurosurgical fellow." He wiped his bloodied hands on his khaki shorts. "She has a faint pulse but wasn't breathing when we found her. My brother's been applying pressure to the wound to control the bleeding."

The lead paramedics nodded at his concise clinical summary. "You've done good work, doctor. We'll take it from here."

"I'm going with you," he insisted. "The local hospital here won't have the neurosurgical facilities needed for this kind of injury. She'll have to be medevaced to a larger hospital, and I can help stabilize her en route."

After a brief hesitation, the paramedics agreed. "All right, get in."

BONUS SCENE 2

OLIVIA

Olivia Tso sat in her cubicle, the room illuminated only by the glow of her computer screen. She was logged in to a secure video chat as Jade, her undercover persona. Across the digital divide was Marge Beaumont, but not just any Marge. This was the Ghost, the shadowy figure who had eluded law enforcement for years.

Olivia had been working tirelessly to gain Marge's trust, a slow and meticulous dance. The Ghost considered Jade an indispensable tech genius, the hub through which all communications for her criminal operations flowed. Olivia's handler, Burns, had warned her repeatedly: They were playing a long game. They couldn't afford to tip their hand, not even if it meant letting some shady dealings go through unimpeded.

Perhaps Marge didn't have any confidantes. Olivia felt the Ghost relished the opportunity to talk to her like a friend. The Ghost had revealed not only operational details, but also private matters. It seemed she had one lingering regret—what that was, Olivia didn't know.

"Jade, there's something you should know. When you're speaking to me, you're speaking to the real me, not my body double."

Olivia's eyebrows twitched almost imperceptibly, a fleeting expression of the surprise she buried. "Body double?"

Marge smirked. "Yes, she's my public persona. She's the successful businesswoman who heads the Beaumont Foundation, shaking hands, kissing babies, and taking all the credit for our 'philanthropic' works. Most people interact with her, never knowing they're not speaking to the real Marge Beaumont."

Still in character, "Jade" chuckled. "You're always full of surprises, aren't you?"

"You have no idea."

As Marge's dark sense of amusement shivered over her, Olivia went through her mental checklist to avoid her body betraying her feelings. This was a monumental revelation. Having a body double made the Ghost even more elusive, a two-faced enigma nearly impossible to corner. Would they ever be able to lock her up?

BONUS SCENE 3

LILY

Mirror Estate's great room exuded holiday warmth, the guests overseen by a towering Christmas tree draped in twinkling lights and shimmering ornaments. Savoring the deep fir scent, Lily Tso edged closer to her friends, Dylan, Kyle, and Tommy, to be heard over the lively crowd. Across the room, Eva Higgins was busy entertaining her newfound cousins, and with a crystal glass of sparkling cider in her hand, she looked the epitome of seasonal cheer.

While Kyle went to get more desserts and Tommy headed off somewhere, likely to flirt with Eva, Lily sidled up to Dylan. "Do you still, you know, get paranoid? Anxious?"

He stepped farther away from the crowd, and she followed. "Yeah, I'm still paranoid. No anxiety, though. Are you having episodes again?"

Only Dylan truly understood her experience, and she was glad to have someone to talk to. She'd had a hard time after their kidnapping ordeal. "I don't know if you'd call it an episode. There was this guy. I swear I saw him everywhere. At the hotel, the restaurant—just everywhere." She twisted her burgundy skirt in her fingers. "But when we confronted him, it turned out he was a hotel guest. Still, at the restaurant parking lot, I just had this strange feeling. Like I was being watched. Or, you know, something bad was about to happen."

"Yeah, I had that feeling all the time the first few days when I got here. But my experience tells me I shouldn't ignore my instinct. Fr. Phil agrees. According to him, our experience somehow sharpens our senses of danger, so to speak. I think it's kind of like your mom. Her instinct is well honed." He took a sip of his wine. "Maybe you ought to talk to Fr. Phil again."

"Maybe I will, but the guy proved my instinct wasn't that right after all."

"Not necessarily."

"What do you mean?"

"Have you asked your mom to check on him? Maybe he isn't what he appears to be. Just ask her."

"Oh, come on, you don't think that guy is some sort of spy. And why would he target me?"

He stared at her.

Then she winced. "You mean... you think someone could be after my mom?" She rubbed a hand over her eyes as a recent incident accosted her. "You know, we didn't get to midnight Mass as early as I told you, because my mom got all freaked out when the lights flickered and then went off before we were to leave. She even gave me a gun and went out to secure the perimeter."

"I'm sure she knows what she's doing. You're safe with her. Still practicing your kung fu?"

"And hand-to-hand combat and shooting and—sometimes I think she wants to train me to be an operative."

"Cool." His grin flashed, crinkling up the sides of his eyes. "You can protect me the next time we get in trouble."

Before she could formulate a good comeback, Kyle returned with more desserts.

"So, Dylan, are you going to see her?" Kyle asked.

Lily frowned. Did Kyle play matchmaker? Who was Dylan going to see?

"I think so. Olivia and your dad seem to think I might be able to get her to tell me things."

Oh, that. Lily plunked a gingerbread star back onto her plate. "Wait. Why would you go see your aunt? I thought she didn't want anything to do with you or your grandmother, except to kill you."

Months earlier when they were both held captive in some unknown cabins, Dylan told her about his aunt and her criminal empire—how she tried to kill him. And now, he was going to try to get her to reveal secrets that Lily's mom, a trained intelligence operative, couldn't?

"I have no idea. She asked to see me. And I'm confident she can't kill me in lockup."

"He's right." Having already finished his cranberry bar, Kyle brushed crumbs from his fingers. "Olivia will be there with you. Even if she had to wait outside. You'd be well protected."

Maybe. But Lily still shivered, the sweet ginger scent now cloying. If Dylan were going to have anything to do with the Ghost, he couldn't be safe enough.

TANGLED SECRETS

A Suspense Thriller

BOOK 4
SNEAK PEEK

PROLOGUE

PARK HILLS PRIVATE SCHOOL

GRACE

In the bustling school auditorium, whispered chatter further tinted the air already thick with the scent of pine from the festive decorations. Grace Benson, her heart aflutter, perched at the grand piano, her fingers ready to dance over the keys. This was her moment, her first time directing the school's Christmas program, and she'd embraced it with both hands.

As the lights dimmed, she took a deep breath, steadying herself. No time for fretting now. The first class, a group of third graders, shuffled onto the stage, their faces alight. From there, the night progressed in a whirl of color and sound. Each class brought their unique flair to the stage, performing dances and songs they'd practiced for weeks.

Then the finale arrived—the nativity scene. She'd taken great care in selecting children from each grade, from kindergarten to fourth grade, to participate.

The stage transformed into a serene Bethlehem scene, complete with a manger and makeshift stable. The children, dressed in their costumes, took their positions with a seriousness that belied their years. Mary and Joseph, played by a pair of fourth graders, stood by the manger.

As she began the gentle, familiar strains of "Silent Night," the children started their performance. The shepherds, a group of second graders, entered from stage left, followed by the wise men adorned in sparkling costumes. The angels, a chorus of kindergarteners and first graders, flanked the stage, their voices joining in the song to create a heavenly sweetness that seemed to lift the entire auditorium.

Smiling, she watched from her piano. The children were more than rising to the occasion—they were shining. Of course, the audience was mostly family members, guardians, and relatives. A lot of them slid their phones up to record when their kids took the stage.

As the evening's last notes faded and the auditorium began to empty, parents approached her, each of them beaming. Their words washed over her, filling her with a warm sense of accomplishment. She greeted every compliment with a humble smile, her heart still racing from the night's success.

Amid the departing crowd, Mrs. Montez, the mother of one of the kindergarten angels, made her way toward her. Her face was alight as she began in Spanish, her words tumbling out in a fluid, lyrical stream.

Caught off guard, Grace managed a smile. "Solo hablo un poco de español," she inserted, her accent betraying her lack of fluency. The woman's eyebrows shot up, a reaction she had seen before. She could almost read the thoughts behind that astonished look—her being Latina often led people to assume she could speak Spanish. After the last of the parents had left and the children were safely in their care, she began to pack her things up.

"Are you ready to go?" Jenny, one of the school secretaries, hollered from the back. "It's dark out. Ned wants to know if you need help carrying things."

"No, I'm good. But tell your husband thank you from me. We're coming back to clean up this mess tomorrow anyway." School closed for the Christmas break until the first week of the new year. But Grace and those who helped with the program had to clean up.

"Okay, I'll see you tomorrow."

With the school quiet now, she stood alone in the empty auditorium. As she locked the piano and gathered her music sheets, a shadow caught the corner of her eye. She turned toward the door. Did Jenny come back?

"Jenny, is that you? Ned?"

Silence.

She was imagining it. That was it. She gathered her things and headed out to the parking lot. After dumping her stuff in the back seat, she got in front and started the car. The drive home was less than ten minutes, but a pair of headlights had stayed behind her since she left the parking lot. She turned into her apartment complex. The headlights stuck with her. Heart pounding, she remembered reading a post on social media about situations like this. Instead of parking, she turned back around, headed to the closest police station, entered the lot, and honked.

An officer came out. "Ma'am, is there a problem?"

"Yeah, a car is following me." She twisted in her seat to point it out, but it was, of course, gone.

He looked to where she pointed. "Stay here, ma'am."

He walked to the curb, checked up and down the street, and came back. "Sorry, ma'am. I don't see any car out there stopping or acting suspicious."

The officer offered to escort her back to her apartment building. She accepted the offer. She knew the car was there. Or perhaps it was simply traveling in the same direction? But why follow her to her apartment complex? Then again, why would anyone follow her?

CHAPTER 1

MIRROR ESTATE

SHEILA

"I need help. I think my husband is a spy," Sheila Mitchell declared as soon as she walked in the door, her urgency seeming to drop the room's temperature a few degrees.

Ron Peters, her ex-husband, and Kyle, their adult son, exchanged puzzled glances. They were both square-jawed men, Kyle about an inch taller than his dad, their careers in the FBI evident in their no-nonsense demeanor.

"What kind of spy? Industrial spy? Corporate espionage?" Kyle asked as he led her to a room off the foyer, gestured for her to sit on the beige velvet couch, and took a seat in a matching chair.

Ron followed and sat in an accent chair across from her. "Has something happened?"

She shook her head, took a deep breath, and clenched her hands in her lap. If anyone could make sense of her fears, it would be these two. "No, I mean like James Bond."

Ron arched his brow. "And what made you think that?"

"It's just—things have been weird lately. Doug has been

taking secret phone calls, disappearing for hours. I found a second cell phone in his drawer."

"I'm sorry, Mom, but, um"—Kyle shifted in his seat—"could he just be, um, having an affair?"

She twisted her fingers together, her knuckles turning white beneath the pressure. "But how do you explain his abandoning credit cards and going cash based altogether? We're not on any credit counseling. And I overheard him speaking in Spanish and some other strange languages. I didn't even know he spoke so many languages. I don't know what to think anymore."

"Okay." Ron held up a hand. "Have you confronted him about this?"

"I'm scared to. What if he's involved in something dangerous?" Her voice trembled. She flexed her shaky hands in her lap and surveyed the luxurious décor. Vaulted ceilings crowned an elegantly furnished front room. A chandelier, worthy of a small palace, sparkled overhead. Voices and the rustle of people milling around drifted from the deeper interior. When had Ron become friends with people who lived in places like this?

Her gaze drifted to the bay windows overlooking an expansive lawn framed by towering trees on acres of land. Clearly, her ex-husband had contacts that existed in a different tax bracket altogether. She frowned. "You're not here on a case?"

"No." Head tipped to one side, Kyle gave her an are-you-serious look. "Back when you asked me, I wouldn't have known we'd be called out on a case. We're here for a Christmas party."

"Oh, I just thought—never mind." It was the day after Christmas, but... During their marriage, Ron was always working. Holidays meant nothing to him. One of the reasons they split.

Her ex-husband braced his hands on his knees, leaning forward, his gaze meeting hers. "Listen, what you told us doesn't seem like much. But, for your peace of mind, we'll look into it discreetly. In the meantime, I suggest you go about your business. Unless he starts threatening you, don't fret too much."

She exhaled, her stomach tightening into knots. How ironic to be here, seeking help from her FBI ex-husband about her current husband, whom she suspected of espionage.

A young man rounded the corner and approached. His smile radiated a disarmingly casual charm. "Grandma sent me," he announced, grinning at Kyle. "She'd like to invite your guest to join in the fun."

Kyle nodded. "Mom, this is Dylan Roche. His grandmother is Carol Marino. Dylan, my mom, Sheila Mitchell."

Marino. The name clicked like a missing puzzle piece snapping into place. She'd heard about M&M Enterprises. Other than real estate development, they were also the parent company of Marino Hotels Worldwide. Their headquarters was in Orlando. So... Mirror Estate, with its sprawling acres and gated luxury, belonged to the Marino family. That's the league Ron and Kyle were in these days.

Dylan's smile never wavered as he led them down a grand hallway. The murmuring voices grew louder when they approached an opulent set of double doors. With a flourish, Dylan swung them open and ushered her into a room pulsing with holiday energy and sweet with sumptuous treats.

As soft strings of a quartet in the corner underplayed the conversations, an elegant older woman sat amid her joyous guests, a commanding presence even as she chatted with a priest with thinning hair. After Dylan introduced Sheila to his grandmother and Fr. Phil and the others, she scanned the room and paused at a familiar face. Simon Roth, the senator who resigned recently. By his side stood a striking Asian American woman—Olivia, his new fiancée, if she caught the name right—and Lily Roth, their daughter, who looked too young to be holding a cocktail. From the way Kyle introduced her, Lily meant something to him. But then, Lily and Dylan looked pretty cozy together. Hmm...

Nearby, another woman caught her attention. Asian as well.

Introduced as Clara, she was deep in conversation with her husband, Dr. Michael Khoury. Their daughter, Faith, chatted with Lily, and their teenage son, Jason, ignored it all, engrossed in his phone. Next to him stood another young man about Kyle's age. Someone said he was Tommy, Dylan's best friend. He and Jason appeared to be playing some games on their phones.

And there was Eva Higgins, Kyle's childhood friend. What was she doing here? Ah, so Clara was Eva's aunt. Small world.

Ms. Marino stood up and stepped forward with a smile. "It's a pleasure to finally meet you."

"The pleasure is mine," Sheila replied, still somewhat overwhelmed by the glittering social tapestry she'd walked into.

After a decent amount of time mingling and engaging in small talk, she felt it was time to go. She caught Ron's and Kyle's attention from across the room and subtly gestured toward the exit. They made their way over to her.

"I should head out."

"Okay. We'll look into your concerns about Doug. You'll hear from us soon." Ron clamped a hand on her shoulder. "In the meantime, try to relax. Have a good rest of the holidays."

"Thanks. You too." Though how would she manage that while anxious about what they might uncover?

Her shoulders already somewhat lighter since she'd given away part of her burden, she made her way to Ms. Marino, who was finishing a conversation with the former senator. "Ms. Marino, just want to say goodbye. The estate is very beautiful."

Ms. Marino stood up again. "Thank you. I hope to see you again soon."

"Likewise." Sheila returned the smile, then gave a polite nod to the senator and the others in their circle.

After saying her farewells, she walked out of the Mirror Estate, her heels clicking against the marbled floors. The grand double doors closed behind her, sealing off a world she was only beginning to understand. As she drove, she rehashed the reason she'd been there in the first place. Was she overreacting? Maybe Doug was having an affair. How oddly relieving that would be. Or would it be? What was worse?

She shivered. Hopefully, Ron and Kyle would discover the answers.

ABOUT THE AUTHOR

S.F. Baumgartner writes fast-paced Christian suspense thrillers. Book 1 of her Mirror Estate series, Living Secrets, was selected as one of the Top Picks in the thriller category at Killer Nashville, 2024. Her love for writing comes second only to her love of reading.

When she's not busy writing about complex characters, secretive operatives, and relentless agents, she spends her time binge-watching crime TV shows, such as NCIS, or playing with her cats. If you enjoy James Patterson's style—specifically short chapters—you'll love her Mirror Estate series.

To be the first to know about any sales, promotions, and new releases, sign up for our monthly newsletter. By subscribing, you'll stay informed about all the latest happenings and never miss an opportunity to explore this captivating world.

ALSO BY S.F. BAUMGARTNER

Mirror Estates series

Buried Secrets, book 1

Living Secrets, book 2

Forgotten Secret, book 3

Tangled Secrets, book 4

Hidden Secrets, book 5

Shadowed Secret, book 6

Stolen Secrets, book 7

Box Set (Books 1-4)

KC & Orlando Prime series

Christmas Murders, a prequel

Fatal Invitation, book 1

ACKNOWLEDGMENTS

I am immensely grateful to everyone who contributed to the materialization of this novel. It truly has been a collaborative effort, and each contribution has been invaluable.

I want to extend my deepest gratitude to my editors and proofreaders: Deirdre Lockhart at Brilliant Cut Editing, Emma Jane from EJL Editing, and Kelsey Darling from Represent Publishing. Their meticulous attention to detail, dedication to refining my drafts, and commitment to catching all errors have been fundamental in shaping this book into its best version.

A special thanks goes to Chelsea Lauren at Represent Publishing for her exceptional work on the interior formatting of the book. Her expertise brought an added layer of professionalism and beauty to its presentation.

I must also express my heartfelt appreciation to the talented designers from 100covers.com. Their creativity and skill in taking my ideas and turning them into the beautiful cover of this book have truly brought its visual aspect to life.

A particular note of gratitude is due to Dr. Tina Tan, Senior Consultant Psychiatrist at Better Life Psych Medicine Clinic in Singapore. Her willingness to answer my questions about amnesia and the immediate aftermath of regaining memories has been instrumental. Her review and approval of the excerpts pertaining to Clara's experience have added a layer of authenticity and credibility to this work.

I cannot forget to thank all the friends and colleagues who helped me polish the blurb and all my ARC readers for their invaluable feedback and support throughout the process.

Last, but certainly not least, I owe a tremendous thank you to my family. Their unwavering support, understanding, and encouragement have been my backbone throughout this journey. Their belief in me and what I do has been a constant source of motivation and strength.

To each and every one of you, thank you from the bottom of my heart. Your contributions, large and small, have made this book possible, and I am eternally grateful.

www.ingramcontent.com/pod-product-compliance
Lightning Source LLC
Chambersburg PA
CBHW021136310726
48971CB00002B/353